Head
First

Claire Kershaw has been diving for ten years, and her love for the ocean inspired many of the scenes in her debut novel, *Head First*. Since graduating from Emory University with a degree in English Literature, Claire has moved to the Pacific Northwest, where you can find her hiking, attempting to keep her houseplants alive, or obsessively reading *NYT* advice columns.

Head First

Claire Kershaw

ZAFFRE

First published in the UK in 2025 by
ZAFFRE
An imprint of Bonnier Books UK
5th Floor, HYLO, 105 Bunhill Row, London, EC1Y 8LZ

A CIP catalogue record for this book is
available from the British Library.

ISBN: 9-781-80418-947-4

Also available as an ebook and an audiobook

1 3 5 7 9 10 8 6 4 2

Typeset by IDSUK (Data Connection) Ltd
Printed and bound in Great Britain by Clays Ltd, Elcograf S.p.A.

MIX
Paper | Supporting
responsible forestry
FSC® C018072

The authorised representative in the EEA is Bonnier Books
UK (Ireland) Limited.
Registered office address: Floor 3, Block 3, Miesian Plaza,
Dublin 2, D02 Y754, Ireland
compliance@bonnierbooks.ie
www.bonnierbooks.co.uk

To my dream come true, for making room for all the other dreams I didn't even know I had.

Chapter 1

'Can you believe this?' Millie thrusts her phone closer to my face.

'Believe what?' I ask, squinting at the screen, attempting to decipher the scientific garble she's pulled up.

We're sitting on my couch while *The Bachelor* is paused in the background.

'Him!' Millie exclaims with a huff. 'Hugh Harris!'

'Oh,' I say, realisation dawning on me. Like Millie, Hugh Harris is a marine biologist, but he's based out of Sydney *and* he happens to disagree with everything Millie publishes. He's a know-it-all. Millie never shuts up about it.

She inches closer to me on the couch, as if bringing the phone as close to my face as physically possible will make me sympathise with her faster. I take the phone out of her grasp and zoom in on an article titled 'Coral Bleaching Is No Longer the Biggest Problem Facing the Great Barrier Reef – and the Butterfly Wrasse Can Prove it'.

I haven't read *The Marinist* since I studied marine biology in college, but I proofread all of Millie's stuff, so I know this article. For the past two years, she's been on the hunt for the butterfly wrasse, a little purple fish with a yellow stripe and a nubby fin on its belly. I thought it sounded cute at first – kind of like Millie's own *Finding Nemo*, but after listening to her drone on and on about how she thinks the species survived its supposed extinction, and what that means for coral regeneration in the Great Barrier Reef, I don't think it's cute anymore. If I have to hear her say one more time that fund-raising efforts to stop coral bleaching should be redirected to stop fertiliser runoff from banana farms, my head will explode.

Millie heaves an impatient sigh, tired of waiting for me to validate her annoyance, so I scroll to the problem area — the comments section.

@HughHarris As a marine biologist with a university degree from the top marine biology programme in the world, I do not agree with Millicent's claims. Considering the rate at which staghorn corals were bleached, there is almost a zero per cent chance the butterfly wrasse has survived. Regardless, the severity of coral bleaching should not be dismissed. Also, **@milliepaxton**, you missed a comma in the second sentence.

@santabarbaraecowarriors21 If biologists **@millie-paxton @hughharris** can't even agree on basic facts – like, let's say, SPECIES EXTINCTION, how do they have the right to tell us what to fund-raise for?!

@greatbarrierreefscuba818 They don't. And **@milliepaxton** lives in Ohio. How would she know?

My mouth falls open. 'I didn't miss a com—' I start to say, scrolling back up to the second sentence of the article. I stop short because, unfortunately, Hugh is right. There is not a comma where a comma should be.

'That's beside the point,' Millie says sternly, swiping her phone back out of my hands. 'He is undermining me in front of *everyone*. And touting his university degree like *I don't have the same degree*!'

'You're right,' I agree, although it takes a herculean effort for me to shake off my wounded pride.

'Not only did he call me *Millicent*, which he knows is not my name — we've been in the same Zoom meeting before — but he's wrong! Coral bleaching *isn't* the biggest threat to marine wildlife — pollution is!'

'He's completely undermining you.' I bob my head in agreement with her. 'Which is a shame, considering you have equivalent degrees and the exact same job title.'

'I know!' Millie yelps, startling my dog, Murphy, who lazily raises his shaggy head off the couch and opens a big brown eye at Millie. 'Sorry, Murph,' she says, scratching him behind the ears. She settles back into her seat.

'He also didn't need to say he has a degree from a top marine biology programme,' I snort. 'What does he think you have? A certificate from www.makemeabiologist. com?'

Millie laughs and then starts typing furiously. 'How about – when I find this fish you can kiss my wrasse,' she mumbles under her breath, her fingers jabbing at her phone.

'Millie!' I cry, grabbing the phone out of her hands before she spontaneously presses 'send'. 'You can't say that! Isn't this something you wrote for work?'

'Fine.' Millie huffs. She crosses her arms across her chest. 'You do it then. You're better at this kind of stuff.'

I raise an eyebrow at her. 'What kind of stuff?'

'The boring stuff,' she answers automatically. She flushes red when she sees the dismayed look on my face. 'You're better at being a professional. And you're better at grammar,' she corrects sheepishly.

'Usually,' I mutter under my breath, still smarting at Hugh's comment about the comma. But Millie is right. I am a self-proclaimed grammar snob. And I happen to be excellent at being boring. I sigh and type out a draft of a respectably passive-aggressive comment.

@HughHarris Just because the butterfly wrasse has not been spotted does not mean it is extinct. I'm not sure what you learned while at university, but I think we can both agree we should not engage in inaccurately creating quotable statistics with no proof to back them up.

Millie reads it, nodding viciously, and gives the OK to send. I feel a wave of pride. *Take that, Hugh Harris!* I think as I press play on *The Bachelor*. We both turn our attention to my small TV, where we have been dutifully watching for the past five seasons. Tonight was the first night ever that we almost cancelled even though both of us were in town. I felt weird watching a reality show while we waited for Millie's results, but she insisted.

We haven't been watching for more than five minutes before Millie heaves a great sigh.

4

No, Millie, I think, panicked, *don't think about it*. After a minute or two of silence, I get up the courage to pause the show and ask, 'What are you thinking about?' I hold my breath. I don't think I want to hear her answer.

'That Mom had the nerve to name me *Millicent*, and you got to be named Anderson,' she huffs. I almost cry with relief.

'Shut up,' I respond, laughing. 'That is the *only* good thing from Mom that I got. You got her ass.' I twist my neck to glance at my behind, which is stubbornly small in comparison to my thighs, no matter the amount of glute bridges I force myself to do at the tiny gym in my apartment building.

'And you got her hair.' I press my hands to my scalp to try to tame the frizz. Millie and I both have curly brown hair, but she manages to keep hers sleek, and mine is an unruly, untameable ball.

I joke about it, but sometimes I think Millie's inheritance of our mother's best traits — her dark curly hair and strong nose — were the first indicators of my sister's first-born personality. She unapologetically takes what she wants.

'Don't say what you always say,' I warn Millie, as she opens her mouth to speak, her full lips forming an O shape.

'But everyone says we look like twins!' both of us repeat together, although I'm using a mocking tone and Millie is deadly serious. I've never told Millie, although I suspect she knows, that being told I look like her is the nicest compliment I get. I could do a lot worse than being a softer version of her, a version with frizzier hair, thicker thighs, less-defined cheekbones and lighter-coloured eyes.

We have this back-and-forth all the time, and only once it's over do I realise that this week, it could have gone much differently. I feel a crushing wave of guilt that I just complained about my hair when Millie discovered a lump in her breast last Thursday. The lump, which Millie, true to form, nicknamed Sal, is the reason I suggested we cancel tonight, but here she is, inhaling a glass of Pinot Noir, insisting there's nothing to worry about.

Millie waves her hand at me, mimicking pressing a button on a remote, impatient for us to continue watching the show.

I press play. The bachelor is laying out a blanket for a beach picnic, and a contestant is popping champagne. She's either blissfully happy about being on a date with the bachelor or someone slipped her mushrooms – I can't tell which. Either way, I feel a twinge of jealousy that there are people out there experiencing that much emotion. Even during my last relationship, sometimes it felt like my dog, Murphy, was the only thing that could pull my heartstrings. Well, except Millie's breast lump, Sal, which has shredded my heartstrings into oblivion.

After a few minutes Millie's phone dings again.

'OMG.' She sits straight up. 'Hugh already commented back.'

'Isn't he in Australia?' I ask, thinking back to what Millie has told me about Hugh Harris. Millie says his accent gives him an 'unfair and unearned' advantage when they both go up for lecturing opportunities on the same circuit.

'It's morning for them,' she informs me, furrowing her brow at her phone. 'Look!'

@MilliePaxton Contrary to your belief, I **learnt** not to 'create statistics' while at university. If you read closely, you would see that I said 'almost'. Your logic needs work. And, just so you're aware, ITLOS plans to certify that the butterfly wrasse is extinct in 2026. Good luck finding one before then. Especially considering, as one savvy commenter pointed out, you live in Ohio.

'He did not,' I gasp. Murphy barks at my tone. 'He criticised my grammar again! Learnt?! That isn't a thing!' I'm infuriated.

'Technically,' Millie reminds me, 'he thinks he's criticising me. And he's gonna wish he never opened his mouth when I find that fish.'

For months now, Millie has been planning a trip to the Great Barrier Reef over her Christmas break. I tune out her rant about the boat she's booked – it's small and nimble, stopping at the reefs that had the highest rate of butterfly wrasse sightings in 2018.

Instead, I click on Hugh's Twitter handle to pull up his profile. His picture is fuzzy – a crop of shaggy blond hair, glasses, and a strong jaw is all I can make out.

'Is he cute?' I ask Millie. I'm irked at Hugh's condescending and haughty tone, but I'm also curious . . . I can't remember the last time I saw someone get under Millie's skin.

'Finally back on the prowl?' she asks, raising her eyebrows.

'As if,' I reply, doing my best to give her a withering glare. I broke up with Zach three months ago, effectively imploding my entire life, and for the past two weeks, Millie hasn't stopped hounding me to see if she can set me up with her new co-worker. She claims two months is 'standard break-up mourning period'. And even though I've tried to explain to her that turning down a proposal is a lot different than a normal breakup and that I don't want another version of the guy I just broke up with — born and raised in Columbus, obsessed with football, hates trying new restaurants, timidly nice — she won't take no for an answer.

Millie snorts. 'Whatever you say. Technically, I haven't seen him in person, just online. But if you're into pompous jerks, then I guess he is.'

I give her a sideways glance. 'Well, shouldn't we respond?' I reach for her phone, ready to defend my honour as a self-proclaimed grammar snob, but it's wedged firmly between her thigh and the armrest of the couch.

'We don't need to,' she says. 'Now do you see why this trip is so important to me? Spotting the butterfly wrasse will be the best comeback there is.' She folds her arms defiantly and leans back into the couch. 'Fourteen days until he's proven wrong.'

When I turn the TV off, Millie stretches out her arms and nudges Murphy's head off her lap. She winces as she stands, a reminder of the procedure she had done last week. The doctors are sending in her sample to determine if the lump in her breast is benign and the results won't be back for three more days. The wait seems excruciatingly long to me, but Millie took it in her stride.

'Andi?' Millie asks, turning to face me. 'I want to ask you something . . .' She wrings her hands and immediately, I'm consumed by nerves. Millie is never hesitant, and I don't like seeing her this way.

'What's up?' I ask, as nonchalantly as possible.

'Well . . .' Millie pauses and starts petting Murphy's head. 'Well, you know my trip?'

'Uh-huh.' I nod, like Millie's given me the chance to forget it. We were talking about it no less than ten minutes ago.

'I was just thinking that if I can't go . . .' She trails off and looks at me, her eyes pleading.

'You're going to be able to go. Didn't the doctor say he thinks, based on the location and stuff, that the lump,' I correct myself, 'that Sal is benign?'

'Well, yeah, but I was thinking today that, just in case, if I can't go, you could maybe go instead of me?'

My mouth falls open slightly and I blink at Millie. 'I can't do that. I'm not a marine biologist. Also, everything is in your name.' The more I think about it, the crazier it sounds. Millie has had some insane ideas in the past – dyeing Murphy's hair green for St Patrick's Day, convincing our dad to eat a weed brownie, but this takes the cake.

'But you got a bachelor's degree in marine science – and you know how to take photos! It'll be easy! And you're scuba certified!' Millie counters, her eyes gleaming, clearly prepared for the argument. 'And everyone says we look alike, and the visa only takes, like, two days to process, you have plenty of time. Plus, it's over Christmas break anyways, so no one at work will know that I didn't go. I'll get a fake tan and pretend that I went . . .' She pauses and swallows. 'Don't tell me I told you so, but a lot of the trip is non-refundable. It was so much cheaper to do it that way. All that money shouldn't just go to waste . . .'

'Millie—' I try to erase the annoyance in my tone '—this is crazy. And . . .' I hesitate because my voice starts to break. 'I don't even want to entertain the possibility that you can't go. Why are we talking about this now when we don't know anything?'

At this, Millie softens. 'OK,' she says. 'We don't have to decide now. It just could be nice for you to . . . you know . . . get out there. And you'd be doing me a huge favour . . .'

I huff. 'I know how to get myself out there, I'm just not ready.'

'Andi, I'm not asking you to be ready for anything *romantic*, I just think it could be good for you to get out of Columbus for a little. So much of your life has changed lately, maybe a vacation will help make sense of that!' she says excitedly, clearly attempting to lighten the mood.

'Ugh,' I groan. 'I don't need a vacation. I'm doing fine.' I gesture at my apartment. 'My house is clean, Murphy is fed. I've hardly cried. I'm fine.'

Millie raises her eyebrows at me in an expression of disbelief that only older sisters can truly master. 'Right,' she says, her voice sharp, 'because all I dream for your life is one that's fine. Not great, not good, but fine.'

I raise an eyebrow at her.

She grins. 'So, you'll think about it? Just in case?'

'Yes,' I lie. *No way*, I'm thinking. *Not a chance.
I'm good here. In my apartment with Murphy.* But as
Millie scoots out the door into the freezing Columbus
November, I can't help but think about the sun of the
South Pacific on my skin.

Chapter 2

I wake up the next morning with an aching jaw and a headache, something that only happens when I've been grinding my teeth all night.

I don't even make it all the way to my cubicle before texting Millie, asking if we can respond to Hugh – *Learnt? Who does he think he is?* But she never responds. The day passes slowly, and I alternate tweaking a slide deck that I need to send to my boss and drafting snarky messages I wish I could send to Hugh. Becca nags me until I reluctantly agree to sneak out of the office with her to get bubble tea. Accompanying Becca on her relentless pursuit of drinks and snacks is the foundation of our friendship. I offer to buy her tea as a thank you for being the only reason I see sunshine most workdays, but she refuses, insisting that I've repaid my debt by listening to her litany of complaints about online dating.

When Becca heard what happened with Zach, she was shocked. She couldn't believe I turned down the chance at a stable, pre-planned future with a nice guy. My explanation that 'I felt trapped,' didn't cut it. 'Trapped by a man is all I want to be!' she exclaimed. I almost offered to give her Zach's number.

When one of my afternoon meetings gets cancelled, I decide to take matters into my own hands and, in an uncharacteristically bold move, I DM Hugh.

Well, technically **@millieandipaxton** DMs Hugh. Millie and I had started a joint Instagram account when we went to India together, chronicling our trip to the 'Golden Triangle' – New Delhi, Agra, and Jaipur. Mostly for our parents, the feed was filled with pink palaces, golden vistas, colourful saris, and giant, lumbering elephants. It was one of my favourite trips I've ever taken – nothing compares to the vibrancy of a New Delhi evening – and looking back at the photos I remember why I used to love travelling so much. I'm so overwhelmed at how long it's been since I've taken a trip – two years, to be exact, the entirety of my last relationship – that I almost forget why I've logged on to Instagram in the first place.

Hugh's Instagram is private, but his bio reads 'marine biologist USYD'. His profile picture is so small that even screenshotting it and zooming in does me no good, all I see is a pixelated outline of a face.

@millieandipaxton I just wanted to let you know that I don't plan on taking logic cues from someone who spells 'learned' 'learnt'.

@hughharris94 It is most effective to communicate with your audience using their preferred speech patterns (I learnt that at university). When one is writing about the Great Barrier Reef (located in Australia, let me remind you) it makes the most sense to use Australian English. Therefore, 'learnt' would have been the correct way for you to write your response. I was just pointing that out.

@millieandipaxton Touché.

@hughharris94 Hmmm . . . you really don't know your audience.

@millieandipaxton ?

@hughharris94 Aussies aren't a huge fan of the French. But, of course, someone from Ohio wouldn't know that.

@millieandipaxton Real original, coming for Ohio like that. Actually, now that I think about it, I would trade Ohio seasons for an endless cycle of natural disasters. *Fire emoji*

@hughharris94 I would say that's a low blow, but I don't expect anything better from an American.

@millieandipaxton Like Australia is that much better.

@hughharris94 We have better healthcare, living standards and lower crime rates.

@millieandipaxton Yet you're still ranked below us for climate action policies . . .

I hear Matteo's footsteps before I see him. I rush to press 'send' before dropping my phone back into my bag, a smile blooming across my face just as Matteo thuds to a stop beside my cubicle. He walks like a lumberjack, even though at five foot nine he's only a few inches taller than me. He fills up the entire space next to my desk.

'What's got you grinning?' he asks, smiling himself.

'Nothing.' I squirm, trying to ignore the insinuation that I haven't been as cheery at work lately.

As if he can read my mind, Matteo's expression softens, and I remember why I liked him so much during my first interview with Sunshine Foods (a giant conglomerate that produces a lot of cereal). I interviewed for an operations job, one that involved a lot of crunching numbers in a cubicle and putting them into a slide to help executives make decisions on how many boxes of cereal to ship to each supermarket. Sunshine Foods was a good opportunity for someone just out of college. I had no idea I would end up sticking around this long.

'I just wanted to tell you good work on this deck,' he says, hoisting a sheaf of papers in the air and waggling them around.

'Thank you.'

'I've been meaning to ask you – are you taking any time off around the holidays? I haven't seen any requests come in.'

I hesitate. I know I should be taking time off, but I have nothing to do with it. Taking time off to sit at home sounds . . . depressing.

'Just let me know when you'll be out.' Matteo's deep voice fills the silence. 'Things slow down during the holidays, no need for you to sit here alone. Heck, even I'll be gone!' He laughs at his own joke. He gestures towards the sea of desks that are already starting to empty out in the post-Thanksgiving, pre-Christmas lull. 'See?'

'Right,' I say, feeling panicked at the idea that everyone seems to think I need a vacation. How many times will I have to say, 'I'm fine,' before they believe me?

'I'll let you know when I'll be out.' I force a smile and Matteo claps his hands on the padded grey walls of my cubicle and walks away. Matteo is the one who hired me, and in the six years I've worked for Sunshine, our relationship has never progressed past colleagues. I know about his two daughters, and he knows I have a sister and live near my parents. He promotes me like clockwork every two years and gives me a 2 per cent raise every year. I never work more than forty-hour weeks and have a great work–life balance. But lately I've been feeling like I have no 'life' worth balancing. Especially now that after our friends sided with Zach in the breakup, I only have Murphy and Millie to keep me company. Sometimes I go running. Maybe I should learn how to knit. With a sigh, I pull up the company calendar.

I have fifteen days of holiday for the year. So far, I've only used three, all of them to go to weddings. I was supposed to take a trip to Italy with Zach, but after I asked him four times if we could spend one weekend planning it, and each weekend he 'lost track of time', and was 'so sorry', and 'please can we plan it next weekend?' I stopped trying to make that happen.

'He doesn't mean to let me down,' I remember confessing to Millie in an attempt to minimise my disappointment. 'Travelling just isn't as important to him. He likes being home.' She had simply nodded.

I force my attention back to the calendar. Sunshine Foods gives us the week of Christmas off, so if I'm going to use my holiday before year end, I basically have to start tomorrow.

Matteo means well, I remind myself, and time off should be a good thing. I can take Murphy for more walks. I can get some stuff done around the house. I can take my time wrapping Christmas presents. I almost cry at how boring my life feels.

I google 'Great Barrier Reef' and watch as the search returns picture after picture of magnificent coral structures, bright pink and yellow, giant clams ringed with purple. I pore over the photos, imagining what it would be like to go to Australia. I spot a bright blue coral that looks like a collection of elk antlers – staghorn coral – the coral Millie's lab studies. *You could take photos of that for her*, the voice in my head says, *you know your stuff. You've been pretending to be more like Millie your whole life. This will be a piece of cake.*

As quickly as I opened it, I close the tab and get up from my computer, looking over my shoulders to make sure no one saw. I'm superstitious, and I feel like if I even admit to myself that this trip sounds fun, something will happen to Millie. I do not want to take that chance.

'Please God,' I whisper, 'let Sal be a good lump.'

Two days later and I'm repeating 'Let Sal be a good lump,' in my head like a mantra. I met Millie at the hospital so we could go to her post-op appointment together, and I can't tell who is more nervous. Millie is scrolling through Instagram from her reclined position on the exam table in the middle of the room, and even though her posture is relaxed, her gaze darts to the door every five seconds.

When we hear a knock, I flinch. I've been jumpier lately, much to Murphy's chagrin. Every time he barks at a squirrel I gasp, and he cocks his head at me in annoyance. And I'm not the only family member that's picked up an annoying habit out of anxiety. My dad has thrown himself into his hobbyist French horn playing and decided to learn all the Christmas carols, starting with 'Silent Night'. I'm pretty sure if my mom has to hear the opening bars one more time she'll scream. She's been in overdrive, texting Millie and me both constantly, dropping off casseroles, baking banana bread and offering to take us out for drinks when we finish work.

I have been attempting to act exactly the same and give Millie a semblance of normal, although I feel like I fend off a panic attack every five minutes.

Millie has rallied all of her positive energy into manifesting a good result. She's doubled down on yoga classes, been drinking green smoothies every morning, and finished all her Christmas shopping. She even had me reset the password to her HealthChart account so she couldn't see the results of her biopsy before she had a chance to speak to the doctor about them.

'There's no sense in paying them if I'm just going to diagnose myself, is there?' she said, when she handed me the log-in credentials. 'Better to not google.'

Since the night we watched *The Bachelor*, she hasn't mentioned Australia again — not once. Before the lump, Millie referenced it every time we were together. If we so much as saw a swimsuit or a cute hat through a window she would squeal, 'Should I get it for Australia?' but since asking if I would go, she's been radio silent.

There's another knock at the door. Millie clears her throat. 'Come in,' she says. Her voice wavers. I take a deep breath and try to steady my shaking hands. Millie plasters a smile on her face, completely committed to a positive outcome.

The doctor sidesteps into the room, his face partially obscured by the sheaf of papers he's holding in his right hand. A shock of white hair sits on the top of his head. 'Dr Taylor,' he announces, as he turns to face Millie.

'Hi,' she says brightly, extending her hand. 'Millie.'

'Ah, so no Millicent then,' he says, making a note on his clipboard.

'Nope. No one calls me Millicent, just Millie.' *Except Hugh*, I think, remembering our conversation from yesterday.

@hughharris94 America's policies are the last thing you should be bringing into this argument . . .

@millieandipaxton Right, because your country is perfect and definitely not still dealing with the fact that it was stolen from indigenous peoples . . . oh wait . . . how could I forget it's STILL stolen because it's still a commonwealth nation? Although I'm not sure how that slipped my mind, considering you have the most royally pompous name ever.

@hughharris94 Your name is literally Millicent.

His grainy Instagram profile picture blooms across my brain. I've been checking to see if Hugh commented on Millie's article again. He hasn't said a word, and something about the pointlessness of reloading the page deepens my embarrassment about giving him so much attention. I've tried to kick the habit of constantly refreshing our conversation and Millie's article, but hating Hugh has been a nice distraction from what's going on with Millie.

As if on cue, Millie speaks. 'This is my sister, Andi,' she says, startling me from my thoughts. I watch Millie stretch her lips into another smile and wonder if the doctor can also tell it's forced.

'Hi. Pleased to meet you,' I say.

'Dr Taylor.' He turns to greet me with a firm handshake. He has even more wrinkles up close. Despite his warm grandpa energy, his hand is freezing. 'I can see the resemblance.' Dr Taylor smiles at us and takes the seat across from me. 'No use in delaying it,' he begins, 'good news, the lump is benign.'

Millie lets out a rush of breath. 'OK,' she sighs with relief.

I immediately fish my phone out of my purse to text our mom.

'We did find something else,' Dr Taylor continues.

My heart clenches and my hands feel clammy. I drop my phone back into my bag.

'When we ran your bloodwork, you tested positive for a harmful variant of the BRCA gene. Do you know what that is?'

I shake my head no, but Millie nods. She's frowning.

'The BRCA genes are inherited from your parents and produce proteins that help repair damaged DNA. But there are harmful variants of the genes. Millice—excuse me, Millie, you tested positive for a harmful variant of BRCA1, which increases the likelihood that you will develop breast cancer at some point in your life. While your scans are clean now, this is something you should be aware of. And—' Dr Taylor looks meaningfully at me '—it's genetic. So, you should probably get tested as well.'

I swallow. My throat feels dry.

'Got it.' Millie fidgets with her hands.

'So . . . what's next?' I ask, filling the silence.

'Well, you have a couple of options.' Dr Taylor folds his hands in his lap and peers over his glasses. I focus on the wisps of white hair that are out of place instead of on his face, which I'm sure is about to deliver more bad news.

'You can do nothing, which is not recommended given your family history and genetic makeup. Or, you can explore taking preventative measures, which is what I would recommend. You could be a good candidate for a double mastectomy.'

Millie doesn't say anything, she just looks at Dr Taylor.

'Double mastectomies are getting more and more common. We separate your breast tissue from your skin and muscle and remove it, which substantially lowers your risk of getting breast cancer. There are reconstructive options as well.' He pauses, and his tone softens. 'Look, I know this is a lot to think about. Why don't I give you two a

21

minute . . .' he pauses, and pulls a pamphlet out of his front coat pocket '. . . and I'll leave this here. It explains BRCA in more detail. I'll come back shortly to answer any more questions you have.'

Millie nods.

'And remember, this is *good* news,' he emphasises on his way out the door.

'Thank you, Doctor,' I manage to choke out, but my voice sounds scratchy and foreign. The room falls into silence apart from the gentle ticking of the clock on the opposite wall.

Millie collects herself quickly, taking a few deep breaths before she starts explaining to me how much research she's already done. It only takes her a few moments to decide. She's going to get the double mastectomy. She doesn't want this hanging over her head. If insurance will cover it, she'll do double mastectomy and reconstruction at the same time.

She's speaking with such force and surety that I can tell she's been thinking about it for days, anticipating this as one of the outcomes of her biopsy. She's thought through all her options and charted the best path forward. I've always been impressed by her decisiveness.

Dr Taylor returns to the room and Millie launches into her plan. Within minutes, he's recommended a surgeon. He reminds me to schedule my blood test with the front desk. He schedules a time to have a follow-up call with Millie.

I'm still in shock when Dr Taylor leaves. We are supposed to get out of the room, leave the hospital, return to our lives, but I can't even seem to get up from my chair.

'Everything's fine,' Millie tells me, 'I have a plan, *we* have a plan.' But I can't shake the feeling that everything's about to change.

The only thing that makes me smile the rest of the day is a message from Hugh:

@hughharris94 I bet you're one of those Americans who pronounces Cairns like it rhymes with barns.

@millieandipaxton Ah yes, because it makes total sense to pronounce it like the film festival.

@hughharris94 Touché.

@millieandipaxton Touché.

@hughharris94 Imitation is the sincerest form of flattery.

@millieandipaxton Sorry, just distracted today. Got some not bad not good news.

@hughharris94 Terrifying to think about how not-bad-not-good news would have to be to distract an American. Another yodeller chaining himself to a Walmart? Did a bear eat Lady Gaga's famous poodles?

@hughharris94 Sorry to hear that though, really.

Chapter 3

I don't see Millie again until after she's got the call. We live five minutes from each other, and she's driven over to go on a walk with me and Murphy.

I know what Millie's gonna tell me, my mom has already called and filled me in. The best surgeon in the Columbus area has an opening. Insurance has approved her for the procedure. Millie has officially scheduled her double mastectomy and reconstruction for 15th December, a day after she was supposed to land in Australia.

'I don't get why all of this is happening so fast,' I say when Millie explains it to me herself. We've stalled on the sidewalk. Murphy is tugging at his leash.

'I don't feel like I have a choice. My body is a ticking time bomb.'

'But . . .' I trail off. I don't know what to say. I got my results from the lab a few days ago and found out I don't have the BRCA gene. I've spent so many years thinking Millie was the lucky one . . . *living* like Millie was the lucky one. But looking at her now, about to miss the trip of a lifetime, it doesn't feel that way anymore. I should be relieved, elated even, but instead I feel heavy with guilt.

'Andi, I've looked into it. I've done all the research. I'm going to have to do it eventually, and the longer I wait, the more likely it is something will get worse. I'm going to get it over with.' Her words are firm, but her voice wavers slightly. 'I won't have a good trip with this in the back of my mind.'

'So . . .' words fail me again. We both know what Millie has come over to ask.

She takes her eyes off Murphy and meets my gaze. 'So?' she asks.

'OK,' I say in a small voice. Just as my heart starts to soar at the possibility of going to Australia, a thought comes crashing into my brain. 'But wait, I'm not going to go to Australia while you're here having a major operation.' I don't voice what I'm thinking – *she'll need me – won't she?*

'Come on, An. I have Mom and Dad.' Millie shrugs her shoulders. 'Please? I have to find the butterfly wrasse. All my work from the last year hinges on it. I'm convinced it's out there. I have this feeling – I just know it.'

'Can't you go once you've recovered? Just call and reschedule. They'll understand!'

'It'll be too late in the season. If the wrasse are out there, the warmer weather is when they're most likely to be spotted. And I don't have the money to throw at another trip.'

'I'll pay for it.'

'That is so dumb. It'll be winter there anyways. It's now or never. I can't wait another year. We have to look before they're certified extinct for real.'

'I can't pretend to be you, Mill. I don't have the training. Can't you send someone from the lab? Send Bianca!'

'I can't send Bianca. I'm not even telling work I can't go. If you find something we can use, I don't want them second-guessing the validity because it's from you and not me. Plus, I can get the tickets transferred to your name really easily. It's not like I'm asking you to use my passport!' Millie glares at me, daring me to challenge her.

I groan. Murphy trots along happily, oblivious to the plans hatching behind him.

'There's just one snag.' Millie glances at me.

My lips form a thin line.

'A snag?' I ask.

'Well, the boat I booked, the small one, it's expensive and non-refundable and I can't change the reservation, I've already called. All they check is my dive certification, and the picture is grainy. We look enough alike. So . . . you'll have to be me on the boat. I know it'll work.'

'I . . .' I falter and stop speaking. I don't know what to say.

'Andi, come on. Don't make me pull the "I'm-the-one-with-the-shitty-gene card". Just go. I haven't seen you happy in ages, maybe this will change something for you.'

I stop short. 'Really?' I ask. 'You haven't seen me *happy*? Did you ever stop to think that's because I turned down a proposal and somehow that made me a social pariah? Or maybe that all of the people I thought were my friends were actually just "couple" friends who don't want to hang out with me now that I'm single? Travelling isn't the problem here, Millie. If I do this, I'm doing it for you, not because going on a vacation is going to magically fix my life.'

Millie glances at her shoes, sufficiently chastised, before saying, 'All I heard was that you're considering going, which is all I ask.'

I huff at her and nudge Murphy along.

'It'll be warm,' she says. 'You'll finally be tanner than me for once. Not to mention, if you find the wrasse we'll get Hugh Harris back for pointing out your grammar misstep.'

Hugh. Much to my own irritation, I can hear his voice echoing in my brain, the way he pronounces 'Graht Bayreer Reef'. I watched a few of his lectures. They were informative, or at least the young women who flocked to the comments section seemed to think so. I thought he sounded condescending and was too dry on stage, but apparently, I was the only one. I was watching them to better prepare for the day when our DMs veered towards marine biology. He still thought I was Millie, and I wasn't about to let it slip that I was her younger sister. I told myself it was only an added benefit that I could find out what Hugh looked like by watching his lectures.

Unfortunately, they were all filmed in a lecture hall on a university budget, so the clarity was lacking. Even his University of Sydney thumbnail was grainy and unfocused, like he took an old picture of his student ID photo and reused it. All I could tell was that he was blond and tanned, with a somewhat crooked smile.

I try not to overthink our conversations. Technically, I'm not doing anything wrong. I'm defending my sister's honour as the outstanding marine biologist she is. And it feels so good, so thrilling, so unlike me to have this little secret. Plus, I like having the last word. And even though I hate to admit it, Hugh is a worthy sparring opponent, despite how annoying his saviour complex is. It's like he can't fathom that anyone else cares as much about the ocean as he does.

I notice Millie looking at me intently, waiting for me to respond.

'But what if I go all the way there and I don't find them?' I ask. 'It'll all be a waste.' I can't believe I'm even entertaining going on my sister's dream trip while she undergoes major surgery. Her eyes water.

'That's OK with me. As long as we tried. And . . .' she pauses, her eyes twinkling '. . . no good tan is ever a waste.'

'Ugh,' I groan. We both know I'm going to go. Even though I've never travelled alone, even though I'm overwhelmingly underprepared, even though I'm terrified.

@millieandipaxton Let's say someone is forced to go to Cairns for two days (no one would give up Columbus for Cairns on their own volition). What would you tell them to do (besides scuba, of course)?

@hughharris94 Depends on whose asking.

@millieandipaxton Me.

@hughharris94 Hmm . . . Unfortunately, we don't have a Rock n' Roll Hall of Fame here, so you may be disappointed.

@millieandipaxton Okay, forget I asked.

@hughharris94 What time of year?

@millieandipaxton Let's say summer.

@hughharris94 Is this your way of telling me you're coming to Cairns in the next month or two?

@millieandipaxton I knew I should have gone straight to Tripadvisor.

@hughharris94 Well, I'm not from there but I've been a couple times. Probably have better recommendations than Tripadvisor.

@millieandipaxton Tripadvisor would have taken me less time.

@hughharris94 Fine. Since you've made it abundantly clear that you like poisoning yourself with coffee, I would tell you to start your day at Cairns Cup. Get a flat white. Then go to marina and do the walking path along the shore, but the Americans usually talk so loudly they ruin the path for the rest of us. You should get up into the rainforest, there's some great hikes (and plenty of places to contemplate how we drove the butterfly wrasse to extinction). And, because I know you'll ask, Vinnie's in Portsmith has great thrift shopping. Although you'd think your fancy university pays you enough to buy new clothes.

@millieandipaxton Woah.

@hughharris94 What?

@millieandipaxton Nothing. Thank you.

@hughharris94 No, really. What?

@millieandipaxton I didn't realise you had actually been listening to me.

@hughharris94 I haven't been. All American girls are the same.

'Mushroom coral!' Millie barks. We're getting pedicures. I'm getting my toes painted a safe, wine-coloured red, and Millie has opted for a sparkly turquoise.

'Ummm.' I rack my brain. 'Lots of lines in a circle . . . um . . . the throw pillow one!'

She nods, impressed, and puts down her phone. Ever since I agreed to go, I've been studying non-stop. I've memorised all the types of coral found in the Great Barrier Reef and can identify them by their photo as well as their defining characteristics. I know almost as much about staghorn corals as Millie does. I know all the fish to look out for, how to take pictures of them without scaring them away, and how to spot their eggs. I've absorbed so much knowledge that I would be able to fool Hugh – that is, if we were still talking. After our last conversation, I replaced my Instagram app with a Marine Biology dictionary so that I remember my real reason for Australia – finding the butterfly wrasse for Millie, and so that I would stop messaging Hugh. If I'm going to find the wrasse, I can't afford any distractions. I also couldn't think of a comeback, but that's neither here nor there.

For the first time since graduating, my marine biology degree is proving useful. I've started feeling a thrum of excitement when I wake up in the morning. I've started humming when I take Murphy out for walks.

'Stop smiling like that.' Millie swats at me, giggling.

'Like what?'

'You're smirking like you're so proud of yourself for getting the answers to my questions right.'

I try to wipe the smile off my face.

'I'm happy for you,' Millie says, her voice dipping into sincerity. I know she means it, but I still can't shake off the guilt I'm carrying for going on her dream trip without her.

'I'll be worried about you,' I reply to Millie, my voice catching.

The day after I'll arrive in Australia, a week and a half before Christmas, Millie's scheduled for surgery. Surgery takes six to twelve hours and she's in the hospital for two days afterwards. The procedure isn't particularly risky, but I'm nervous. Millie's kept her cool. She's even scheduled a spray tan before she goes back to work so everyone will think she went to Australia. She doesn't want to have to answer anyone's questions or be on the receiving end of their pity.

'I'll be fine. It's good to see you so . . . so happy.'

I glare at her. 'It always comes back to my lack of happiness, doesn't it? I'm fine. I've told you that.'

'You know what I mean,' Millie murmurs, flipping a page in her magazine. 'You're fine, but . . .' She trails off, letting the words hang in the air with meaning.

Sometimes I forget Millie is my older sister. She's so exuberant and carefree, and she takes up so much of the spotlight that she feels like the baby. But sometimes she spouts out pearls of wisdom that remind me she's lived more life than I have.

'I know,' I acquiesce. My voice comes out in a whisper.

'Really, Andi,' Millie presses, 'when was the last time you were this happy? Not content, *happy*? Even with Zach I didn't think that . . .' She stops talking, leaving the unsaid words in the air. Even with Zach, she didn't think I was happy. I try to shrug off the implication, I don't want to go down the rabbit hole of wishing I knew sooner, wishing I could have avoided all the hurt.

'Let me think about it,' I say, partly to get Millie off my back. I settle into my chair and turn on the massage function.

I avoid analysing my last relationship . . . thinking about before it instead . . . maybe during our trip to India. I open my mouth to answer but a memory stops me. I was a senior in college taking my final marine biology lab and I knew I was acing it. I was so ecstatic I felt invincible. Millie was employed at the lab doing research and frequently TA-ed our class, but that day she was pulled into other work. I felt so *free* and so powerful without her there. I finished my lab first and with a perfect score. For the first time I felt like I was where I was meant to be, like I could carve my own space in a narrow field. I was excited for my future.

And then Millie came back. I saw her out of the corner of my eye first, ducking into a neighbouring classroom, her lab coat swishing behind her. Then she popped into our classroom and whispered something to the professor, who burst out laughing, beaming at Millie. She was so at home, so commanding, and I felt all my excitement evaporate. Millie wasn't someone I could compete with.

'India,' I finally say.

Millie nods. 'I thought you would say that. And this will be even better, trust me.' She winks.

I'm so intimidated at the thought of pretending to be Millie that I'm not sure if I believe her.

Chapter 4

Murphy knows something's up because he's following me around the house like he did when he was a puppy. It started after I brought him his favourite bone from the gourmet store down the street that I usually reserve only for his birthday. Murphy played with it for all of ten minutes before he turned his gaze to me, full puppy-dog eyes, as if he knew the bone was only a way to soften bad news.

That afternoon was when everything really sunk in. I told Matteo I was going away for the holidays. He clapped with glee and leaned into my cubicle in excitement.

'Where? Where?' he asked, his hands clasping together at his belly.

'Australia.'

'Wow,' Matteo breathed. 'That's really *going away*. Becca! Did you hear Andi's going to Australia?'

'Yes!' Becca calls, her head popping up from her desk. 'While I'm rotting through the holidays with my sister's new baby, she'll be in paradise! I'm thrilled for her!'

I roll my eyes in Becca's direction as Matteo laughs. 'Much to Becca's dismay, my family does think I need to get out more. So, here I am, finally taking a vacation.'

Millie and I had agreed not to explain the situation to anyone. She wanted to keep her health issues private, and I was worried that somehow it would get back to her work that she never went. Once she transferred the tickets, I tried to convince Millie to explain everything to her boss. After all, she *does* have health leave. So, she would still have plenty of time off to undergo surgery and recover. But she pointed out that if they knew I was the one who went on the trip, because I'm not a working marine biologist for the University of Ohio, the lab wouldn't be able to use any photos I took or, more importantly, officially count any sightings of the butterfly wrasse, making the trip a complete waste of time.

'Good for you,' Matteo said, patting the wall of my cubicle. 'And we only have the end-of-year statement to prepare for before you go!'

'I can help you with it!' Becca calls again from her cubicle. I forget how much noise carries in this office.

'Thank you, Becca,' I yell in her direction before turning back to my work at hand – another deck that would be used for one meeting and then never looked at again. Operations strategy sounded exciting six years ago, back when I was fresh out of college – I could use the statistical research part of my marine biology degree and the career path was stable. But the work has become repetitive and stale, the last thing I want to do is churn out another deck before my vacation. Every single time I make a deck I question what I'm doing, dedicating all my time to a company that makes cereal. In fact, the only time I don't feel like I'm wasting my life away is when we do volunteer events like planting trees or last summer when I oversaw the intern programme. At least when I do those things I'm impacting something bigger than me.

I watched Matteo walk away and felt a sudden burst of nostalgia for my years working here, always the same, completely safe. The feeling fades as soon as I remember that my break is only a couple of weeks, not forever – I'll be back here, getting tea with Becca and making decks for the spring campaigns before I know it.

The day I leave for Australia, Millie comes over at ten. She squeals upon arrival. We're leaving for the airport at eleven – my flight takes off at 1.30. Three hours to Dallas, and then fourteen to Cairns. My stomach dips at the thought of being trapped on a plane for fourteen hours. I've downloaded more romcoms than I'll be able to stomach, including *Notting Hill*, *Just Go with It* and *The Proposal*. And, for good measure, to make Millie proud, a documentary about coral reefs. I even screenshotted Hugh's Cairns' itinerary. My phone storage is full, and my suitcase is zipped (barely), but I don't feel ready.

'Are you ready?' Millie asks, launching herself onto my crisply made bed.

I shake my head. 'I don't think so?' I back-flop onto the mattress next to her. Both of us stare at the ceiling.

'Me neither.'

Lying next to her on the bed I feel an overwhelming sense of pressure. I want to do this for her so badly. The only emotion that can overcome my guilt at being the sister without the BRCA gene is my hope that I can do something, anything, to make it better.

After the surgery and a night in the hospital, she'll be released, where she will recover, wrapped in gauze, for three to four weeks. She won't be able to lift her arms over her head. She'll stay with our parents and Murphy, although she won't be able to walk him in case he pulls on the leash. The week I'm gone will be her worst week. She will be exhausted and sad, and living in a body that doesn't feel like hers. It doesn't feel right to know I'll be living her dream at the same time.

'I'm gonna find this stupid fish,' I say, more to myself than to her.

'I know you are,' Millie says calmly, still staring at the ceiling. 'And I'm gonna have boobs that never sag.'

My laugh comes out strangled because I'm trying not to cry. I scoot closer to her and tuck my head onto her shoulder. 'I love you.'

'I love you too.'

As much as I think I prepared, I don't even make it onto the plane before I realise I forgot something. I'm on the jet bridge when I go digging in my toiletry bag for my hand sanitiser and pull out my face sunscreen instead. Looking at the bottle, I realise what I've forgotten. I forgot reef-friendly sunscreen.

Millie doesn't even buy sunscreen that isn't reef-friendly. Any marine biologist worth their salt wouldn't dare do that. Unless I can find the right kind of sunscreen before I get on the boat, everyone will know I'm a fraud, let alone the guilt I'll feel using a product that could damage the environment I'm supposed to have dedicated my life to studying and preserving. I'm supposed to board a shuttle to the pier as soon as I land in Cairns, and there is zero chance that I'll be able to find reef-friendly sunscreen at Dallas airport.

I resist the urge to smack myself in my forehead with the heel of my hand.

'Are you OK?' the flight attendant asks as I scooch by her onto the plane.

I gulp. 'Mhm,' I say, hoping she thinks I'm scared of flying and doesn't register that I'm about to have a full-on mental breakdown.

What was I thinking? I ask myself as I sink into my seat. I'm in the window, squeezed next to a man with a giant Kindle on his lap. He is paging through a romance novel in exceptionally large font, something I would usually find amusing, but I'm so stressed that it doesn't bring a smile to my face.

How am I going to convince people that I'm Millie if I can't even remember the basics? *Why did I think this would be a piece of cake?* I begin to regret spending more time studying the coral and fish than reviewing scuba basics. Millie kept telling me, 'It's just like riding a bike,' but it's been almost five years since my last dive. Not to mention I'll be on a boat with total strangers, and I'm travelling all the way there and back alone. I'll have no one to stop me from making a complete fool of myself. No, worse, a complete fool of my sister.

I close my eyes to keep from crying. If Millie thinks I can do this . . . then I can do it . . . right? As the plane takes off, a familiar thought hits me, one I've had a thousand times before: *I wish I was her*.

I ease her scuba certification card out of my wallet. The photo is small and grainy. I can pass for her easily, the same way I did for those eleven months when she was twenty-one and I used her ID to get into bars.

I only indulge myself for a moment before a shake of turbulence brings me back to my senses. How dare I wish I was Millie, how could I have the indecency to want to trade places with her, when I am jetting off to Australia and she is getting ready for what will probably be the worst week of her life?

The plane shakes some more, and I find myself promising to myself, and whatever universal power is keeping the plane in the air, that if we get on the ground safely, I will do Millie justice and take advantage of this opportunity.

I don't want to keep wasting my twenties wondering when I'm going to be happy. I was happy in school when I was studying the movement of the ocean. I used to be excited to travel, thrilled to see new places, so elated to find out what was *next*. I loved feeling like I had choices. But then . . . I chose Zach and pretty soon it seemed like that was my last choice, suddenly my future was planned. Before I knew it, my friends were his friends, couples the same age as us, content to spend every Saturday at the same trendy brewery on the edge of town. Up next was a house in the suburbs and a baby named Theo.

Now that my future with Zach is gone I should feel happy but instead, I feel frozen, like now I have too many choices, and I don't know if I'll choose the right one.

As I settle back into my seat, fear washes over me. But now I'm not sure if it's because I'm going halfway around the world all by myself to masquerade as my sister while she undergoes major surgery, or if I'm terrified because I know that by the time I come back, my life will never be the same.

Chapter 5

One day before the first dive

The flight to Dallas is short. I watch one movie, read a couple of chapters of my book, and try to temper my panic. When I'm standing in front of the boarding gate for Cairns, I text Millie and my parents that I'm about to board my flight. Once I'm in Australia, I won't have service, and I'll only be able to talk to them on Wi-Fi, which I won't have on the boat. I try not to think about the fact that I'll have no idea how Millie's doing until I'm back on land.

'You're gonna be great,' Millie texts back immediately. 'You'll find that butterfly wrasse. I know it!'

'Hugh's gonna be sorry,' I respond. Instantly, I regret it. Hugh should be the last thing on my mind, especially considering I hadn't talked to him in almost a week. I watch Millie's three dots appear in our chat, realising that she might think it's weird for me to bring Hugh back up. Thankfully, all Millie does is love the message and send back multiple muscle arm emojis which are code for 'you got this'. I breathe out a sigh of relief.

I am turning to make one final bathroom run when the intercom crackles. Everyone around me looks up, boarding is supposed to begin any minute. We wait as the gate agent behind the microphone, a middle-aged woman with perfectly coiffed hair, speaks.

'Could a passenger by the name of Andi Paxton please come see me at the counter?'

Heat rises in my cheeks. *Is this about Millie switching the tickets? What if they don't let me board?* I feel like I've just been called to the principal's office. I half expect someone next to me to say, 'Ooo, Andi's in trouble,' but no one around me seems to care – everyone returns their attention to their phones. I make my way towards the gate agent, falling in line behind a young couple whispering to each other.

I all but gape at the woman in front of me, who has managed to tie a silk scarf around her hair flawlessly. She looks like an old Hollywood movie star. I think back to when I've practised tying a bandana around my hair and all I ended up doing was making myself look like I got lost on my way to shovel hay. The gate agent peers around the pair and motions for me to come forward.

'Andi Paxton?' she asks, as I skirt around them. They don't move an inch to let me pass them by, the woman is too busy looking at her phone. The gate agent shoots me a sympathetic look as I wiggle around.

'Don't worry,' she says kindly, 'nothing's wrong.'

'Phew,' I sigh out.

'Passport?' she asks.

I slide it over and she begins rapid-fire typing into her computer.

'We have notes in the system when there's a last-minute ticket change due to exceptional circumstances.' She drops her voice to a whisper. 'It says here that your sister had to cancel due to unexpected health issues.'

I feel my eyes start to fill with tears, a lump forming instantly in my throat. I nod.

'My sister is my best friend.' The gate agent smiles kindly. 'And we had an extra seat in first class.'

'First class?' I gasp, I can't help myself. I laugh as a tear spills onto my cheek. Wait until Millie hears about this.

She smiles at me and slides back my passport and a ticket. 'I'm glad it seems like you'll enjoy it.'

Dazed, I pull my luggage behind me and swerve around the couple. The scarved woman gives me a thorough up-down, appraising my haphazard outfit like she wants to stop me from being in first class on appearance alone. I hear them approach the table to ask if the gate agent has been able to complete their upgrade.

'Unfortunately, not at this time,' the gate agent replies calmly.

'But you just upgraded *her* to first class.' The scarf-lady points at me. I scuttle further away from them, wanting to disappear into the faded airport carpet.

'You asked to be seated together, and there was only one seat left in first class.'

The woman huffs and turns to go, but not before giving me a pointed glance.

Her partner remains behind, asking the gate agent if there's anything he can do. After another minute of bargaining, he turns to go, lugging a mysterious and heavy-looking black box after the woman in the scarf.

When I land in Cairns it's morning. My first-class experience was nothing short of blissful, even if I did spend an inordinate amount of it watching videos of Murphy as a puppy and wondering if he missed me. The food was so good I didn't even finish my own snacks and when I reclined my chair all the way down, I almost let out a scream of excitement. Thankfully, I didn't see the glamorous woman and her boyfriend again. Now that I know first-hand how wonderful a first-class upgrade is, I see why she was so disappointed.

I clear customs and try to tamp down my yawns. I glance down at the notes I'd written on the plane. The flight gave me time to make a game plan and I resolved to spend the next six days accomplishing two things: 1) finding the butterfly wrasse for my sister, and 2) using this time with no distractions, no work, space from a routine that used to be filled with Zach and our friends, to think about what I really want in life. I know I don't want to stay at Sunshine Foods forever, and I also know I made the right choice breaking things off with Zach, but that's about it.

Before I take my phone off Wi-Fi, I get a text from my parents wishing me well. Becca has sent me a barrage of texts, including *I miss you already loser!!!* and *Can you get an Australian hunk's number for me please??? Tell him I'll marry for a visa!* I reply to them both before sending one last message full of hearts to Millie. I start to weave my way through the airport, towards the open air, hoping to find sunscreen on my way out.

Not a single store seems to be selling the sunscreen I need but my frustration clears as soon as I step outside. Instantly, I'm hit by a wave of humidity. I breathe in long and slow, a huge smile covering my face as I am blanketed with warmth. Compared to an Ohio winter, it feels incredible, blissful, even. It's early enough that there's still dew sparkling on the grass lining the parking lot. The airport is small, palm trees lining the building. I spot the sign for the shuttle to the docks right away.

I'm nervous and tingly that I'm about to be deep in a lie. I remind myself that I know everything about my sister *and* that these people don't know her at all. They will have no idea. I place her ID strategically at the front of my wallet in case I need it when I board the boat. I step in line behind the other tourists queueing for the bus. An older couple takes their place behind me. They bicker softly until one of them laughs. When I glance behind me, they're holding hands. I feel a tug at my heartstrings – they have what I want one day.

We barely have to wait five minutes before they start to load us onto the bus. I'm last to board because I need to physically kick my suitcase into the space underneath the bus (it barely fits, and I feel my face heat with embarrassment). But I end up with the front seat to myself, and as I unpack my water bottle to take a large sip, I think to myself, *I did it. I actually made it all the way to Australia. I'm about to dive the Great Barrier Reef.* Just as I'm about to take another sip, cheersing myself as I do so, a straggler boards the bus and throws his backpack between us before taking his seat. I jump at the sudden movement and spill water down the front of my shirt. *Great*, I think, giving the man serious side-eye. He's fiddling with his wallet, so he doesn't even notice. I roll my eyes. I know I'm one of them, but why do American tourists seem to suck so much?

As soon as we pull out of the parking lot and onto the main road, sunlight streams through the windows. I dig out my toiletry bag to rub some sunscreen onto my face, no sense in getting burned before my trip even starts, and try to enjoy the ride. Air is rushing through the cracked windows and it smells like the ocean. I can barely contain my excitement.

We haven't even been driving for five minutes before I notice the man next to me is staring at me. Well . . . not exactly at me . . . he's staring at the toiletry bag that's resting in my lap . . . *really* staring at it. I watch him studying my bag, weirded out that he's taken such an interest in my lap, but he doesn't notice. He has shaggy blond hair and tanned skin. He's wearing a loose-fitting slate-grey T-shirt. He looks . . . familiar . . . but I can't place him. I quickly remind myself that I'm extremely jet-lagged and know nobody in Australia. Maybe he looks like a famous person.

I stare at his nose, which slopes perfectly straight, like the profile outline of Prince Eric from *A Little Mermaid*.

He catches me staring and we make direct eye contact. I feel the back of my kneecaps prickle with sweat. Suddenly, my heart is pounding, and my throat is dry. I clear my throat awkwardly and look away. I resolve not to let my new-found singleness make me extremely nervous around every hot guy I encounter. I remind myself of my goals – *not even perfect Prince Eric noses will distract me.*

Before rotating my shoulders to completely face the window, I steal one more look at his eyes, which are a dark, grey-ish blue that reminds me of a rain-storm. They're not the aquamarine that Prince Eric has. They're almost the colour of the skin of a dolphin. And he looks angry.

It clicks. He reminds me of Hugh Harris. I dismiss the thought as soon as it crosses my mind. *There's no way.* It must be the jet lag.

I almost ask if there is something I can do to help him but think better of it. Maybe he had to sit next to a crying baby on his flight. I look out the window instead. We are passing palm trees that sway in the wind. In the distance are huge, vividly green mountains. Some are shrouded gently in fog. The whole place is lush and breathtaking. Occasionally, water appears in between buildings. It's bright blue and calm. I'm in paradise.

The bus clanks over a huge pothole, sending his backpack and my bag straight up in the air. I attempt to catch my toiletry bag and fumble, sending it straight into his lap. He looks at me with fury, his eyes even darker than they were a second ago, his brow furrowed.

'Here.' He thrusts it into my hands. He has an Australian accent, so it sounds like 'heeya'.

'Thanks.'

'You know they make reef-friendly sunscreen, right?'

I almost point out that he's so tanned it looks like he's never used sunscreen in his life, but instead I diplomatically say, 'OK.'

'And yet you brought that.' He gestures to my bag.

I am grateful Australians speak English, but man, this guy is hard to understand. He sounds like he's trying to talk with rocks in his mouth. It takes me a moment to decipher what he's trying to say, which is: *Why do you have non-reef-friendly sunscreen when you're at the biggest reef in the world?* Instead of thinking of a response, I panic. I stare at him, blinking, thinking, *Oh my God, how is this already happening? I've barely left the air-port parking lot and they already know I'm a fraud.*

He raises his eyebrows at me and the space between his eyebrows crinkles. As I clock his disgust, my thoughts shift from embarrassment to annoyance. *Is this guy serious?* He continues staring at me. 'I forgot my other sunscreen,' I say finally, unsure of why he thinks I owe him an explanation.

He nods but I can tell by his face he doesn't believe me. 'I'm serious!' I double down. 'I really did. I looked for a different kind at the airport before I came.'

'Sure,' he says. He turns his attention forward.

'What, you don't believe me?' Immediately upon asking, I blush. I don't know why it's important to me that a stranger believes I wouldn't willingly bring reef-harming chemicals to the Great Barrier Reef. Maybe because he's Australian, and I don't want to enter the country and get off on the wrong foot. Maybe because he is undeniably very cute. Maybe because I'm pretending to be some-body who would never make the mistake I just did.

'Sure,' he mumbles.

All right, asshole, I think.

We sit in silence the rest of the bus ride. I try to focus on absorbing every bit of scenery. I take a picture to send to Millie. I double-check I have her ID. I try not to look at who I've now labelled as 'angry suntan man', even though, despite his temperament, he's nice to look at. He's muscular in a gentle sort of way. Not like he goes to CrossFit, but more like he goes on runs and helps his neighbours move their furniture when they need it.

We're in line to get off the bus when I see his back-pack. He's so much taller than me that I'm face to face with the logo: University of Sydney Marine Biology Lab. *There's no way* . . . I think, shaking off the unease in my chest.

I debate asking if he knows Hugh but think better of it. He's so unfriendly, if I tapped him on the shoulder, he would probably have a panic attack at the idea of talking to me again. Plus, I realise, I don't want Hugh to know that I was using the wrong sunscreen.

Chapter 6

Day of the first dive

I walk in a large circle before I realise I'm completely lost. I'm looking for Coral Sea Dreaming's boat, but I can't seem to find it anywhere. All the other bus passengers have either disappeared inside the port building or are lining up outside their boats. Even the old couple have found their way to where they're supposed to be. The only other person that looks as lost as me is angry suntan man.

I huff and sit down on a bench to pull up my email and see if that will give me any direction, but I can't connect to the Australian network, and my phone is stubbornly refusing to show any of my inbox without connectivity. Angry suntan man looks as stumped as me, but I figure he must have service – he is Australian after all.

Lugging my bag around the docks has made me slightly sweaty, and I wipe at my hairline before turning to him. 'Excuse me?' I try to ask sweetly, hoping he will forget our bus conversation for long enough to help me out.

He stares at me with his grey-blue eyes. Gentle lines have appeared across his forehead.

'I'm wondering if you can look something up for me. I'm looking for Coral Sea Dreaming, and I can't seem to spot their boat anywhere.'

His expression transforms from confused to crestfallen. 'You're on . . .' He pauses and coughs once, like he's dislodging something from his throat. 'You're with Coral Sea Dreaming?' His accent elongates the name, making it sound like 'coral sea drayming'.

'Yeah . . . are you?'

He grunts, which I assume is an affirmative. A pit of dread pools in my stomach. *How can the one person who spotted my sunscreen mess-up be on my boat? Aren't there, like, a thousand boats here?*

'Can't find that bugger anywhere,' he says, not meeting my eyes.

'Have you tried their website? I would but I haven't got any signal,' I offer.

'Yes.' His tone is curt. I can feel him thinking, *Obviously*, but he doesn't say it out loud.

I start to introduce myself, outstretching a hand in his direction, but just as I do, his phone vibrates in his hand and a voice starts sounding out directions. 'I think it's this way,' he says, hoisting his backpack onto his shoulders and leaving my hand hanging limply in the air.

'It's Millie,' I mutter, slowly testing out my new identity, but he's too far ahead to hear me, so my hand returns limply to my side.

We work our way through the docks, ducking under signs and stepping over mounds of seagull poop. Angry suntan man takes a sharp turn to follow a narrower dock. He's a whole head taller than I am, which makes navigating through the signs nailed to swaying sailboats much faster. Instead of squinting at them, I follow his broad shoulders. Soon we're all the way at the end of the pier.

We stop in front of a small sailboat, maybe about fifty feet long. '*CORAL SEA DREAMING*' is written in large blue lettering across the side. Benches line the back of the boat in a large square around what must be the captain's chair. A man and a woman are sitting on one of the benches, their hands intertwined. Her head is resting on his shoulder and he's showing her something on his phone. In unison, they both start to laugh.

I can't help but think about Zach. *That could have been us.* I wonder if we ever actually looked like that. We didn't exactly share a sense of humour. I shake my head. I don't want to think about him now. For the next five days and four nights, I am Millie. My first goal is to find the butterfly wrasse. Thinking about the life I left behind comes second.

Clouds dot the sky, but I feel my shoulders starting to sunburn anyway, and I pivot my attention to the cover over the back of the boat that protects the benches and the captain from the sun. I glance at angry suntan man, who looks remarkably less angry and instead like he may start to enjoy himself. He's got a smirk on his face that reads, *Aren't you gonna thank me?* I don't thank him. Instead, I ruminate on how annoying I think his tan is. I bet he isn't in a rush to put on sunscreen.

The boat is a flurry of activity. I see a woman with a messy bun ducking in and out of the room on the middle of the deck. A dark-haired man is flitting from bow to stern and back again. I know based on Millie's registration that the boat can fit twelve, but looking at it now, I don't see how. All I can see is a flat white deck, a large white sail, the captain's chair at the back, surrounded by benches and covered by an overhang, and in the middle of the boat, something that looks like a small cabin.

An extremely tanned barefoot man with blond dreads and dark sunglasses deftly manoeuvres past us and jumps onto the boat with the agility of a jungle cat. Angry suntan man and I exchange a look. I can tell he's also wondering what's going on. A second later the man with dreads pops back out onto the pier and greets us.

'I'm Aaron,' he states, like that explains everything. 'I'll grab your stuff.' He reaches for my suitcase and flings it on board like it's weightless. I cringe at the memory of having to kick it into the compartment underneath the bus.

'I don't need to show you ID?' I call after Aaron, but it's too late, he's already climbing aboard with my bag. He picks up angry suntan man's next. Only once he's stored our luggage does he pop back out onto the deck. 'Shoes into the bin,' he says, looking down at us and gesturing at a large storage container on the dock. 'No shoes aboard.' We shrug and both chuck our flip-flops into the container.

'Welcome to *Coral Sea Dreaming*,' Aaron announces, stretching his arms out wide. 'I'm your captain.'

The woman with the messy bun pops up next to him. 'And I'm your first mate, Vanessa,' she says in a lilting Italian accent. A stray lock of dark hair whips around her cheek. 'I'll check you in in a minute. Feel free to make yourself comfortable.'

I smile back at her. Aaron and Vanessa seem chill. There is potential for this to be the restart I need. The shrill caw of a seagull cuts through the air. Buoyed with excitement, I toss my backpack onto the boat and step over the side.

I take a few shaky steps across the boat, which is lurching gently even though it's securely tied to the pier.

I settle onto a bench under the covered overhang next to Aaron's chair. I hug my backpack close to my chest. I take inventory of my home for the next five days.

The boat is clean, which is what I was most worried about. The deck doesn't feel dirty underneath my feet, just textured and grippy, which I assume is to help keep people from slipping. Everything smells a little damp and a little like salt, but it's a nice, reassuring smell. The bench I'm sitting on is comfortable, a worn-in vinyl material that's cracked in spots and a faded light blue.

I realise that the room I was seeing before is really a doorway with steps that lead to the sleeping quarters. Apart from what I feel like is the captain's room, the rest of the boat is small. When I think about it, I realise I've never been trapped anywhere this small in my life. From the back to the front of the boat there's just two narrow walkways on either side of the centre platform. The scuba equipment is set up at the front of the boat. I can see a line of air tanks. The platform in the middle of the boat looks like an ideal place to sunbathe. But I can't help but notice that there's nowhere to go if things go sideways. If anyone figures out I'm not Millie, I'm totally stuck.

In an attempt to stop myself from getting claustrophobic, I look out at the horizon and take in the crystal blue water and the gently sloping mountains. I will probably never be somewhere as pretty as this again. The thought both calms and depresses me.

When my gaze swings back to the boat, I find angry suntan man looking at me intently. He quickly looks away, but after a beat his stare returns.

'What?' I ask, exasperation creeping into my voice. 'Am I in your seat? Are you going to lecture me about sunscreen again?'

'What?' he says, the line between his eyebrows appearing again. 'No, you're not in my seat. I was actually going to ask if you want to go get suncream. Vanessa said we have fifteen minutes before check-in starts.'

'Oh,' I manage to get out. *Maybe he isn't 100 per cent asshole after all . . .* 'Yeah. That would be nice.'

'There's a place at the edge of the pier. Let's go,' he says gruffly, ducking underneath the overhang and making his way back to the ladder.

'You don't have to take me,' I stammer, but he's already jumping off the boat. I rush to catch up to him, scurrying down the ladder as fast as I can, forgetting that I'm barefoot until I wince at the hot dock underneath my feet.

'Shoes?' He hands me my flip-flops. I barely have them on before he's striding towards the edge of the pier.

'Coming!' I call, but he doesn't even turn around.

I follow him the entire way to the store, tracking his shoulders as he dodges past tourists and sailors. A small terrier barks at us as we pass, and I wince as my thoughts turn to Murphy. He loves the beach. He would be right at home here. I'm panting by the time we get inside, and I have to wipe a line of sweat from my forehead. A bell above the door chimes. He's stooped in front of a shelf of sunscreen.

'This one is best.' He hands me a large tube.

'Thank you.' I look at him and he looks away.

'No problem.' He shrugs. 'Better for the reef.'

'Right.' I swallow.

The sun blazes on my skin as soon as I step back outside. I glance at my shoulders. They look pink. *How is it possible I'm already burning?* I think. I squirt some sunscreen onto my palm and try to rub it on my shoulders while we walk towards the boat, but my tank top makes it awkward, and I end up looking like I'm trying to give myself a hug. I smear sunscreen across my chest and huff in frustration. I'm forced to stop and drop my bag as I try to rectify the situation.

I have one arm underneath my tank top and my other arm bent sideways over my head. I look up to see angry suntan man glancing over his shoulder with a bemused expression.

'Do you need . . .' he trails off, his lips quirking up into a smile.

I watch his gaze linger on my belly button now fully exposed to the sun, my shirt having ridden up as I wormed my sunscreened hands through it.

'Uh, it's OK.' My cheeks flame with embarrassment I wriggle my way back to a normal position as fast as I can. 'I think I got it.'

My voice seems to snap him out of it, because he flushes red and his lips compress back into his usual grim expression. He turns around and starts marching towards the boat.

'All right, team,' Vanessa announces, bouncing into the captain's room. We've made it back and are sitting on opposite sides of the boat. He hasn't looked at me once since we returned. When I thanked him again for taking me to grab sunscreen, he merely grunted.

'Let's start on our paperwork.' Vanessa hands out clipboards and pens. 'We're waiting on two more, there's only six of you on this trip. Well, plus,' she starts counting on her fingers, 'me and Miguel and Aaron. So, we are nine.' She nods towards the doorway and the stairs. 'After we're done, I'll show you the sleeping arrangements.'

The paperwork is simple. We state our scuba certification dates and credentials. I write out Millie's information, which terrifies me, because she's a lot more experienced than I am. Even though I watched a lot of YouTube review tutorials on how to set up gear and calculate decompression time, I still don't feel prepared. I make a mental note to try and casually ask Vanessa or Miguel if they'll review the equipment with me.

There's an additional page that outlines our itinerary:

Day 1: All aboard at 10 a.m. Midday Dive + Late Afternoon Dive (Treasure Cove)

Day 2: Morning Dive + Afternoon Dive + Night Dive (Treasure Cove West, Wonder Reef)

Day 3: Morning Dive + Midday Dive + Late Afternoon Dive (Queen's Point)

Day 4: Fitzroy Island Day Excursion + Turtle Rehabilitation Centre

Day 5: Morning Dive + Lunch. Disembark at 3 p.m. (Capricorn Reef)

Millie had painstakingly prepped me for all the dives but seeing them on paper while hearing the seagulls caw behind me feels different. She wrote out notes on each dive site, instructing me on what to look for and when and where the last butterfly wrasse sighting occurred. She bundled all her notes up for me in a little book that she tucked into my suitcase when she dropped me off at the airport. I started crying when I read the first page on my flight to Cairns, because she scrawled in her giant, loopy cursive: *You're gonna be great, sis.*

I make a mental note to cross-reference Millie's list with the itinerary they gave us. I can't do any research on my own if the sites are different, but at least I would know not to put too much stock into the notes she left me.

I had forgotten about Fitzroy Island until I see it on the page. Millie had told me about it briefly, but I hardly did any research because there's no scuba diving involved. Fitzroy is off the coast of Cairns, only accessible by boat. From what I remember, it's mostly comprised of rainforest and the Turtle Rehabilitation Centre. Even though I've hardly been on the boat for more than ten minutes, I'm relieved we'll have a chance to stretch our legs on dry land.

I skim the itinerary one more time before folding it into a neat square and tucking it into my back pocket.

Nine chances to find the butterfly wrasse.

I'm about halfway through the rest of the forms when I hear the unmistakable sound of a pen scratching angrily across paper.

Angry suntan man is writing furiously. Something about the way he's hunched over his clipboard makes me want to finish faster than he does. I pick up my pace, hoping I can hand Vanessa mine first. He finishes before I do and hands his clipboard to Vanessa with a triumphant grin. My skin prickles in annoyance. I finish next, and I wait for her to sign and initial his form before I hand her my sheaf of papers.

'Ah,' she says, upon reading my name, 'you're the two marine biologists.'

I smile and nod proudly. Angry suntan man shoots me an incredibly surprised look. *Ha!* I think, before my brain reminds me that I am not, in fact, a marine biologist. And that as a fellow marine biologist, angry suntan man will be very confused as to why he had to help me procure reef-friendly sunscreen. *Dammit.*

My stomach flips when I realise the repercussions of what Vanessa said. If angry suntan man is a marine biologist . . . he's Hugh. The man who just took me to buy sunscreen is Hugh Harris. *No*, I think quickly, *he can't be Hugh*. The universe can't possibly have made this trip even more complicated.

Plus, Hugh is . . . I think back to our DMs . . . back to what Millie has told me about him . . . he's snarky and haughty and an insufferable know-it-all. I push down my next thought: angry suntan man is all of those things too.

Vanessa opens her mouth to say something else, perhaps formally introduce us, but before she can another two people come aboard. The first one up the ladder is lugging a massive black container that looks so heavy duty it could have come straight off a military cargo plane. I recognise the container first, racking my brain for why it's familiar.

'My camera,' the man explains breathlessly to us, gesturing to the massive box. It dawns on me as his partner scales up the ladder behind him.

The scarf lady from the airport and her partner are on my boat.

I press myself into my seat hoping to disappear completely. I fumble for my sunglasses and slide them onto my face. *She won't remember my name*, I reassure myself. *She won't hate me for taking her first-class seat. She won't notice that I'm now going by Millie.* For the first time in my life, I'm thankful for how unremarkable I look. Dark curly hair and light eyes, full cheeks, average height. There are a million people that look like me. Plus, I switched into my jean shorts at the airport, so I'm not even wearing the same outfit.

She doesn't appear to have changed and is now sporting the silk scarf stylishly knotted around her neck, somehow not looking like she just walked off a flight. Her companion is slightly bent over, panting, and she edges around him to perch on the edge of a bench in the shade. She gives the group of us a little wave, and I notice as her gaze lingers on angry suntan man. Then her gaze passes to me, and I sink further back into my seat just as her companion fumbles with his box and it thuds to the floor.

'Shit!' he exclaims loudly. Angry suntan man rises from his seats to lend a hand, but the man waves him away. Vanessa sternly lets him know that the captain's room is no place for his camera. Following Vanessa's instructions, he fumbles his camera down the stairs to stow it below deck. I think about the little black waterproof camera Millie gave me. *What could possibly be in this guy's box?*

When he appears back on deck, our dive group is finally all together. Camera man and the scarf lady, the two lovebirds across the way, angry suntan man, and me.

The couple across from me finish their paperwork right when Vanessa bounds back up the stairs. I wait while they hand her their clipboards and then force myself to spring into action the way that Millie would. Typically, I would introduce myself last, I'm not the most overeager socialiser. But Millie would want to chat immediately, and being friendly with everyone will help me when I eventually ask them to keep an eye out for the butterfly wrasse. 'The more eyes watching, the better,' Millie drilled into me before I left.

'I'm Millie,' I announce, jumping up from my chair.

'Hello! I'm Pippa,' the girl says with an easy grin. She has a soft British accent and seems kind. I like her immediately. 'This is my boyfriend,' she announces, turning to the man next to her.

'Andrew,' he says. He has a deep voice and a strong stance, like he's preparing to captain the boat in an emergency. I flash them both the biggest grin I can muster.

Their attention turns towards angry suntan man. He is looking right at us, his mouth in a thin line, but his eyes are obscured by his sunglasses.

Andrew sticks out his hand. 'Hey, mate, I'm Andrew.'

Hugh's expression shifts, losing its surliness. He looks peaceful and happy . . . almost friendly. I watch his shoulder muscles ripple under his T-shirt as he stands up. I notice his eyes have gone from greyish to a brighter, more cerulean blue.

'Hugh,' he says, as he extends his hand to shake theirs. He smiles an easy, wide, slightly crooked smile that he certainly never gave to me.

My stomach drops.

'I'm so sorry,' Pippa says, voicing my exact thought. 'I didn't quite catch that?'

'Hugh,' he repeats, louder and more clearly.

I'm glad he's looking at Pippa and Andrew because my mouth is hanging open. If I'm honest with myself, I suspected he was Hugh from the moment I read his backpack. But I didn't *want* him to be Hugh. I don't *need* another complication. I was hoping if I pretended he wasn't Hugh then he could just end up being some guy borrowing his friend's backpack. But if he is Hugh Harris then where are his glasses? Doesn't he wear glasses? And why didn't Millie tell me he was *this* cute?

Hugh Harris, the man hell-bent on proving Millie wrong, is on my only opportunity to prove her right.

When is he going to realise that I'm Millie Paxton?

What if he realises that I'm really Andi Paxton?

What if scarf lady remembers that I go by Andi?

If Hugh gets so much as a whiff of trouble, he'll see right through me. And he already witnessed my sunscreen debacle.

My heart is racing, so I take a deep breath and channel Millie. I cannot screw this up for her.

Finding the butterfly wrasse is all that matters.

'Hugh,' I mutter under my breath, 'you're going down.'

Chapter 7

Nine dives to go

I listen to Vanessa explain the boat in a daze. I vaguely register the words 'life jacket'. I avoid looking at Hugh, wondering if I can successfully avoid him for the entirety of our trip.

I don't remember the name of the camera-toting man although I'm pretty sure the scarf-wearing woman's name starts with an N, something pretty and feminine sounding, like Natasha. The name Hugh Harris runs through my mind on what feels like a continuous loop.

We pull away from the pier. I force myself to take in my surroundings, looking everywhere except where Hugh is seated, which is on the same bench I am, but as far away from me as physically possible. He scoots away from me again, and I'm tempted to lift my arm and check and see if I remembered deodorant. I either smell, or he has put two and two together and figured out who I am. He won't want to talk to me either. He thinks Millie hates him.

And he knows as well as I do that there can't be that many marine biologists named Millie studying the Great Barrier Reef, can there? For once, I agree with Millie, cursing my mother under my breath for giving us such untraditional names. *Millicent? What was she thinking? What happened to Rachel or Sarah or Hannah?*

We leave the marina in our wake, the cluster of tall buildings and ships getting smaller and smaller. The mountains frame the background, huge and soft, trees rounding out their edges, so the peaks look like scales of a friendly dragon, and not like the jagged spines of a triceratops. As I relax into the rhythmic pounding of water against the side of the boat, I can't help but smile. The water is crystal clear and where it meets the shore it turns a brilliant shade of aquamarine. The beaches of Cairns sparkle a bright white as we pull away. Grey rocks and palm trees dot the shore, swaying gently in the wind. People are already setting up chairs on the beach, and there's a group playing volleyball, sand spraying up around their feet as they run back and forth. Sandwiched between the vivid, electric blue sea and the lush, sloping mountains, Cairns is a tropical paradise.

But despite the view, the further we get from land the more my anxiety rises. Five days on a boat with Hugh Harris. Five days of not knowing how Millie's surgery went. Five days of reckoning with the fact that I'm now single with hardly anything at home to return to, and that after being on a boat for five minutes I'm already happier than I have been in two years.

Vanessa and Miguel hand out instant coffee packets and pour hot water out of a tumbler. I accept both gratefully. The mix of the coffee and the sea breeze starts to clear my head. At some point I forget about Hugh. The water is bright blue and is getting choppier the further away from the marina we get. The waves have got a little bigger and the boat has leaned into a gentle swaying rhythm. I find myself smiling into the distance, at the swaying palm trees getting smaller and smaller.

This is the feeling I search for in yoga classes. Being so content where I am that I can fully be in the moment. When I've checked my troubles and worries at the door and for an hour, I am fully present. I am only able to be fully present right now because there is no service or Wi-Fi and no option for me to exit the boat. But I sink into it, and it feels strangely blissful.

I create a reminder in my phone for three months from now, when I know I'll be slogging through a dreary Ohio March, that reads: 'Do a yoga retreat.' Then I create another reminder, this one for January, that reads: 'Start doing more yoga to prep for yoga retreat.'

'Millie?'

I look around in confusion, wondering where my sister is.

'Millie?' Vanessa asks again. She's staring straight at me. I'm about to shake my head, I can feel my spine stiffening and my neck muscles preparing to communicate *Nope, you've got the wrong girl*. But thankfully, my tongue regains movement and I parrot, 'Yep!' and try to ignore how much it must have looked like I was having a neck spasm. I spot Hugh giving me a weird look. I ignore it. If he's not going to address that we might know each other, then neither am I.

Vanessa has already disappeared down the stairs and into the cabin. I follow her because no one else has got up and it appears I have been summoned.

'Watch your head!' she calls. Just in time, because I'm centimetres away from banging my forehead on the metal door frame. I grab onto the door with my hand and lower myself down into the first level of the ship's cabin.

I take about six stairs down and land in a small area with three beds. Bunk beds stack on one side and the opposite wall holds a mattress piled with notebooks and papers and maps. There's duffels and backpacks littering the space, along with various hats and sunglasses. There are dark-tinted windows that look out onto the deck. It feels homey and must be where the crew sleeps.

I follow Vanessa down another ladder further below deck. It empties out into a room with a table and a booth around it, backing up to a galley kitchen. The table is littered with suitcases and backpacks.

'Grab yours?' she says, making her way down a narrow hallway.

I lug my suitcase behind her, following her into an impossibly narrow room with four bunk beds. It smells slightly mildewy but seems to be clean, with worn wood bedframes and a patch of peeling paint in the corner.

'Is this OK?' she asks.

'Um,' I hesitate. Millie hadn't mentioned I would be sharing a room with strangers. There isn't even space in the room to put down my bag. If I drop it, I'll have to lay it on a bed. It's so cramped I feel like I'm having trouble breathing. As if Vanessa can sense I'm about to start hyperventilating, she steps back and lets me stand in the room myself. I feel marginally better.

'The other two rooms just have a queen bed, and we think the couples should take those. So, if all right with you, you'll share with . . .' She pauses and consults her clipboard.

Not Hugh, I think.

'Hugh!' she says brightly.

'Um . . .' I trail off again. I have no idea what to say. Millie would say no, but I hate confrontation.

'If you don't feel comfortable,' Vanessa says, leaning in closer, her voice dropping to a sympathetic whisper, 'we can figure something out. Sometimes we throw all the men in the bunk room, but—' she glances at her clipboard '—usually the couples take the bigger beds.'

She must read the concern on my face, because she adds, 'I thought this was explained in the waiver when you signed up, there's usually a warning about the room situation because the boat is so small.'

'Oh no, it's fine,' I say quickly. The last thing I want to do is bring attention to myself, and I can manage to share a room for four nights. I'll take the top bunks, and Hugh can take the bottom ones. Given how tiny it is, we'll only be in this room to sleep and change anyways. 'This is great.' I force a smile.

'Wonderful!' Vanessa makes a notation on her clipboard and then proceeds to show me the bathroom, which is so small it takes practically no 'showing'. There's a toilet and a showerhead jammed right next to each other. There isn't even a mirror. When I stand up inside of it, my head almost grazes the ceiling. I wonder how Hugh will fit inside, and then I realise that he probably won't. The shower looks more like it was built for dogs than for humans, the faucet only comes up to my neck.

'I know it's small,' Vanessa acquiesces, as we climb the ladders back up out onto the deck, 'but a small boat is the only way we can get to the best reefs.' She smiles at me, her bun spilling out all over head, and, despite the news that I'll be crammed in a room with Hugh Harris for the next four nights, I can't help but mirror her excitement. That's what Millie had told me too. The best scuba diving in the world.

Derek and Natalie are the man with the camera and the woman with the scarf. I commit to remembering their names this time around. Derek is a hobbyist aquatic photographer and Natalie is his girlfriend. She hasn't taken off her large sunglasses, so I never know if she's looking at me or not. But she seems observant, her gaze constantly roving around the room. I stay quiet, trying not to draw any attention to myself.

Thankfully, Pippa does most of the talking for the group of us. After Aaron let us know the trip out to the reef was three hours, she started chatting away. When she asks Derek and Natalie how long they've been dating, Natalie shrugs and says, 'A couple of months,' and Derek says, 'We're in the honeymoon phase,' while beaming. I wish Millie was here because the difference in their reactions is so stark that I don't think they'll last much longer than this trip, and I desperately want someone to gossip with.

I decide to avoid Natalie, at least for today. She seems forward and smart. And I'm nervous she's the type to notice I'm going by a different name, and want to address it. So instead, I focus on Derek, making the mistake of asking him about his camera and getting trapped in what felt like an hour-long lecture on the pros and cons of underwater cameras and why this one in particular was the best money could buy. I find out that he works for a tech company, which confirms my worst fears: Derek is a very smart man from Texas who acts like a frat boy and buys the most expensive toys he can. Once again, I wish for Millie, but I see Pippa stifle a giggle when Derek asks if I want to see some of his old dive photos, and I feel a sense of relief that there is someone like-minded on the boat with me.

Throughout the conversation, if you could even call it that considering I hardly said more than three words, I see Hugh glance once or twice in my direction. We have settled into a familiar seat pattern. Hugh and I are on the same bench, Derek and Natalie are on the bench in the middle, and Pippa and Andrew are across from Hugh and me. We form a U-shape around Aaron, who presides over us from the captain's chair.

At one point, Derek launches into an explanation of how cameras are instrumental in researching marine life. He accompanies this monologue with an explanation of the marine life present in the Great Barrier Reef. During his lecture, I see Hugh shift in his seat more than once. I see him fight back a smile out of my peripherals. It's good to know at least one person is enjoying this conversation.

The more Derek mansplains, the more annoyed I get. I force a smile at him through clenched teeth, trying to ignore Hugh's amusement. *At least I'm being social! How was I supposed to know I was signing up for a lecture from someone who knows less than I do?* And, in my defence, it was hard *not* to ask him questions, given he lugged his camera back upstairs into the captain's room and had his feet around the box like he was protecting a human life inside of it.

Mercifully, at some point Vanessa interrupts Derek to ask what his camera is doing on deck. She is not amused that he's already gone against her rules. I turn away as she stares him down, trying to stifle my own laughter. I hear Derek tell Vanessa that the 'sea breeze is good for drying out the equipment after all the humidity in Cairns'. I can practically see Vanessa's eyes roll all the way back into her head. 'But it's an *underwater* camera,' she points out.

I look around for another conversation to join but Pippa and Andrew are holding hands and watching the shoreline get smaller and smaller, Aaron is poring over a map and saying something into a radio, and Hugh has stood up and walked over to the railing to look out to sea. His hair has been ruffled by the ocean breeze and looks even more shaggy than it did when we met. We go over a larger wave than usual, and I watch as the veins on his forearm pop when he grabs the railing of the boat to steady himself.

He turns around and we make direct eye contact. I feel so caught in the act of staring at him that I immediately stand up, which forces me into an awkward situation of pretending like I have somewhere to go. Reluctantly, I make my way towards the front of the boat, where Miguel is readying our scuba equipment. The sun is beating down and the heat is unrelenting once I'm out of the shade. The aluminium guide rails are hot to the touch. I can't wait to get into the water. To get to Miguel I have to pass Hugh, which turns out to be impossible given how much space he takes up and how narrow the sides of the boat are.

'Excuse me,' I say, attempting to edge around him but not wanting to touch his backside.

He shifts his torso completely so he's parallel to me, effectively cutting me off from where I was headed.

We stand, in a stalemate, warily glancing at each other.

'I was just going to sit back down,' Hugh informs me.

'I was just going to talk to Miguel,' I reply. Neither of us move.

'Oh, is Derek's marine biology 101 class over?' he says, his expression unreadable. 'I have to say, I was happy to see you listening so closely. You do have a lot to learn.'

My heart skips a beat. *So he* does *know who I am.*

'Oh wow, you certainly are something.' Hugh cocks his head. A muscle in the side of his jaw ticks. 'I've never met someone who is *more* annoying in person than online.'

'What can I say? I don't like to disappoint.'

I scowl.

'Speaking of disappointments, did I hear Vanessa say we're rooming together?' he asks, with no preamble and certainly no smile. His mouth is still a perfectly straight line.

I check the box in my head that he in fact *does* smile at everyone but me. My scowl deepens. 'Yes.'

Hugh returns my scowl with one of his own. 'Just my luck,' he mutters, turning back towards the sea.

'OK, you don't have to be such an asshole,' I mumble. It comes out a little louder than I intended.

Hugh whips back around. 'I just need rest, that's all. I didn't know I would be sharing a room. Some of us have important work to do.'

I raise my eyebrows. 'I'll do my best not to get in your way, then.' I turn to go, just as Hugh starts to crack a smile. He glances pointedly at the space I'm taking up in the walkway.

'You kind of already are.'

I glare at him.

'If you'll excuse me, I'm going to go see if Miguel needs help,' I lie, knowing I won't actually be able to help Miguel in any way. I pray Hugh doesn't try to follow me.

Thankfully, he steps aside to let me pass, still smirking.

I huff out a breath as I walk towards Miguel, keeping a hand on the rail for balance. The ocean feels choppier from the front of the boat, so I scurry as fast as I can towards Miguel's bustling movements.

'Hey! I'm Millie,' I introduce myself. He's humming softly, arranging tanks and what looks like black bulky life jackets neatly in a row.

'Miguel.' He shakes my hand in between swift movements. He smiles broadly, setting me instantly at ease. He has a thick accent I can't place, but it's definitely not Australian.

'You're so steady on a boat,' I observe. Only once it's out of my mouth do I realise how dumb I sound. Of course he's steady on a boat, this is his job.

But, to my surprise, he smiles bigger, thrilled. 'I just started, so I'm still getting my sea legs.'

'Oh! Did you just move here?'

'From Colombia.' He runs a hand through his wavy dark hair, pulling a lock of it behind an ear. 'I think I'm finally getting the hang of it.'

71

'It seems like it.' I clutch the railing to make sure I'm out of his way. We chat about the weather and the trips he's done in the past. He's cute, with an easy charm about him. This is his fifth trip. The question I'm desperate to ask is wriggling to the front of my brain. He's so nice and we're alone, so it seems like the perfect time.

'Hey, Miguel,' I say, interrupting him checking the air pressure on an oxygen tank.

He looks up, sensing the trepidation in my voice. His eyebrows press together, and his dark eyes grow big with worry. The colour drains from his face.

'Are you going to be sick?' he asks, reaching out a hand to steady me.

'Oh, no, I feel fine!' I say quickly.

The colour quickly returns to his cheeks, and he laughs. 'I'm not good with puke,' he confides in a whisper, 'it freaks me out.'

'Me too!' I agree. 'Someone else puking usually makes me sick.' Miguel and I share a conspiratorial look that says, *Nobody better be puking on this boat*. Satisfied, he returns to checking air pressure. 'What's up?'

'I was actually wondering if you could give me a refresher. I haven't dived in a while, and I want to make sure I have a good handle on the equipment.' I'm so nervous to ask that I stumble over some of my words, but Miguel doesn't notice.

'Sure thing!' he says. 'Come back up here when we're closer to the reef, in another two hours or so, and I'll run over everything with you.' He holds my stare for a beat longer than normal, and I wonder if he's like this with everyone on the boat.

'Thanks,' I say, breaking eye contact. I can't help but feel a wave of relief. Miguel was nice about it, flirty, but nice, *and* no one else from the boat heard me ask. A marine biologist needing a dive refresher isn't exactly in Millie's notes for how to blend in.

I turn around to head back towards the benches to sit with the rest of the group and bump straight into someone's chest. It's so unyielding that I practically bounce backwards off it. And it smells slightly of cedar.

'Ah!' I cry out, although I am the only one who seems to be affected by our collision, seeing as the chest is immobile. I curse the narrow walkways of the boat. I'm bound to be bumping into people all week. I blink up into the face of the man I just hit as a deep voice grumbles back.

'No worries,' Hugh says, but he doesn't move. Our torsos are so close we are centimetres from touching.

I feel my throat go dry again. 'Ahem,' I cough, sounding like a drowned cat. I take a step back from him but there's so little space I only create six more inches between us.

Hugh opens his mouth to say something, but I cut him off. 'Oh don't tell me,' I say, crossing my arms in front of my chest, 'you're going to point out that I'm in your way again, when really you just pick the most inconvenient place to stand.'

Hugh's face cracks into a smile. My stomach flips.

'Technically, I was here first,' he says, his eyes not leaving mine. 'But no, that isn't what I was going to say.'

I feel my face softening. 'OK,' I mutter. 'Forget I brought that up then.'

'I was going to ask if you were OK with taking the top bunk . . .'

I squint up at him. *Technically, I already wanted the top bunk . . . but he doesn't need to know that.* 'Why?' I ask. 'Does the top bunk make you seasick?'

Hugh's face remains impassive. 'No,' he says slowly.

'I'm fine with whatever.' I shrug, deciding to take a cue from Miguel. 'I'm *really* comfortable on the water. I'm sure you'll get the hang of it soon. It's just like riding a bike.'

'I'm not uncomfortable on the water,' Hugh says quickly, his lips pressing together.

'Whatever you say,' I say in a sing-song voice. 'But to answer your question, sure. I like being on top anyways.' I smile at him sweetly, feeling proud of myself, and make my getaway, scooting by him and towards the benches.

'I'm sure you do,' he calls after me, his voice lilting into unknown territory. As I process the double entendre I perfectly set him up for, heat blazes through my body. I can feel his gaze on me as I walk away.

Sweat prickles the backs of my knees. I remind myself that Hugh's attention is *not* a good thing. If he finds out I'm not Millie and reports it, anything I find on this trip will no longer be credible.

I shake the thought out of my head. We haven't even broached the subject of the wrasse yet, I reassure myself. Plus, he's already admitted that he has to focus on work. He may not ever want to discuss it. But my stomach feels unsettled. By the time I sit down on the benches, I can still feel the way his chest felt against mine when our bodies collided. My heart rate hasn't slowed all the way down yet. First Miguel and now Hugh. I haven't been that close to a man that I wasn't dating in two years.

'Focus, Andi,' I say under my breath. I check my phone. Millie's surgery is in sixteen hours. I need to remember what's important.

Chapter 8

Urgency overtakes our small boat when Aaron starts instructing Miguel and Vanessa where to drop anchor. Suddenly, the three of them all seem to be yelling, while the rest of us stare at them, open-mouthed. They move in unison, calling out commands I don't understand, and gently our boat lurches to a stop. Waves rock us gently up and down.

We stopped seeing other boats about a half-hour ago. Now I can barely make out specks on the horizon, it's just us and the open ocean. Millie will be happy to hear they really do deliver on their promise and get to the most remote reef entry points possible. As soon as the anchor is dropped, Aaron plops happily back into his chair, and Vanessa starts rolling up the sails, barking at everyone to start preparing for our first dive. Miguel has given me a very comprehensive briefing on the equipment, and I'm feeling infinitely more confident than I did when we set sail.

I go below deck to change, which turns into a flexibility challenge, given how little room I have in our cabin to wrangle my clothes off and my suit on. Hugh's stuff isn't on a bunk bed yet, and I wonder if he decided he would get more rest sleeping under the stars. I pop on my bikini, which is a collection of simple black triangles that cover me up as much as a bikini can. I wonder if I should have brought a one-piece instead, but as soon as I see Pippa and Natalie my worry fades. Pippa's in a flowery bikini with a stylish square neck and high-waisted bottoms. I make a mental note to ask her where she got it. She's also sporting a cute straw hat. Natalie's in a strappy one-piece that criss-crosses across her chest and around her waist, pulling her in and pushing her up in all the right places. I stare at her, wondering how on earth she managed to get that on in the tiny cabins we have to change in.

'She's like Harry Houdini,' I imagine quipping to Millie. I'm desperately trying to remember everything that happens so that I can tell her when I return, even jotting some notes down in the journal she left with me, but I already know I'll forget things. I can't wait to tell her Hugh Harris was on the boat. I don't know if she'll be mad or manically happy – probably both, and probably dependent on whether or not I spot the butterfly wrasse.

Soon, the boys have changed into suits as well and, as much as I don't want to admit it, Hugh's forearm was a pretty good indicator of what the rest of him looks like. I try not to stare as he rubs sunscreen on his face. His abs ripple as he maintains his balance on the rocking boat. He's strong. All over. Like a vegan who does an Iron Man every year. He's sporting a deep tan, which I still find incredibly annoying. Why did I have to come to Australia's summer during Ohio's winter?

'Sunscreen's over here!' Vanessa yells, pointing to a bag full of bottles of sunscreen she's carried up to the captain's room. Hugh looks up towards Vanessa and catches my eye. He looks at the bottle in my hand and smirks. I wince at the memory of trying to slather it over my shoulders myself. Thankfully, Pippa is nearby to help me cover my back.

'I saw you talking to Miguel,' she says, while she rubs on sunscreen. 'He's cute!'

I laugh. Pippa reminds me of Millie, always on the lookout for something fun to talk about.

'He is cute,' I admit. 'But being nice is his job. And, anyways, I'm here for work,' I say definitively, hoping if I say it enough times out loud, it'll crystallise in my brain. The only thing I am here for is the butterfly wrasse.

Andrew asks Pippa for help before she can say anything else, and I take the opportunity to duck downstairs for a moment of peace.

I need to reset my focus before our first dive. I squeeze past the tiny kitchen and the table that is bolted to the floor. I make my way down the narrow hallway, almost bumping my head on the ceiling. Hugh's bag is now resting on a lower mattress. It's a sleek navy duffel bag. I resist the urge to peek inside it, and instead, grab for my phone.

I stare at the screen blankly, thinking about my sister. If she was here she would be making a joke, probably one at Derek's expense, and her laughter would ease my nerves. I scroll through my camera roll to find a selfie she sent me right after she dropped me off at the airport. She's giving the camera a thumbs-up, beaming. I try to channel her positive energy.

I open the book of notes she gave me quickly and review what she's written down about Treasure Cove, our first dive sight. The last sighting of the butterfly wrasse was in 2017, on the west side of the reef.

'Have fun!' she'd written in big letters. 'It's your first dive! ENJOY IT. And don't use up your oxygen too quickly, then they'll know you're a rookie ;)'

A sharp knock on the door startles me so much that I drop the notebook.

'I'm busy,' I call out, picking up the notebook and shoving it back into my backpack as fast as I can.

'It's me,' Hugh says loudly. Then he coughs. 'Hugh.'

I roll my eyes. 'Come in,' I say, crossing my arms across my chest. 'I was just leaving.'

'Great.' Hugh sighs, stepping inside.

I turn to leave, but Hugh has blocked the exit. He's bending over his duffel bag, clearly looking for something. A wave gently rocks the cabin and the muscles on his back tighten as he steadies himself. A pair of plaid boxers spill out as he searches for whatever he's looking for and he stuffs them back in with such haste that I can't help but smile. He keeps pulling out clothes and setting them on the bed. The room starts to fill with his smell as he unpacks, woodsy and grassy, and I take a deep whiff of it, relishing a chance to not smell saltwater, mildew, or sunscreen.

It's the first time we've been in our room at the same time, and the standing room is so small that we're practically touching. I shamelessly let my gaze linger on his butt, which I hate to admit is really nice. The temperature in the room feels like it's risen five degrees in two minutes. Somehow, Hugh is blocking my way for the third time in the past hour. I'm totally stuck as I wait for him to finish whatever he's doing, but I realise that I don't really mind.

'Don't you have somewhere to be?' he mumbles.

'Well, I can't really get by you, can I?' I motion towards the door, which he has completely blocked with his body.

'Aha!' Hugh says, pulling out a small bottle of eye drops. He stands up, the crown of his head grazing the ceiling, and I watch his six-pack ripple.

I feel out of breath, even though all I've been doing is standing.

He runs a hand through his hair. 'You said you had somewhere to be? Or, don't tell me, I'm in your way again?'

There is nothing more annoying than someone who knows how good-looking they are. 'Classic,' I manage to murmur, glancing as his eye drops. 'It must stink to need so many things to help you get used to being on the water.'

Hugh glares at me with venom. 'Saltwater irritates my eyes.'

'You irritate my eyes,' I say, before pointedly scooting around him to leave the room.

I turn to see how my retort landed as I step out into the narrow hallway and catch Hugh's eyes glued to my backside. He looks up and our eyes meet. *Two can play this game*, I think, before swaying my hips ever so slightly. Hugh's eyes dart back to my waist. Electricity zaps through my body.

I turn and walk back down the hallway towards the steps upstairs. Halfway up the ladder, an ocean breeze ruffles my hair. I resolve to put Hugh, and his woodsy-smelling, strong-gluted, aquamarine-eyed body out of my mind. I'm here for one thing only.

When I come back on deck, Vanessa is handing out stinger suits, which we are wearing instead of wetsuits because the water is warm and there's jellyfish. I've never been so thankful to squeeze myself into tight-fitting Lycra. I feel both protected from the sun and from comparison to Natalie and Pippa. Before I know it, they're lining us up to assign buddies.

I realise too late that the couples are buddied up together and that means I'll be left with Hugh. My eyes flicker to his face and, as if he could feel my gaze, his eyes immediately flick up, meeting mine. My stomach twists in what must be nerves. I don't know how much longer I can pretend I don't have a clue who he is, and buddying up for dives won't help me do it.

Hugh's mouth opens, and I find myself terrified of what he's about to say. Will he finally admit he knows who I am? Say he's already going to be spending enough time with me in our room and he wants a different partner?

Thankfully, before he says anything, Miguel steps in and says, 'I'll take Millie for the first dive.' I smile at him, and catch Pippa trying to hide her grin. Miguel offering to be my buddy leaves Hugh with Vanessa. Hugh's mouth closes and falls back into a line. I feel so grateful to Miguel that I feel weak in the knees, which I try to convey to him in a smile, but I think I smile too big, because Miguel looks at me like I'm insane.

As soon as Miguel turns his gaze elsewhere, Pippa catches my eye and winks at me. 'Oh stop,' I whisper, elbowing her gently. Neither of us can stop grinning. We're giddy with excitement, or nerves, I can't tell which.

Miguel and Vanessa run through the equipment with the entire group, passing it out as they quickly refresh everyone's memory. Everyone has their own buoyancy control device (BCD), which is a fancy, industrial grade life jacket, a weight belt, an oxygen tank, a regulator that you breathe in and out of, plus an emergency regulator in case the primary one breaks. We all have little computers that help measure how slow we need to ascend and descend, and gauges that tell us how much air we have.

I sit down at my assigned station. The crew has given us each a number and I have number six. Andrew on one side of me with number five and Hugh is on the other at station number seven. Hugh and Andrew slip their BCDs on easily, immediately starting to tug at their straps. Mine won't unclip though, so I can't get it on. Hugh raises his eyebrows at me but makes no move to help me out.

'Ugh,' I cry in frustration, after tugging at my buckle for the tenth time.

'Here,' Andrew says, leaning over, 'want me to try?'

I nod.

He unclips it in one go.

'Figures,' I mutter.

Andrew laughs. 'I'm sure you loosened it.' He flashes me a smile that instantly puts me at ease.

'Thanks.'

'Don't mention it.' He smiles at me before turning his attention back to his equipment.

After I notch a weight belt around my hips to help me achieve a neutral buoyancy in the water, Miguel and I check each other's set-up, as buddies are supposed to do. Miguel's movements are steady and confident as he runs through the checklist. We each have enough air in our tank – about 200 PSI. Our BCDs work, inflating and deflating through a little hose with a red button, which will sink us down underwater and provide a flotation device in case we need it. We're sitting so close that for the first time, I notice that Miguel's eyes are flecked with gold. A lock of hair falls forward, escaping from behind his ear, and he tucks it back with a flourish before confirming that our regulators work. We take a test breath, our inhales and exhales sounding like Darth Vader. We check each other's clips to make sure we're safely secured into our life vests, and then we're ready to take the plunge into the water.

'You got this.' Miguel smiles at me encouragingly. 'I'll be next to you the whole time.'

'Thanks.' I meet his eyes, and they are so bright and full of confidence that I glance away, wondering if he'll see right through me and realise just how anxious I am.

We are all clustered on the front of the boat with our gear assembled. I take a sideways glance at Hugh, who is buddy-checking Vanessa, taking his time checking every buckle on her life jacket. Suddenly, I'm itching to get in the water, to beat him into the waves. Miguel is helping Derek though, so I am forced to wait on the aluminium bench and watch Hugh and Vanessa step into the ocean. I don't even want to know how happy Hugh is that he's beating me into the water. I swear I see a triumphant smile peek out at me from beneath his mask before he takes the plunge.

Andrew elbows me in the side. 'How are you feeling?' he asks me, beaming.

'I'm excited,' I respond, not wanting to acknowledge that my primary feeling is anxiety. I'm worried I'll use up my air too fast, which Millie says is the number one way to spot a novice. And I'm worried I won't find the fish.

'Me too!' Andrew hoots. 'I cannot believe we get to do this – it's going to be brilliant!' He fist pumps the air and Pippa cackles.

'You are so embarrassing,' she says playfully, rolling her eyes.

But Andrew's energy is infectious. I can already feel my nerves loosening a bit. 'This is gonna be fun,' I agree.

Once Miguel is ready, I walk up to the break in the railing where we're supposed to take a giant step in. I hear Derek behind me walking Natalie through his camera set-up for the second time.

'Always keep your eyes on me,' Miguel instructs, 'and remember what I taught you.' He goes through the hand signals. 'A fist over the head means OK. Use your fingers to communicate your PSI number so we know how much air you have left. And enter the water feet first, none of those flopping in backwards, head-first entries unless the water is completely calm.'

I nod and make the OK sign with my hand. Like I would try to backflip into the water with an oxygen tank strapped to my back. Feet first is good. Feet first is comfortable.

But as soon as I think it, I feel a twinge in my gut. Feet first is comfortable, but I don't know if comfortable is what I want anymore. Maybe, I think, by the end of the trip I'll have learned the head-first entry, the one with the backflip.

'One hand on your mask, another on your regulator,' Miguel instructs, interrupting my thoughts. 'Now take a big step, feet first.'

I do as instructed and lift my foot, which is burdened by a massive flipper, up and off the edge of the boat. Slowly and all at once, I step into the water.

Boom. Water rushes into my ears and around my face. I breathe into my regulator, and even though I shouldn't be, I'm surprised when it works, supplying oxygen even when I'm face down in the water. My BCD is inflated, so I pop right up to the surface and swim away from the side of the boat. I give Miguel the OK sign by bopping my head with my fist. Hugh and Vanessa are bobbing up and down a couple of feet away from me.

'You good?' he asks, his tone more perfunctory than caring. His regulator is out of his mouth, so I take mine out to respond.

'Yep.' I take a deep breath and plunge my face into the water. It's mild, only a little cold, and crystal clear. I can see all the way to the sandy bottom. I can't contain my excitement. I pop my head back up, grinning. Being in the water is ten times better than being confined to the boat. I take a minute to let my eyes skim over the top of the ocean, really letting it sink in that there is no one in sight, it is just our small group floating in the largest reef ecosystem in the world.

Hugh is beaming too. For the first time since I met him, he seems fully consumed by a true emotion. He's not pivoting from sarcastic to sincere or from helpful to asinine, instead he's full of pure joy.

It takes a minute for everyone else to jump in. Derek is last because he had to make sure his camera was set up correctly, and by the time he's in, we're all antsy to descend. We grab a mooring line, which stretches from a nearby buoy all the way down to the bottom of the ocean and deflate our BCDs. Slowly, we sink from the surface to the ocean floor, popping our ears along the way. We move hand over hand down the mooring line, and with each foot we descend, the ocean seems to get quieter. The only sound I can hear is my own breathing in my regulator. I'm in heaven.

Everyone takes their time adjusting their buoyancy. I have to inflate my BCD a little to counteract the weight belt, and soon I'm hovering about two feet off the ground. I kick my fins back and forth to keep myself steady. Andrew has a hard time figuring out his buoyancy and keeps floating up too fast, which prompts Vanessa to point at him and jerk her thumb downwards in a 'get down here now' manner. Andrew proceeds to sink and float like a yo-yo. I fight off laughter at Andrew's blissful ignorance that Vanessa is extremely frustrated.

Thankfully, he seems to find the humour in his own difficulty, at one point throwing his hands over his head in a surrender gesture. Once Andrew is closer to the bottom, we start kicking towards the reef. Vanessa leads the way, and I stay near the back of the pack with Miguel. I'm grateful our swim towards the reef is gradual because I'm already so overwhelmed, I feel like I could cry.

The bottom of the ocean is pristine white sand littered with sea cucumbers. They look like giant slugs, but the closer I look, the more I realise they're kind of pretty.

Some have horns all over their sides, some are purple, some are green and some are spotted. We can see the reef looming in the distance. It's massive. I've only scuba-dived in Florida and the scale of this reef compared to the Florida Keys is blowing my mind. It reaches from the ocean floor almost to the top of the water. It must be thirty feet high. I'm in awe.

When we reach it, we swim around the wall slowly. There's coral everywhere. Mushroom, staghorn, bottle-brush and brain. Some of the staghorn coral is a brilliant, electric blue. I'm so overwhelmed by it that I pause to stare, and Miguel has to nudge me to keep up with the group. Vanessa shows everyone a type of coral that retracts its bright purple petals when she claps her hands in front of it. It looks like a magical underwater show made just for us, and I'm thrilled.

There are bright yellow, pale pink and neon shades of green. It feels like every surface is a different type of coral. My brain can't make sense of the amount of texture it's trying to take in – some corals are soft and spongy, some are spiked, some have sprouted circular orbs that dangle on the edge of what looks like tentacles. There are shelves of coral that look like interlocking spiderwebs. There are forests of coral whose branches look like dozens of trees. There are rolling fields of coral that look like swaying sea grass.

We swim over a giant clam that's as long as my body. It's cracked open, and I can see the water slowly pumping in and out of its purple membrane. We pass an anemone, and two orange-striped clownfish guard it. Miguel sticks his finger towards the anemone and one of the fish swims at Miguel with what looks like anger. I giggle, releasing bubbles that float up towards the surface.

We continue swimming in a giant circle. Derek is looking at everything through his camera, which I feel must take away from the experience. I see Hugh give Derek a couple of looks and wonder if he's thinking the same thing. Andrew and Pippa are excitedly pointing things out to one another, their hands flailing in all directions as they take everything in.

We stop at another giant wall, comprised of all different types of corals, and everyone seems to find something different to focus on. For the first time, I force myself to look at the fish *and* the coral. I am overwhelmed in the best way. I can't remember the last time I felt like this.

I pull out my camera and look for the butterfly wrasse, which frequent staghorn coral. I try to stay as motionless as possible, and I watch as fish dart around me. There are tiny butterfly fish that have yellow stripes down their backs and flit around so gracefully it seems like they are dancing. There are angelfish, swishing their broad dark blue bodies, cardinal fish and cod. I see my personal favourite – the humbug damselfish – which is black and white striped, half-heart shaped, and ridiculously cute. Plus, who doesn't love a fish named humbug?

I don't spot any butterfly wrasse. They're distinguishable from other types of wrasse because of an extra fin they have on their underbelly, which helps levitate them just off the coral, so that they can feed off the coral's mucus. They are purple, with a yellow stripe down their back. And Millie said they are small and fast. I try not to get in my head about not seeing one. After all, it's only the first dive. And they might not even exist.

I manoeuvre myself in a circle to check out what the other divers are looking at, and as I turn around, I bump into Hugh. He has been hovering right behind me. He recovers his balance faster than I do. I make a mental note to tell him that he needs to stop getting in my way.

I move my hands in front of me frantically like I'm a bad synchronised swimmer until I regain my balance. If he was trailing me to spy on my diving quality, I'm not doing a good job of proving that I'm the marine biologist I say I am. I'm glad he can't see me blush. Despite the chill in the water, I feel heat radiate through my body.

I swim by Miguel's side as we slowly turn around, heading back towards the boat. On our way, we interrupt a school of blue tang surgeonfish (better known as Dory in *Finding Nemo*). They flash their fins in a vivid cloud of bright blue and yellow. I notice that Hugh's regulator isn't spouting bubbles anymore and I wonder if he's holding his breath too. There is an incredible magic to the ocean. I'm not ready for this dive to be over. It seems like everyone feels the same way because we're swimming back slowly, drinking in every coral we pass and every flutter of fin that passes us.

I don't see a butterfly wrasse, but the dive doesn't feel like a loss. I'm proud of myself for how many fish species I recognised and how much I remembered about the different types of coral. Maybe everyone will believe I'm a marine biologist after all. Maybe Millie was right, this will be more fun than India. I grab onto the mooring line and deflate my jacket in preparation for the slow ascent. The last thing I want to do is leave the water.

Chapter 9

Eight dives to go

We pop up above the surface. Everyone is grinning from ear to ear.

'Wow,' we all say to each other and to ourselves. 'That was incredible.'

We inflate our BCDs and bob on the surface. The water laps at our chests. I lick the salt off my lips. The humidity soothes my mouth, which is dry from breathing in straight oxygen. Everyone is quiet. There is a collective feeling of astonishment and joy. It feels like the moment during a concert where the entire crowd starts singing the lyrics to the same song. I relish knowing that I am just as affected by what we just saw as the strangers next to me.

Miguel and Vanessa scurry up the ladder first, pulling themselves out of the water easily, and lowering down a bucket for the rest of us. One by one, the group takes off their fins, shucks them into a bucket hanging off the side of the boat, and hoists themselves up the ladder with effort. Hugh and I are last.

'You go.' I gesture at the metal rungs bobbing in the ocean waves.

'Ladies first,' he replies. Even though he's technically being polite, it feels pointed. I glare at him, but he doesn't budge, his eyes sparkling an electric blue, water dripping off his eyelashes. Tired of waiting, and desperate for a drink of water, I haul myself, cloaked in heavy scuba gear, up the ladder while he watches.

We towel off and huddle in the shade of the captain's room, balancing our lunches on our laps. We're all seated once again on the worn vinyl, in our usual seats. Hugh and I are as far away from each other as we can be while still sitting on the same bench. Vanessa is eating with us, sitting next to Andrew. Miguel and Aaron are busy elsewhere.

The group quiets as we start to eat. The crew whipped up a series of grain-forward salads, a remarkable feat considering how small the ship's kitchen is, and worlds better than the PB&J I was expecting. A bowl of fresh pineapple sits on Aaron's chair.

'That was incredible,' Andrew says to Vanessa between mouthfuls.

'This year is the best it's been in years,' Vanessa tells us. 'The reef is just starting to recover from a bad bleaching event a few years ago, and the coral cover is coming back.'

'Cool,' Andrew says, 'so the worst is over?'

'Not exactly,' Vanessa sighs. 'Global warming won't magically improve. And pollution is still a big problem,' she says, 'fertiliser from the nearby banana farms is really harming the reef.' Vanessa gazes at the horizon. I nod vigorously. *Vanessa is saying exactly what Millie thinks!* I glance at Hugh. He's pointedly staring at Vanessa. He's not smiling.

Andrew looks sombre.

'Garbage is also a big problem,' Vanessa continues. She inclines her head towards the ocean. 'Almost every dive I go on, I find plastic.'

'So, the coral bleaching could come back?' pipes up Natalie, surprising me, and by the looks of it, Hugh as well, with her interest on the subject.

Vanessa sighs and nods. 'Every year we roll the dice on whether it will get worse,' she says.

Natalie sits back in her seat, her expression blank. She whispers something to Derek, who nods. I wonder what she's thinking. I glance at Hugh and he makes eye contact with me, raising his eyebrows triumphantly before settling back into the bench.

Any hope I had that to look for the butterfly wrasse in peace disappears. He knows I'm searching in hopes it will divert some fund-raising efforts towards pollution, and he thinks I'm not going to find it.

I want to ask Hugh if we can just agree to disagree, and not talk about it, so I wander to the front of the deck, hoping he will follow. There's a platform on the hull of the boat that's raised (it's right over the portion that's below deck), and it's large enough to fit two or three people. I climb on top of it and sit myself up against the window to the crew's room to stretch my feet out. The sun is bright, and I'm thankful I put on a large T-shirt before lunch. There's a zero per cent chance I can make it through these few days without getting sunburn.

There's a hammock right next to me that stretches from the window to the mast for the large sail, but I don't want to be the person who claims the hammock immediately when it's clearly the best seat in the house, so I stay put.

I gaze out across the ocean and take a deep lungful of salty air. The morning fog has completely lifted. White boats speckle the horizon, all of them appearing after we surfaced from our dive. They're still far enough away that they're just dots, and Aaron said they probably won't come any closer.

'So, what did you think of our first dive?' Miguel asks me excitedly, interrupting my train of thought. He's paused in front of me, mid-walk to the front of the boat.

'I loved it.'

He bobs his head in agreement. 'What's not to love?'

'I can't think of a thing,' I lie. *Hugh Harris being on this boat is something I don't love*, I think. *I am living a lie, and he is too close for comfort.*

'Have you been to this part of the world before?' Miguel asks. His hands are full of equipment that looks heavy, but he's carrying it like it's air.

'No,' I shake my head, 'but now that I'm here . . .'

'Let me guess, you don't want to leave,' he fills in for me.

'You caught me!' I put my hands up, laughing. 'Who can I bribe to get citizenship?'

Miguel laughs. 'Hey, I was that way too.' He shrugs. 'It worked out for me.'

'I can't actually abandon my home to live a life of adventure . . .'

Miguel tilts his head, the smile on his face only getting bigger. 'Why not?' he asks, his voice lilting with charm.

Before I can answer, Aaron calls his name. 'Think about it,' he says, 'life is short!' Then he rushes towards the cabin, equipment in hand.

I stretch out under the hot sun, thinking. Why couldn't I live in a place like this? I could fly Murphy here . . . he would hate the flight, but he *could* do it. I couldn't leave Millie though . . . or my parents . . . I shake the thoughts from my head, I might as well not daydream about the impossible.

I lean back into the platform and relax under the hot sun. If I can't make this permanent, the least I can do is enjoy the present. I should be taking a nap and getting some rest to better prepare myself to find the butterfly wrasse. I can hear Derek grumbling about reassembling his camera, which apparently has to be cleaned in freshwater after every dive. I don't know how Natalie doesn't lose her patience.

'Did you hear that?' Pippa whispers as she climbs up onto the platform next to me.

'Derek?'

She giggles and nods. 'It's insane!' she says. 'He knows Google has brilliant pictures of the reef, right? Like taken by Nat Geo or whatever? I showed my mum some before we came. I don't know why he thinks he could take better. He might as well save himself the trouble and print those out.'

I let out a full-on laugh. 'Pippa,' I say, still laughing, 'it's probably about the "memories".'

She rolls her eyes at me. 'He's giving all of us something to remember, that's for sure. You know he brought filtered water from the mainland just for the camera bath?'

'No,' I gasp.

'Yep,' she says. 'I'd have to off Andrew if he was ever that mad about a toy.'

Pippa and I keep chatting, although it's mostly her giving opinions of the people on the boat. Aaron: mysterious, she's *desperate* to know how old he is. She bet Andrew he was older than forty-five. I glance back at Aaron. With his eyes obscured by sunglasses, he could be anywhere from twenty to fifty.

Pippa continues with her assessment. Vanessa: a total badass. Miguel, she *loves*. Especially for me. 'The diving instructor,' she gushes, 'perfectly cliché!'

I squirm in my seat. 'He's too boyish to be my type,' I demure, 'and he flirts with everyone.'

Undeterred, Pippa carries on, excited. 'And I hear you and Hugh are marine biologists! I want to know everything. How many dives have you been on? What was the coolest thing you saw today? Is this your first time here?'

I laugh at her enthusiasm. 'I've never been here before,' I confess, 'but Hugh is Australian, so he has a couple times, I think.'

'Brilliant! I heard that—'

I'm curious to hear what she has to say about Hugh, but Andrew interrupts her in the middle of her sentence, calling from the captain's room to see if she'll help him put on sunscreen.

The sun and the gentle rocking of the boat make me sleepy as soon as I'm left in peace. I'm about to drift off when someone else scrambles onto the other side of the platform. Lazily, I squint out of one eye to see who it is. I'm hoping it's Pippa, but I would even settle for Andrew, who seems like the kind of guy to come out here to take a nap.

But as I open my eye I take in a large, tanned foot, a muscular calf and a bulging thigh. I know it's Hugh. I turn my head away from him and pretend to be asleep. If Hugh had come out here fifteen minutes ago, I would have been ready to confront him, but now I just want him to go away.

I hear the telltale crinkling of a book being opened and I can't resist finding out what it is. I try to turn my head back towards Hugh as slowly as possible. I open one eye slowly. The cover is colourful, and I can make out *The Changing Tides of—* before I am forced to open one eye fully to read the entire cover.

'I knew you were awake.' Hugh snaps his book closed and places it down next to him. My view of the title is obstructed by his torso.

'Hm,' I grunt. I don't know how to approach this situation.

'So,' he says. He has sunglasses on, so I can't tell what colour blue his eyes are, which is my main indicator of his mood. So far, they've been dark when he's angry, grey when he's confused and light blue when he's happy. Pretty much the darker they are, the angrier he is. I wonder if I ever thought this much about anyone else's eyes. I don't think I have.

'So?' I reply.

'Millie Paxton,' he says.

I hesitate. I don't want to lie, so I try to think of something I can say that isn't confirmation of his statement.

'Hugh Harris.'

'Nice to meet you in person.' He lowers his sunglasses to the bridge of his nose. He's staring at me so intently that his gaze feels hotter than the South Pacific sun.

'I wish I could say the same.'

'I knew you were a typical American girl, but I have to say I'm surprised you follow the stereotype so completely.'

I smile at the mention of our DMs before I register what he said. Confused, I cock my head at him until he gestures at my T-shirt. When I glance down, I can't help but burst out laughing. I packed a few of my dad's old shirts for the trip, all oversized and worn down to a threadbare, light layer, perfectly doubling as swimsuit cover-ups. This one happens to feature a drawing of French fries dancing across a McDonald's logo.

'Oh my God!' I press my palm into my forehead. 'I swear, I did not pick this on purpose.'

Hugh's abs contract with his laughter, deep and rumbly. 'I figured it may not belong to you considering it looks older than you are.'

He's right, there are holes along the hem and the seam of the left shoulder is coming undone.

'It's my dad's,' I explain.

'So it runs in the family.' He raises his eyebrows.

'I am not going to apologise for being patriotic,' I say, pushing my sunglasses further up my nose. 'I happen to like this T-shirt. It's appropriately vintage, not like you would know.'

Hugh's wheezing with laughter now.

I glare at him.

'What?' he asks, seeing the annoyed look on my face. He wipes a tear from his eye. 'I'm not even laughing at the T-shirt anymore. I just can't believe I'm stuck on a boat with you of all people. And we're sharing a room!' He dissolves into laughter again.

'And I can't believe you're able to contort your mouth into something that isn't a frown.'

'I'm capable of quite a few emotions,' Hugh informs me, although his mouth settles back into a line.

'And I'm surprised you've found a happy one considering Vanessa just proved my point,' I retort.

'Is that what you heard? I heard her say coral bleaching is still an issue.' Hugh raises his eyebrows at me and for the first time, maybe because his sunglasses are back to covering his eyes, I notice his lips. They're slightly chapped from sun and wind. His bottom lip is fuller than his top lip in an almost feminine way, but the strong line of his jaw balances it out. He has blond stubble sprouting across his chin.

'And I heard her say that corals are healthier.'

'Just because they're healthier doesn't mean the problem is fixed.'

'It does mean that it's not the primary problem anymore,' I argue. I've spent enough time listening to Millie to know the high-level logic like the back of my hand. 'Hugh, Vanessa said it herself, the pollution from fertiliser is killing the reef. We have to bring attention to it.'

'We already have attention on the reef, though, why do we need to pivot it elsewhere, especially when coral bleaching is proven to move people to donate? Why risk people not donating at all?'

'But that's just it! Coral bleaching has been so overused that it doesn't move people as much anymore.'

'Where are your data points to back that up?'

'I don't need data points,' I growl, although I wish I had service to text Millie and ask her what exactly the data points are. 'I need a fish to prove to the public that they need to be focusing on something else.'

'Well, you're not gonna find it,' Hugh says smugly.

'Well, you're being condescending.'

'That's all you've got?'

'Ugh!' I huff. 'Look, I was going to ask you if we could just not talk about it. Can we agree to disagree?'

'OK,' Hugh says, his tone changing ever so slightly. 'What do you propose we talk about?'

'Hmmm . . . seasickness? Eye irritants?'

'I have a better idea. How about the benefits of reef-friendly sunscreen?' Hugh says.

'Oh sure, that sounds like the best path to friendship. I'm sure talking about the one thing I forgot will help me forgive you for humiliating me online repeatedly and disagreeing with everything I stand for.'

Hugh blinks, and for a moment I wonder if I've taken things too far.

My worry dissipates as a smug expression crosses his face. 'Wow, talking about forgiveness already? I didn't expect that from you, Millie. You seem too stubborn to forgive.'

'I think I may have spoken too soon,' I say quickly. 'Once I find the wrasse, and you apologise, then I'll forgive you. Until then, don't distract me. I have important work to do.'

'OK then,' Hugh says, but his voice is light. 'I'll leave you to your *important work*.' He gestures at the book in my hand, *Beach Read* by Emily Henry. I want to punch myself in the face. Even if I tried, I couldn't have found anything that looked less like work. I make a mental note to drag my copy of *The Marinist* magazine upstairs next time.

'Can you just leave me alone? I'm trying to get some rest.'

'Sure thing,' Hugh says, sitting up and lazily stretching his arms out towards the sun. 'I'll leave you to your dreams – which is the only place you'll ever see a butterfly wrasse.'

Before I can think of a retort, he's gone.

We're about to start preparing for our second dive when I reach up to touch my head and realise I made a huge mistake by not braiding my hair. My messy bun is now an actual mess. I try to run a comb through it and feel my comb start to bend with the tension, which is a bad start. I bump my elbow into the wooden frame of the bed and let out a yelp. Reluctantly, I drag myself upstairs onto the open air of the deck. Working on knots in public is embarrassing but better than having broken elbows. Painstakingly, I tease my hair into sections and comb them out one by one before pulling them into two tight French braids that run straight down the back of my head.

Hugh pops his head around just as I'm finished.

'Vane—' he starts to say, before realising that it's me he's talking to. He pauses for a beat and opens his mouth. 'Nice braids,' he finally says, in a tone that makes it very unclear whether he was complimenting me or making fun of my braids.

'Thanks?' I ask.

He cocks his head to one side and retracts his head from my vantage point. Then, seconds later, he appears again. 'Also, looks like you missed a spot.' He says, pointedly glancing at my shoulder. Then he goes back to his book.

I look at where his gaze had lingered, and sure enough, right on the top of my left shoulder is a bright pink sunburn. Somehow, I managed to adequately apply sunscreen everywhere but there.

Thinking about Hugh looking at me so closely, my face flushes red, even brighter than my burned patch of skin. Since our conversation earlier we had barely spoken, and he's managed to get under my skin more than once.

About an hour ago, I had been chatting with Pippa, who was eager to pick up where our conversation left off. We were sitting in the shade sharing a bench, both of us taking a break from the sun but neither of us wanting to sit in our teeny rooms.

She jumped in right away, asking what the lab was like, and what the career trajectory was for a marine biologist. She was shocked to hear that there were more women than men in the field and lamented the sexism in her own workplace (sales) and how she sometimes was the only woman in meetings.

'When Andrew wakes up, he'll want to talk to you about the octopus population here,' she told me, 'he's completely obsessed.'

Andrew popped his head upstairs just as Pippa stopped talking.

'Andrew,' she called him over excitedly, 'I was just telling Millie how much you want to see an octopus.'

'Oh yeah.' Andrew grinned. 'I just love them. I really hope we'll get to see one, it's one of the main reasons we decided on this place for our holiday. I read there are loads of them here.'

'Maybe on the night dive?' I suggested. Octopuses are notoriously shy, and I didn't want to get Andrew's hopes up but if there was ever a chance to see one, this would be the place to do it.

'Millie is a marine biologist, just like Hugh,' Pippa explained excitedly.

Andrew tilted his head. 'You are?' he asked. 'But Hugh said . . .' He trailed off.

'Hugh said what?' I asked. My stomach flipped. *Does he know?*

'Well, I thought you both were, but then I was talking to him about it, and he said you two didn't exactly have the same job . . .'

'Oh,' I said, trying to stay chipper while I panicked internally. 'I don't know what he meant but we are both marine biologists.'

'Oh, I'm so sorry.' Andrew blushed. 'He said something about the lab and the field, and I got completely confused. We don't get a lot of marine biologists in Clapham.'

'He's just overexcited,' Pippa teased affectionately, laying her hand on Andrew's arm. 'Honestly, he's been so thrilled he's been half-witted ever since we got here.'

'Well, what do you expect? It's probably raining cats and dogs at home right now,' Andrew said jovially. 'Anyway, I would love to hear anything you know, Millie.'

I was so relieved that Hugh was making a snide comment about where Millie worked, and not that he thought my marine biology skills were lacking, that I let the awkwardness slide. I told Andrew everything

I knew about the blanket octopus, a rare species where the females are thousands of times the size of the males and the blue-ringed octopus, which is small, spotted and extremely poisonous.

Andrew and Pippa loved it, soaking in every detail. Millie will be thrilled to know how much quizzing me paid off. Andrew's curiosity endeared me to him quickly, even after the comment he made about his conversation with Hugh.

I almost confronted Hugh about it, wanting to know why he felt the need to distinguish between Millie's job and his job, but I didn't want him to know it bothered me. The last thing I need is for him to realise how much of my brain space he's taking up.

'Stinger suits on!' barks Vanessa, bringing me back to the present moment. She gets more spirited and bossier with every passing hour, which I find to be a huge relief because the further we are from shore, the less confident I feel in myself. I hurry downstairs to put my brush away, my braids bouncing against my back as I go.

I'm barely back upstairs when Vanessa's voice rings out again.

'Miguel, you're with me now,' she yells in Miguel's direction.

I pause with my stinger suit halfway up my torso. If Vanessa is with Miguel, then . . . I look around and see Hugh staring at me.

'Pippa,' I say in my sweetest voice. Her stinger suit was hung up next to mine and she has one hand on the railing and the other trying to yank her foot through the ankle hole. 'Are you partnering with Andrew for this dive?'

Pippa laughs. 'Unfortunately, yes. No one else wants to partner with the one person who can't get their buoyancy figured out.'

'Great!' I say, false cheer emanating from my throat. I look in Hugh's direction again, but he's gone.

I scurry over to the scuba tanks as fast as I can. I catch the tail end of Hugh's conversation with Vanessa, which I'm positive is him trying to convince her that they should be dive buddies. He is giving her a smouldering look that I've never seen before. His hands are gripping the railing, and his forearms are bulging. He smiles at her, flashing his straight square white teeth. There's no denying it, he looks hot. Vanessa seems strong-willed, but this might break her.

'Sorry!' she trills in her sing-song Italian accent. 'First dive was an exception. Instructors are usually paired with each other, it's easier for us to keep an eye on the whole group when we're not worried about our buddies.'

'Dang it!' I mutter under my breath. Both turn to look at me.

'Millie! Perfect! You two, together,' Vanessa commands, pointing at me and Hugh.

Miguel catches my eye and mouths something that looks like an apology, shrugging sheepishly in Vanessa's direction.

Reluctantly, I sit next to Hugh on the bench and we strap ourselves into our life vests. His expression is serious, like he's gone into work mode. We go through the motions, checking to make sure our air tanks are full and testing our regulators. Then, without speaking, we both turn towards each other to perform the buddy checks.

I wrap my fingers underneath Hugh's jacket straps and yank down to make sure they're snug. I can feel the heat from his body through his stinger suit. He's as still as a statue, and I yank a bit harder than I have to, seeing if it'll break his flat expression, but he doesn't react. I check his air pressure. I press on his regulator and his backup. I inflate and deflate his BCD. I try to be collected and professional, but I'm terrified I'll miss a step and he'll notice. When I finally drop my hands and settle back onto the bench, Hugh reaches over to begin his check.

'Regulator,' he says, pressing the button. He's murmuring in a low voice, and it sends chills up my spine.

'Air pressure.' He picks up the gauge and his fingers brush my waist.

'BCD.' He slides his fingers into the space between the strap and my chest. His face is so close to mine I can count the freckles on his perfectly sloped nose. I stop breathing. He's moving excruciatingly slow, like he can sense my discomfort.

'You don't have to be so thorough.' My voice comes out of my throat in a low growl.

'Just because I don't respect your work doesn't mean I want something to happen to you,' Hugh murmurs back, 'then I'd have to be the one to drag your body to the surface, and it'd be a whole big hassle . . .' His voice is gravelly but has a teasing note. I stare out at the water, aching to jump in and clear my head to shake off this encounter. How can I be attracted to him and so aggravated by him at the same time?

'A hassle,' I muse, unable to resist calling him out. 'Not a loss though, especially considering I'm just someone who works in a lab. We're not the same kind of marine biologist. You are *far* more important.'

Hugh's eyebrows raise in surprise as he processes my comment.

He glances at Andrew. 'That isn't what I meant,' he says in a low voice. 'We just have a different attitude towards the field. Don't act like you haven't realised that.'

'No, we do n—'

'You guys ready?' asks Vanessa, interrupting me.

'All good!' Hugh says suddenly, snapping back into his normal voice. He straightens up and straps on his mask.

'Yep. All good,' I say, but Hugh's already walking towards the break in the railing. In one swift motion, he sits on the bench and leans backwards, catapulting head first into the calm water in a perfectly executed backflip. I follow, feet first, like Miguel taught me. Hugh's presence is driving me insane. *Different attitudes? What does that even mean?* I take a giant step into the ocean thinking: *Focus, Andi, you cannot let Millie down. Hugh is playing games with you, and you promised yourself no distractions.*

But all I can think about when I pop up in the water is how badly I want to continue our conversation. And how impossibly good Hugh's hair looks when it's slicked back with seawater.

Chapter 10

Our group hits the mooring line in unison. We're faster and more efficient than before, largely due to Derek having his camera assembled ahead of time. We descend. Andrew can't control his buoyancy, again, and Vanessa does the same thumbs-down motion, prompting both Hugh and I to laugh. We watch the bubbles escape out of each other's masks. I like the way his cheeks scrunch up when he smiles. But then Hugh's voice echoes in my head, telling me I'll never find the wrasse, and my smile vanishes.

I push the thought out of my head as we kick towards the reef, making our way into shallower water. I find comfort in the wheezing breath in and out of my regulator. There's something about being underwater that feels completely meditative. There's a sensory blockage. You can't smell. You can't taste. You can't feel anything but the water slowly seeping through the stinger suit. You can only hear your own breathing. You are just taking in what's around you, totally immersed.

Hugh stays right next to me, always within arm's reach. His closeness is stifling, and I can't shake the feeling that I'm being observed, even though every time I glance at Hugh his gaze is trained in front of him. I worry he's looking for proof of why we're 'different'. *It's hard to focus on the reef with Hugh at my elbow*, I think, *I wish I had Miguel back.*

Hugh and I are second in line after Derek and Natalie. Andrew and Pippa are behind us. Our dive follows a similar trajectory to the one before, even though we descended at a different point. Soon, we come up to a looming coral wall.

Vanessa quickly finds a giant lobster hidden in a rock crevice, and we all take turns looking at it. It's the biggest lobster I've ever seen, bigger than a small dog, and it's brown and white striped. Given its size, it must be ancient. Lobsters can live over one hundred years, and I wonder if this one is a centenarian. Its antennae seem to be countless, and they poke out from everywhere. Around the hole the lobster has chosen for its home there are hundreds of blooming corals. There's a bubble-gum pink one that looks like it's made out of sponges, and a bright magenta coral, home to a cluster of orange fish that don't seem to be bothered by the lobster's antennae at all.

Once we've all cycled in and out of the best vantage spot for observing the lobster, Derek stations himself in front of it and starts to take photos. He's so immersed in his photography that Miguel has to tap his carabiner on his air tank to get his attention so that we can move on. The clanging echoes through the water. We keep moving as a group, following Vanessa.

As we round the bend, I pull my focus away from Hugh's impeccable diving technique – arms locked in front of him, gently kicking, completely at ease – and zero in on the staghorn coral instead. I want to make sure I've done everything in my power to do Millie proud.

I don't see any fish resembling a butterfly wrasse. I see cod, angelfish, parrotfish and gobies, but no wrasse.

There's a cluster of brain coral at the base of the structure that captivates everyone's attention. Brain coral is mesmerising on its own, it looks like a giant, endless maze, and each ridge is made up of a thousand little polyps, but this coral has an added bonus – above the coral there's a colony of what look like translucent worms. They are wriggling and every so often catching sunlight. They look like they are dancing. It's breathtaking.

Vanessa starts kicking and motions to the group to keep moving. Derek, as usual, is still taking photographs. As we pull away from the brain coral, Andrew starts to lose his buoyancy again, this time floating upward with so much speed that Miguel has to grab him and pull him down. Even Natalie is laughing this time, I spot bubbles trailing upwards from her mask.

We swim through a clearing and Vanessa finds a flounder in the bright white sand. I don't know how she spotted it; it's so perfectly camouflaged. She pokes at it with her finger and it wriggles and changes colour, flushing from pale white to a light brown with spots. We watch it in wonder as it swims across the ocean floor.

I'm still watching the flounder flap its fins against the ground, skirting over rocks and hugging the side of coral structures, when Vanessa swims away. Andrew and Pippa follow. Hugh stays by my side, patiently waiting. I normally would love having someone this attentive to dive with, but all Hugh's perfection is doing is making me insecure about my dive skills. I can still see Vanessa, so we swim leisurely after her retreating figure. Out of habit, I turn my head to try and spot Miguel behind me, but I don't see him or Derek or Natalie.

I tug on Hugh's arm and lift my hands, palms outstretched in a 'what's going on?' expression.

He makes the same gesture back to me. 'I don't know,' his eyes are saying from behind his clear plastic mask. We turn to swim faster towards Vanessa, Andrew and Pippa. There are rules to diving, and the first is not to get separated from your buddy and your guides. If you do, you are supposed to ascend to the surface and inflate something called a 'flare' which shoots up from the water and is bright orange. We can still see the three of them, so we don't ascend yet. They're approaching a curve of a rock structure, about to be out of sight. Both Hugh and I kick faster.

Out of the corner of my eye I see movement. Big movement. My heart rate picks up but my legs slow down. I freeze in the water. I feel my heartbeat through my whole body.

A shark is swimming along the bottom of the ocean, towards Hugh and me. It's about five feet long, and its eyes are pale and terrifying.

'Hugh,' I try to call out, but my voice gets absorbed by my regulator. I grab at his ankle and barely brush it with my fingers. He starts to turn around, sees the shark out of his peripherals, and his movements slow. Then, much to my disbelief, his legs kick in a giant scissor motion, propelling him away from me.

I'm unable to regain feeling in my legs. The shark swims closer. My blood runs cold. 'Kick, Andi,' I say to myself, trying to return movement to my feet. The shark has slowed down and lurks just a few feet away, its giant pale eyes staring at me.

With a flick of its tail the shark sways closer to me. Suddenly, I feel a heavy hand on my forearm. With a gentle tug, Hugh pulls me forward, his body appearing between me and the shark. Instead of kicking towards Vanessa, Hugh had manoeuvred in a circle, maintaining a calm momentum, returning to push me forward. I regain movement in my legs and try to strike a balance between swimming fast and swimming frantically. If sharks can really smell fear, I'm a goner. Despite Hugh as a bulwark, I'm terrified.

Hugh propels me forward once more without any sense of urgency, a gentle hand encouraging me along. Together, we kick in Vanessa's direction. I start to relax in his grip, grateful for the way his body feels next to mine.

His hand lingers on my forearm, warm and stable. I resist the urge to layer one of my hands over the top of his. I want to feel even closer to him. I try to catch his eye, but he's focused on Vanessa's shadowy figure.

I remind myself that Hugh would have watched out for anyone he was diving with, even Derek. I force myself to remember that I have a job to do, a job that I cannot let thoughts of Hugh distract me from. But for a moment I wonder if this is what's under Hugh's stubborn exterior. Someone who looks out for others. Someone who helps them find sunscreen. Someone who saves them from sharks. Someone who's *nice*.

As if he can read my mind, Hugh drops his hand from my arm as soon as we get closer to Vanessa. I turn to see if the shark is still following us, but all I see is a flick of its fins as it disappears into the gaping wide blue of the ocean. We reach Vanessa, who looks behind us for Miguel and Derek. When she realises we are alone, she immediately motions for us to ascend, her gestures impatient. She is not happy.

As soon as we break the surface, I take my regulator out of my mouth. We're closer to the boat than I thought we were, popping up only about twenty-five yards from where it's moored.

'Are you OK?' Hugh asks me, his regulator floating in the water.

My teeth are chattering, but I'm not cold. 'I . . . I guess,' I stammer. I put my face in the water to check the ocean floor below, terrified that I'll see the shark lurking underneath my feet. When I look up to take a breath, Hugh is looking at me intently, worry creasing his brow.

'That little guy scared you, huh?'

'Little guy? He was huge!'

Hugh laughs. 'And you thought I was the one who was nervous in the water.'

I glare at him, but only for a beat. 'Thank you,' I say, quietly, so I don't know if he hears it above the sound of the ocean waves.

'Don't mention it,' he whispers back. We share a look and I have a surge of optimism that maybe this trip could turn around, that maybe I'm not bunking with the worst possible option, but my thoughts are quickly interrupted by Vanessa clearing her throat. I turn to see her glaring at us, the look in her eye a clear warning that Hugh and I should never have let her out of our sight.

'I'm sorry,' I say immediately.

'This is really important, guys,' Vanessa says through clenched teeth. 'I cannot lose you. I am responsible for your safety.'

'I know.' I hang my head. 'I'm so sorry.'

Vanessa huffs air out sharply through her teeth. 'If everyone can't keep up, we'll have to separate.' She shakes her head, staring out at sea. 'Miguel will take the slow group,' she finishes quietly, almost to herself, 'as punishment for whatever he's doing right now.'

'That's not necessary,' I rush to say, 'it won't happen aga—'

'We ran into a shark,' Hugh says, talking over me. 'Millie got a little flustered, I had to turn back to help her. It won't happen again for me. I can keep up with the fast group.'

Hugh speaks louder than I do, and Vanessa nods at him in something that looks like belief, before turning the brunt of her gaze on me. She doesn't say anything but she doesn't have to for me to know what she's thinking – I can't handle a shark, and she'll put me in the slow group because of it. Before I can plead my case further, she swims away from us, shouting for Aaron to lower the bucket for fins.

My mouth gapes open as I watch her go and I choke back a surprised gasp. It took Hugh less than sixty seconds to blame the whole thing on me. Although he isn't technically lying, he did tactfully omit that we were already falling behind Vanessa before the whole shark incident. And he did it so that *he* could get ahead. So much for *nice*.

'You're gonna blame everything on me?' I hiss at Hugh, narrowing my eyes. 'We were losing them before we even saw the shark!'

'I don't see how you can be upset with me for telling the truth. You didn't expect me to go in the slower group because you couldn't handle a shark, did you?'

'It wasn't my fault we fell behind Vanessa! I need more time to look for the wrasse!'

'Well . . .' Hugh trails off. 'It kind of was your fault.'

'We were already losing her before we saw the shark.'

'I guess.' Hugh shrugs. He starts to make his way towards the ladder. We've been making our way back to the boat, kicking back from the point where we ascended. Vanessa has already clambered up.

'Bloody hell!' Andrew pipes in. 'You saw a shark?'

I huff. From the deck, Vanessa is shouting at Aaron to look for Miguel, Natalie and Derek. She's furious that Miguel let them get so far behind. Pippa has already wrapped herself in a towel.

'That wasn't cool,' I say to Hugh.

'Hey—' Hugh throws his hands up in mock surrender '—I didn't do anything except tell the truth. Honestly, I should have let you face the shark yourself. We're not exactly searching for the same thing here, remember?' He adjusts his life vest casually, shifting his shoulders back so he sits a little straighter in the water.

'That doesn't mean you get to throw me under the bus to Vanessa!' I hiss. 'Don't take away my shot to prove you wrong because you think that I will. That just makes you cowardly, don't you think?'

I can't remember the last time I was so angry. I'm seeing red. I get a mouthful of seawater because I'm too busy glowering at Hugh to pay attention to the waves. He stares down his nose at me. I'm forced to break eye contact when I turn to the side to cough out the water that went up my nose. So much for looking like I know what I'm doing. By the time my gaze comes back to Hugh, he's stifling laughter.

He takes a deep breath before speaking. 'Point taken,' he says calmly, 'I'll be better next time.'

'Next time? There's not gonna be a next time! I'm going back to Miguel.'

'So you *do* want to be in the slow group?' A wicked smile plays across Hugh's lips.

'Ugh!' I groan.

I haul myself up the ladder and out of the water as fast as I can. I don't want to be in it and next to Hugh another second. I'm embarrassed at how much he's getting into my head. I won't be able to bear it if I have to return home to Millie empty-handed, especially if the reason has anything to do with Hugh Harris.

I grab my towel and stalk downstairs to the safety of my cabin. Only once I'm inside do I remember I share it with Hugh. 'Ugh!' I yell at the wall.

Chapter 11

Seven dives to go

I wish more than anything I could talk to Millie. Her surgery is in ten hours. It's all I can think about. I check the time on my phone so frequently during dinner that Pippa whispers to me, 'What's going on?' She knows I have no service – none of us do – so my obsession with my phone is notable. I quickly tuck my phone back into the pocket of my jean shorts and reply, 'Nothing.' She shoots me a curious look but returns to her meal.

We are huddled around the table in the belly of the boat, eating fried black bean burgers with the leftovers from lunch. There is a U-shaped bench around the table which most of us have squeezed onto, and four chairs surround the table on the opposite half. I marvel at the ability to fit functional furniture into such a small space. Everything is a little worn down by the sea but all of it works, and the bench is comfortable despite the gentle back and forth of the sea.

The group is silent apart from sounds of chewing. I'm not sure if Aaron is the best cook I've ever met or if we're all just starving from the activity. Judging by the way everyone else is shovelling food into their mouths I'm assuming it's the latter.

It's our first real meal together with Miguel and Aaron included, and Vanessa wastes no time attempting to drive the conversation forward in what feels like a corporate group bonding exercise. First, we go around and say our names and where we're from. When I say Columbus, Ohio, I notice the corners of Natalie's mouth tighten. *Don't ask about our trips*, I think, crossing my fingers underneath the table.

'Who had the longest trip to get here?' Vanessa asks next.

I remain silent, hoping Pippa and Andrew will speak up. London must be a longer trip than I had.

'Isn't Ohio the furthest away?' Natalie asks, peering at me across the table. Since we boarded the boat, I've managed to avoid her completely, although I've seen Pippa talking to her once or twice. Pippa was laughing, a sign Natalie might not be as bad as I thought, but I still couldn't shake my paranoia that they were discussing me.

'Did you come straight here from Ohio?' asks Miguel, his soft brown eyes connecting with mine. 'That must be an eighteen-hour flight.'

'No,' I respond, 'I had a connecting flight.' I want this conversation to end more than anything in the world. The last thing I need to relive is beating out Natalie for a first-class seat and the more we discuss it, the more worried I am that she is going to ask why, at that time, I was going by Andi.

And if Hugh picks up on anything being amiss, he's made it very clear he's not the type to let it go.

'Where'd you connect through?' chirps Pippa through a mouthful of salad. She's trying to be nice, but I want to throttle her.

'Dallas,' I say quietly.

Natalie cocks her head at me, a habit of hers I find extremely unnerving.

'We were on the same flight,' she says with a tight smile.

I try to return Natalie's grin, but I panic. 'I have to go to the bathroom,' I say, cutting her off and clambering off the bench, squeezing down the hallway towards the miniature restroom.

I lock myself inside and steady my hands on the walls to take deep breaths while my heart rate slows. I try to tamp down the feeling in my gut that Natalie is out to cause trouble. *She has no reason to care about my name*, I remind myself. *She doesn't care about me.*

I unlock the bathroom door once I hear laughter, and I'm confident the conversation has moved on, but I can't seem to shake the uneasy feeling that's perched in my gut.

I get back from the bathroom in time to hear Vanessa ask us to pick our Great Barrier Reef 'mascot'. We work our way around the table. Derek chooses a stingray, Natalie a seahorse, Pippa a surgeonfish, Andrew a clownfish (which got a laugh, because they each picked the *Finding Nemo* characters). I waffle on what to choose and land on a flounder because they blend in. When Hugh proudly announces that his mascot is a butterfly wrasse, I choke on a piece of black bean burger. Pippa slams a palm in between my shoulder blades, and it dislodges. I immediately turn beet red and murmur a quick 'thank you' to Pippa before staring at my plate. I refuse to look at Hugh, although I can tell by the way his shoulders are trembling in my peripheral vision that he is laughing. I clench my hands into fists under the table.

Pippa, sensing my agitation, pours me more water from the communal pitcher and hands me a full glass. In contrast to my mixed emotions about Hugh, most of which are extreme annoyance, I love Pippa already. She's perceptive, friendly and has a shrill laugh that seems to be constantly echoing off the walls of the boat. She's always next to Andrew but simultaneously gravitating to my side. When she sat at dinner, she put some much-needed space between Hugh and I, another notch in my reasons to like her company.

I have done my best to avoid him since he got me in trouble with Vanessa. Who, after the Derek drama had died down, pulled me aside to tell me that I 'had to be more careful', and that she 'was going to have to recommend shorter dives if I couldn't keep up'. I saw Hugh watching our interaction out of the corner of my eye. As far as I can tell, Vanessa didn't give him the same lecture. I have never wanted to punch someone so badly.

Now, we're listening to Aaron tell us about the time he captained a boat for a famous reality TV star to go diving on the Great Barrier Reef. I catch him hinting that the reality TV show in question was *The Bachelor*, but despite how interested I usually would be in the story, I can't focus. If Vanessa is serious, and she restricts my dive time, that means less opportunity to spot the butterfly wrasse. Despite my effort not to pay him any more attention, I can't help but glare at Hugh.

As my eyes narrow in on the slope of his nose, I see Miguel looking my way out of my peripherals. He looks down at his plate and I do the same, busying myself with my few remaining bites of food. I wonder if he is like this with everyone – I've already seen him laughing plenty with Andrew.

Derek interrupts Aaron to tell a story about how his boss and the famous guy Aaron mentioned have some sort of rivalry over a factory in Vegas. I watch Vanessa's spine stiffen ever so slightly. She gets up to clear our plates, graciously manoeuvring around us as she takes things back to the kitchen. I don't think anyone else notices the slight side-eye she gives Derek. She may dislike me, but after what happened earlier, she dislikes him more.

Miguel, Natalie and Derek shot up their flares right after we got back on the boat. They seemed to surface just in time, right before Vanessa really blew her lid. She pulled Derek aside immediately, wagging her finger at him like an angry schoolteacher, mentioning his camera repeatedly. Her voice returned to normal at the end of their conversation. Derek looked close to tears until she switched to a gentler tone and said, 'I'm glad you're OK.' I had forgotten until that moment that everyone on board pays Vanessa, so there's probably a protocol where she can't yell at Derek. I almost wished he had gotten yelled at. What he did was worse than me! Hugh and I technically never even got lost. Plus, if you can't keep up with the group when you're taking photos, then you shouldn't be taking photos.

Surprisingly, given his acerbic personality, Hugh was making quick friends with Andrew, who seemed to think he was hilarious, and it appeared he had even won over Miguel. He had an easy conversational way about him, and a sincere way of listening to people – his head would gently lean to the right, his eyebrows would furrow a centimetre closer together and the blue of his eyes would deepen.

I shake my head to free my thoughts from Hugh. Now that he's proven himself to be someone who isn't a team player, and who is clearly distracting me and sabotaging my mission for my sister, I can't afford to waste any more time thinking about his eye colour.

After dinner, Vanessa teaches us a card game called Hook Line Sinker, where everyone places bets and takes card tricks. She keeps count of points on a massive notepad. Hugh picks it up quickly and I get into it too – soon me, Hugh, and Andrew are competing for top spot. Andrew wins and hoots with pleasure, getting up from his chair to do a victory dance that sends everyone into bouts of laughter.

When the game is over, everyone seems to scatter. Natalie claims the sea weather dries out her skin, so she heads downstairs to do a face mask. I'm not ready to be in a small cabin with Hugh, so I huddle on a towel on the platform by the hammock, and Pippa joins me for a glass of wine.

Andrew, Derek, Miguel, Hugh and Aaron are all chatting over beers on the benches near the captain's chair. Every now and then I hear Andrew's boisterous laugh and Hugh's low chuckle. Goosebumps rise over my legs, but I don't know if it's the breeze off the ocean or the sound of Hugh's voice on the wind. I have a big sweatshirt on, the only one I brought on the trip, and I pull it over my knees to keep the chill off. It's my ex's sweatshirt, from a small town in Michigan where he used to vacation with his family. I stole it after the first night we slept together and never gave it back. I've had it for so long I often forget it wasn't originally mine.

Pippa asks me about Ohio, but I deflect. I haven't perfected talking about Millie while calling her Andi yet, and I don't want to try to lie, especially when I'm drinking wine. Instead, I ask Pippa about Andrew. She confesses they've been talking about getting engaged, and we chat about how they met and where they live. They're moving in together soon, and Pippa's nervous about sharing a bathroom.

'Sometimes he's in there for hours, I swear,' she says, both of us collapsing into giggles. 'Multiple times a day!'

Eventually, we grow uncomfortable reclining on the hard shell of the platform and we stand up, resting our palms on the railing and gazing out at the dark ocean. The moon is bright, and the sound of the waves is peaceful.

'I love it out here,' Pippa says, gesturing with her hands towards the ocean. Just then we hit a wave, and she fumbles, her plastic cup falling out of her hand and down towards the water.

No! I think, as I watch it fall in slow motion. Immediately, my thoughts go to Vanessa, who pulls a piece of plastic out of the reef on every dive. I may have brought toxic sunscreen but I'm not going to let a piece of plastic float about the Great Barrier Reef if I can help it. I can see the cup perfectly clearly, bobbing in the moonlight. Before I know it, I've stripped off my sweatshirt, and I haul myself over the railing and into the ocean.

Only once I've slammed into the cold water do I realise what I've done is incredibly stupid. There could be any number of sharks lurking under my feet.

'Millie!' Pippa shouts.

I locate the cup in seconds, the water is still, and I hear Aaron ask Pippa what's going on. He shouts at me to get to the back of the boat, where there's a ladder, and Pippa scurries to bring me a towel.

'What were you thinking?' Aaron asks, as I pull myself out of the water. 'You know you can't launch yourself into the water in the middle of the night.' My teeth start to chatter. 'She dropped pla-a-stic,' I stutter out, holding up the waterlogged cup.

'Ah.' Aaron flashes me a sympathetic smile. 'Good on you, then. But don't go about repeating that. Go get in the shower.' The rest of the boys are crowded around Aaron. Andrew gives me a high five. 'Great save,' he says. Miguel squeezes an arm around my shoulders. Even Derek high-fives me.

Pippa is quick to grab a towel. 'That was quite dense of me,' she says.

'It was an accident.' I smile at her and my teeth clack against each other. The temperature on the ocean drops over ten degrees each night, and, boy, can I feel the chill. On my way downstairs, I turn to apologise to Aaron for jumping in without a life jacket and I meet Hugh's eyes. He stares at me for a beat too long, unblinking.

A shiver runs down my spine. I head to get cleaned up.

After my second shower of the night, I go upstairs to hang my clothes to dry on the deck. My hair is dripping wet, so I decide to sit on the platform for a while. I curl up underneath the protection of my sweatshirt while the evening breeze dries out my hair. I'm only outside for a couple of minutes before the group of men disbands, everyone heading to bed.

Andrew comes over on his way downstairs. 'Millie,' he says softly, pausing at the top of the staircase. 'I just overheard Hugh explaining to Derek what you both did . . . that both of you are marine biologists. I'm sorry I said earlier that your jobs were different. I realised afterwards that telling *you* what *you* do for work was probably insulting. I usually don't mansplain so badly, I promise. Pippa is right . . . I've been overexcited for days.' Andrew gives me a sheepish grin and waves goodnight as he retreats towards the captain's room, leaving me puzzling over his comment.

Hugh basically admitted to what he told Andrew earlier . . . that we were 'different', and now he's defending me to Derek?

I decide Hugh's taken up too much of my brain space today, so I stare up at an endless blanket of stars instead of replaying our conversations. I feel an almost primal need for my sister. Seven hours until surgery. I say a little prayer, to the universe, or to the ocean, or to the butterfly wrasse I so fervently hope exists, that everything goes smoothly.

I feel so far away from everything I know. I'm about as far from Ohio as I could get unless I was launched into space. I don't feel like I have any direction anymore. I hardly have a pull back home except for Murphy and Millie. My heart squeezes at the thought of Murph. I miss him.

Thinking about returning to my life, my dead-end cubicle job, my parents who don't expect anything from me except stability, fills me with dread. How am I supposed to go back after *this*? How am I supposed to muster up excitement to get tea with Becca after swimming through the brightest coral reef I've ever seen? How do I hold a conversation with Matteo about the American Girl doll he bought his daughter for Christmas after being hunted by a shark? How do I join the Columbus dating scene after watching Hugh's muscles ripple underneath his worn grey T-shirt . . .

He's getting in my head, I think, angrily, *and he's so good at it he could be doing it on purpose for all I know.*

I glare out at the ocean, listening to the sound of waves slapping against the boat. Maybe the sea will bring me some clarity. I still have four days. I try to map out constellations, but I don't recognise any. I've long since uncrunched my legs from under the sweatshirt, and the cool breeze off the ocean feels good against my sun-kissed skin. My goosebumps are gone. I feel like my body is the end of a live wire. Everything is nuclear with colour, with emotion, the stakes are high. I feel like I'm actually living life correctly, for once. I feel terrified admitting it, but I love this feeling. I love feeling so alive.

This is the most in touch I've been with my emotions since I can remember. And it's the most I've *felt* in so long that I start to cry. I cry with worry for Millie and with anxiety for myself. I take in a deep gulp of air, my lungs preparing for a sob, when I hear someone clear their throat.

'Oh, sorry. I didn't know you were out here.' It's Hugh. Of course it's Hugh.

I want to retort 'Where else would I be?' or ask him what game he's playing, talking about me behind my back, but I know my voice will betray me. It will come out cracking and hoarse. I worry the moon is so bright that he'll be able to see the tears on my face.

'I'll just . . . head back in . . . I didn't mean to interrupt,' he says after a beat, but he lingers for a moment too long.

I want to ask him to sit. If he hadn't thrown me under the bus with Vanessa, if he had just protected me from the shark and left it at that, I would have asked him to stay. But after how much he's managed to get in my head after only one day, he's the last person I trust to see me like this – so vulnerable. I can't bring myself to say anything. Eventually, Hugh turns on his heel, his frown catching in the moonlight, and disappears around the corner.

Chapter 12

Moonlight is shining so brightly into our cabin that I can see our room like it's daylight.

Hugh is next to me in my twin bed, our noses almost touching. He's gazing at me with something like adoration. *What is happening?!* I think, confused but liking it more than I care to admit. *How did we get here? Did he apologise for throwing me under the bus? He better have because he's certainly a di—* But then Hugh kisses me, so slowly, and so deeply that my toes crinkle against the sheets, and my confusion flies out the window. *OK, so this is what's happening . . . and I love it.*

I wrap my hands around Hugh's biceps and let them travel up his shoulders, fluttering against his tanned skin. His tongue is in my mouth, and I return the favour hungrily, biting gently on his lip. I feel him tense beneath me. 'Andi,' he breathes, whispering my name in the darkness. A shudder ripples through me, and there's a heady pulse between my legs.

Hugh pulls away and kisses my neck, his lips searing a path towards my shoulder. I moan, gently, and his mouth returns to mine, his hand sliding around my waist towards the small of my back.

I wrap both hands around his neck and throw a leg over his torso, pulling him even closer. I feel possessive and aggressive, like even if I spread myself over every inch of his body it wouldn't be enough. Even though we're in a tiny room I want it to be smaller. I want every piece of myself to be pressed up against him.

He mimics my movements, his hands grabbing my ass, his lips on my neck. I feel him harden against me. Then he brings his lips closer to my ear and nibbles gently on my ear lobe. I can't help myself. I whimper. He whispers in my ear, 'I want you so badly,' and I feel like I'll explode.

I dance my fingertips down his chest, going lower and lower before flirting with the waistband of his plaid boxers. I skim my hand over the top and hear his sharp intake of breath. I glance at his face. He slides his hand from my low back and cups my breast, brushing his thumb over my nipple.

'Andi,' he breathes again. 'You're so sexy.' And that's when I realise what's off. Hugh doesn't know I'm Andi. Hugh *can't* know that I'm Andi. I scramble away from him in a panic, forgetting where I am and smack my head directly into the low ceiling of our cabin, which jolts me right out of my dream.

'Ow!' I cry loudly. My vision swims. I shake my head to clear it and gingerly bring my fingertips up to my forehead. Then I hear a grunt from below me and remember that I am sharing a room with Hugh. *What if I made noises while I was dreaming? Can he tell I just had a sex dream about him? Oh my God, oh my God, oh my God*, I think, listening carefully for any movements on the bunk below me. Thankfully, I only hear the sound of Hugh's breathing, a peaceful and steady inhale and exhale. I take a deep breath in, trying to slow my racing heart, and register that the room smells not unpleasantly like Hugh.

I gotta get him out of my head, I think, as I quietly clamber down my bunk. But watching him sleep isn't exactly helpful in that department. His eyelashes flutter against his cheek, his bottom lip is full and pouty, and his hair is delightfully mussed. *Snap out of it!* I remind myself. I had done well last night, sneaking in after he was already in bed and thankfully avoiding any potentially awkward encounters. *I will not argue with him today*, I promise myself. *Today, I will focus.*

Rubbing my forehead, I grab my sweatshirt and my phone from the opposite mattress, where I'm storing all my stuff, and clamber upstairs. My eyes are puffy from crying last night and I'm glad I have some privacy in the cool morning air to try and regain some normalcy. I'm the first one out on the deck, and it feels so good to be out of the confines of our tiny room, and instead in the middle of a great expansive ocean.

The boat feels clean and fresh in the morning, and the smooth white laminate feels cold on my feet. It's only just dawn, and there's a grey light all around. I take a deep breath of the salty air. Only because no one else is awake, I take the hammock, gingerly climbing into it. It rocks slowly with the boat's movement. The sun starts to rise over the water, filling the sky with deep orange, then bright, almost neon pinks. Against the bright blue of the water, the sunrise is breathtaking. I stare at it for so long that when I look away, I have a bright spot in my vision. I take a picture on my phone, including the edge of the hammock so I can remember that there is a paradise somewhere, even if it's half the world away.

Then I remember that Millie's had her surgery.

I feel a little sick to my stomach at the thought. The desperation of wanting to know if she's OK gets to me, and I start to cry again. A tear escapes down my cheek as I watch the sunrise. I hadn't factored in what waiting for Millie's results would do to my mental health on the trip.

'Please God, let Sal have gone gracefully,' I whisper, the ocean breeze carrying away my words.

'Sal?' Hugh asks, clearing his throat. I hadn't heard him climb up onto the deck, and now he's standing at the edge of the platform beneath the hammock.

'Ohmigod,' I say quickly, the scenes from my dream come back to me and flood me with embarrassment. I sit straight up, causing the hammock to swing violently from side to side. 'Ah!' I scream, attempting to regain control of it before it dumps me over onto the platform.

Hugh smiles a sleepy, crooked smile and reaches out a large hand to steady the hammock. 'I got you,' he says.

I can barely stand to look at him so closely, his lips, his eyes, even the curve of his shoulders are doing something to me that I don't want to admit. I want to stay mad at him for being rude and self-important yesterday. It felt like as soon as I made the mistake of thinking he was a nice guy, he wasted no time in proving me wrong. I pointedly look at the sunrise.

'How's your head? From the sonic boom that came from your bunk it must be hurting.'

'It's fine.' I brush my fingers over my forehead, gingerly feeling the bump. 'Oh shoot, I woke you up, didn't

I?' I decide I don't care after the words leave my lips, but it's too late.

'I was already awake,' he says, but his eyes crinkle in a way I haven't seen before. I wonder if that's his tell that he's lying. 'Who's Sal?'

'Why do you care?'

'Hm,' He sits down on the platform and dips below my line of vision. I peer over the hammock and watch him interlace his fingers behind his head. 'Well, if I can figure out who Sal is, and really get in your head, then I have a better chance of you never finding the butterfly wrasse.'

I feel tears pooling in my eyes. I know he's joking, but it doesn't feel funny to me. Finding the wrasse is all I can do for Millie, and I'm so worried about her.

'Millie?' Hugh asks, his voice softer. 'I was just kidding, I'm not a complete butthead.'

I try to sniffle quietly, but I can't. I sound like a pig as I rattle air through my nose. 'I know,' I whisper.

Hugh reaches a hand up towards the hammock and pats me on the shoulder. 'Hey, I also came up here to apologise.'

'For what?' I sniffle again, refusing to look at him. 'For shaming me because I forgot my sunscreen? Being a smart ass online *and* in person? Giving Andrew the idea we were somehow differently qualified and then changing your mind? Purposely distracting me because you don't want me to succeed? You know what—' I turn, gathering steam '—you know you're hot and more successful and Australian, and you're weaponising it.' I'm so close to tears that my bottom lip trembles.

'OK.' Hugh puts his hands up in a surrender gesture. 'It is way too early for these kinds of accusations.

Firstly, you're not so bad-looking yourself and you have also been a kind of a smart ass, I did change my mind, and . . .' He pauses and shrugs. 'I kind of thought that the joking was just . . . our thing?'

I decide to think about Hugh saying I'm not bad-looking later. 'Being rude and unfriendly is *our* thing? I would never have been such an ass about sunscreen,' I point out. 'And you can't just say we have different attitudes towards the field, whatever that means, and change your mind.'

'If I do remember correctly you were a bit of an ass about my seasickness. And I actually *helped* you find the appropriate sunscreen?'

'Well . . .' I hesitate. Hugh is right, I have been an ass about him being seasick. 'I didn't know you actually got sick.' I glance down. 'I was teasing. And, in fairness, you were mean to me on the bus about the sunscreen. You started it.'

'I wasn't mean!' He scoffs gently. 'And even if I was, you would do the same thing if you were me. That sun-screen hurts the ocean.'

'I know.' I hang my head. 'I'm sorry I even said any-thing. We can go back to being our usual rude and unfriendly selves now.' I can feel Hugh's eyes on me without having to look up.

'Look, I'm up here to extend an olive branch of for-giveness then, considering there are too many things I'm supposed to apologise for.'

I sigh. 'Oh, lucky me to be forgiven. And what, may I ask, is making you so magnanimous as to offer me forgiveness?'

'Woah. Too early in the morning for big American words.'

'OK,' I reply, 'I'll dumb it down for you. What gives that you suddenly want us to be friends?'

'Last night. When you jumped in the water to get that cup, I saw how much you cared. And for the record, that's what made me change my mind about our attitudes. I'm not proud to admit it but I didn't think you were as committed as me to the cause.' Hugh says the last bit slowly, choosing his words carefully.

'Of course, I'm committed.' I turn around to face him. 'Why would I be out here if I wasn't? We don't all have the luck to be born on the same continent as the thing we want to study, you know. Just because I can't be out here all the time doesn't make me "less committed". You can't use your geographical privilege to say you're better than me.'

Hugh hesitates, scratching the stubble on his chin. 'Fair point,' he admits. 'I didn't think about it that way. Anyways, it's cool to see someone care as much as me.'

'Hmm,' I grunt, but I'm softening, and he can tell.

'I'm not saying I'll stop making fun of you.'

'I suppose that's all right with me.' I sink back into the hammock. The light is still soft over the ocean. The sun will be blazing in a couple of hours. I let a big sigh escape from my lips.

'So, do you want to talk about it?' Hugh asks. I can hear him settling against the platform next to me.

I open my mouth to answer that I don't. I know that I should keep what I'm going through private. I know that even though Hugh says he wants to be friends, he still doesn't think the wrasse is alive. I know that I should be surrounding myself with people that will help me, that believe in me.

But I also do want to talk about it. I desperately want someone else to know why I'm so worried. I want to share my burden with company so that I don't feel so alone in this great big ocean. And if that person is Hugh, on a sailboat, with a Great Barrier Reef sunrise in the background, then so be it.

'It's my sister Mi—' I stop myself just in time. 'My sister,' I say quickly. 'She got some weird news a couple of weeks ago, that she has a gene that predisposes her to breast cancer, and she got a double mastectomy this morning. I knew it would be hard not knowing how her surgery has gone, but I didn't realise it would be this hard.'

'Woah. I—I'm really sorry to hear that.'

'Yeah.'

'Was this what you were talking about the day you got that not-bad-not-good news?'

I look up from the frayed hem I'm tugging on the sweatshirt sleeve. Hugh and I have been so hostile since we met in person that sometimes I forget we actually know a good bit about each other. His message that day making fun of Americans was the only thing that brought a smile to my face.

'Yeah,' I admit. 'Well remembered.' I feel like I should say something else, but I have nothing to add. I'm worried if I share too many details, I'll slip up worse than before and say Millie's full name.

'I'll be right back.' I turn my head in time to see Hugh push himself up and head towards the cabins. I watch as he disappears out of my sight. *Have I been completely naive? Why did I think Hugh could handle my problems? Why would he care about my sister? He doesn't even know me.* So much for being friends.

Grumpily, I get out of the hammock and sit on the platform, crossing my arms over my chest. I don't feel like swaying in the breeze anymore.

I stare at the water, hoping for a turtle or a pod of dolphins to appear so that later I can make Hugh feel bad for leaving me after I opened up to him, but no matter how hard I stare at the ocean, nothing appears.

'Millie?' I hear Hugh call softly.

'What?' I growl. I purposely keep my face angled away from where his voice is coming from.

'A little help?'

I turn to find him balancing two very full cups of steaming liquid, one tea and one coffee. The liquid is dangerously close to sloshing all over the sides, but miraculously, despite the rocking of the boat, Hugh has kept it under control.

'When I get bad news my mom brings me tea, but I know you like coffee so . . .'

I can't be mad at someone who brought me coffee, so I smile and gratefully accept the cup from his outstretched hand. The steam curls up towards the sky and is instantly borne away on the breeze. 'Thank you,' I say, scooting over to make room for him.

'I'm sorry about your sister. If you want to talk about it, I'm here. And, for the record, I'm also sorry about what I said to Vanessa. I didn't know she was going to get mad at you. You're already Miguel's favourite anyways.'

'Oh, come on.' I raise a single eyebrow at him. 'He's like that with everybody.' I pick at a loose thread on my sweatshirt. 'And you certainly didn't seem sorry yesterday,' I mumble.

'I know—' he throws the hand not holding his tea up in defence '—I know I didn't seem that sorry. I genuinely didn't know she would actually threaten to shorten your dives. It clearly wasn't our fault the groups got separated. If I'm honest, I think Miguel and Vanessa screwed that up.'

'You think?' I gaze down at the steaming coffee and gently blow on it. 'I felt like it was my fault.'

Hugh shakes his head. 'It wasn't.'

'Well,' I say, attempting to hold onto my annoyance but it's draining out of me. 'It's OK. I want to put it behind us. I need a clear head today.'

He smiles, slightly crooked and cheeky and genuine.

A laugh escapes my lips.

'What?' Hugh asks, a wrinkle appearing in between his eyebrows.

'I just realised this is probably the Hugh everyone else has got . . . you're kind of nice.'

'I am nice.'

'And happy.'

'That too. I'm more than just a hot, Australian face, Millie.'

'We'll see about that.' I laugh.

Hugh's eyes dance turquoise. 'So, I take it we have a truce then?' he says.

'Truce,' I confirm. Then I remember the shark isn't really why we weren't friends in the first place. 'Except the wrasse,' I say. 'I'm finding that fish. Whether you like it not.'

Hugh holds his cup of tea in front of his mouth, but I see a grin bloom behind it.

Chapter 13

'Nice sweatshirt.' Hugh nods at the unravelled hem I'd been picking at earlier. Self-conscious, I tug the sleeves further down towards my hands. We're sitting next to each other now, both gazing out at the sea towards the sunrise. We've spent the last couple minutes in companionable silence, watching as gulls swooped into the water. Every so often I steal a glance at him out of my peripherals, and one time I catch him looking back at me. We both look away as fast as we can, focusing on the turquoise horizon. He's squinting, but his eyes are a clear bright blue this morning with golden flecks around his irises. He's a little sunburned around his cheeks and on the slope of his nose. He looks even more like Prince Eric in profile than he did yesterday. The sun is about two feet above the water now, and Hugh says he started to hear rumblings of movement in the cabin while he was making tea.

'Is this something Americans do? Wear extra-large clothes?'

'Well, it's actually not mine.' I blush, although I can't pinpoint whether it's the implication that I'm wearing men's clothes or Hugh's gaze that makes me uncomfortable.

'Oh.' His eyes widen. 'I see.' He coughs awkwardly and recovers his normal expression. We sit in silence for another minute before he says, 'I have to say it's impressive that you found someone who can put up with your snoring.'

'What!' I exclaim, heat creeping up my neck. 'I don't snore!' *Snoring is better than moaning in my sleep*, I think. *At least I didn't do that.*

Hugh's lips twitch. I can tell he's trying his hardest to keep a smile at bay. 'If you say so,' he says.

'Also, I'm not . . .' I stammer. 'I haven't found . . .' I trail off again, not wanting to admit to snoring. 'I thought we were in a truce,' I complain, half whining.

'You're right,' Hugh says, hands up in mock surrender. 'You don't snore. Truce.' He winks. 'So, tell me about the owner of the sweatshirt. If it's not yours, is it someone special's?' Now, it's his turn to blush at his own naked curiosity, and he fixes his gaze onto his half-empty cup of tea.

I stifle a laugh. 'Well . . .' I hesitate. 'It's my ex-boyfriend's,' I begin. I'm continuously surprised at how easily 'ex' rolls off my tongue. 'We actually broke up pretty recently . . . it wasn't great.' I roll my shoulders back and take a deep breath. It suddenly feels like every word I choose is heavy with importance. 'He was right for me at the beginning. He was – he is – patient and safe. He's reliable. I needed that in college, and right afterwards, when I didn't know what I wanted to be doing. But I know myself better now and . . . well . . .'

When I stop talking, even the gulls are quiet, the ocean seems to be holding its breath. 'This sounds stupid but it affected more of my life than I thought.' I sigh. 'I'm hoping this trip will give me some time to focus on myself.

So I'm single but . . .' I stop talking, leaving the rest of my thoughts left unsaid.

'You're focusing on yourself,' Hugh supplies, his voice even. His eyes are still glued to his tea.

'Trying to,' I say in a small voice.

Hugh stills. I glance over at him, but his face remains impassive. Suddenly I'm extremely aware of my body. My breathing slows, but my heartbeat pulses at my temples. His leg is so close to mine that if we were to get jostled our limbs would touch. I spot a big wave in the distance, and feel a thrill dance up my spine. Neither Hugh nor I say anything as it approaches. We are both completely still. The wave is almost underneath the boat. I am so focused on the possibility of our limbs tangling together that I am holding my breath.

'Morning!' Andrew calls out, plopping down beside us right as we crest over the wave. We all jostle into each other, and any tension between me and Hugh dissipates.

Andrew launches into a barrage of questions, wondering how we slept, if we had breakfast yet, if there was more coffee. Watching Hugh respond with complete normalcy, as if Andrew hadn't just interrupted a moment, is all I need to convince myself that letting that conversation continue would have been a bad idea. *I wish Hugh wasn't on this stupid boat.* I know why he is though – if Millie knows this is the best dive trip a marine biologist's salary can buy, then Hugh knows it too. I remind myself that I can't keep letting Hugh distract me just because he keeps me on my toes and appears in my dreams. *Nothing can get in the way of me finding this wrasse.*

We have three dives today, three more tomorrow, and one more after Fitzroy Island. Plenty of chances.

'How'd you guys sleep?' Pippa asks, poking her head above board. Soon, Natalie and Derek follow. I overhear Pippa comment on how nice Natalie's skin looks (she's right, it's glowing) and Natalie responds with something that makes Pippa laugh. I'm wondering if I should bring my coffee over to them, if maybe I'm being too cautious about Natalie remembering my name is really Andi, but my anxiety keeps me rooted in my seat.

Luckily, Vanessa and Miguel dive straight into work, saving me from my indecision. They ready equipment for our morning dive and remind us we should eat something before we go.

'But you're not supposed to swim right after you eat,' says Derek, with a genuine look of confusion on his face.

'I think that rule is just for kids,' Natalie whispers to him, nudging him with her elbow.

I stifle a laugh and I see Hugh's shoulders shake out of the corner of my eye.

After a lengthy safety briefing, which feels like it's aimed solely at Derek, we change into our suits and strap on our equipment. I lurk next to Miguel, hoping he'll sense my presence and ask me to be his buddy, but I have no luck. Hugh is watching me out of the corner of his eye. I wait until Miguel says, 'Derek, you're with me,' jamming his thumb towards his chest for emphasis before I reluctantly turn towards Hugh.

'See?' I whisper, inclining my head towards Miguel. 'No favouritism here.'

Just then, Miguel shoulders past me, pausing to say under his breath, 'Maybe next time we can be buddies again.'

As soon as he's out of earshot, Hugh bursts out laughing.

'Shut up,' I hiss.

'You better play nice, or I won't be saving you from any sharks today,' Hugh says with a gleam in his eye. I glare at him by way of response.

We've done this before, the dance where we check one another's equipment, but when Hugh leans close to me to check my air pressure, I find myself holding my breath. And when he slips his fingers under the strap of my BCD, the pressure of his fingers causes heat to race into my belly.

I can't tell if he's trying to distract me. Or because we declared a truce, he is sincerely attempting to be a good buddy. My mind keeps circling back to our conversation earlier.

As soon as I'm off the boat and in the expanse of crystal blue water, my head immediately clears. Effortlessly, everything is pulled into focus, my breathing slows, my heart race stabilises. My weird tangle of maybe-this-isn't-hate-anymore feelings for Hugh, my worries about Millie, my deep missing of Murphy, all vanish from my mind as we start to descend.

The group is quick this morning. It feels like everyone can't wait to get to the reef. Vanessa has to motion to us twice to descend slower. There are strict rules on how fast you can descend and come back up, and all of them depend on how quickly the body acclimatises to pressure.

We all have computers with us that do the calculations, and I know if I looked at mine it would read the same warning Vanessa is giving — our descent is too fast.

But none of us are looking at our computers. Hugh is eyeing the looming shadow of coral in the distance. I can see his smile underneath his mask. I follow his gaze.

We're on a different part of the reef this morning, and both Miguel and Vanessa had seemed excited about the conditions and the location when we were on the boat. We find out as soon as we're underwater that they were right to be excited.

We aren't descending on a mooring line. Instead, we all bring our BCD hoses over our heads and press the deflate button, slowly sinking down towards the sandy bottom. We're only about thirty feet underwater, and the sun filters down, dappling the ocean floor.

Derek doesn't have his camera, and Natalie is making the most of his attention by pointing out a school of sweetlips fish that darts by us. I've been keeping an eye on Natalie, but she hasn't made any effort to talk to me since last night. I bring my attention back to the sweetlips fish. Their bodies are patterned in a black-and-white zigzag that makes them look like an optical illusion, and they have bright yellow lips, yellow fins and yellow tails. One by one, our group stills, watching as they flick their fins to pass us.

The sound of water in my ears is calming, a whooshing noise that eventually fades to the background, but never goes away. My regulator is a loud and comforting reminder that I'm breathing. Scuba-diving is my favourite form of meditation, I think. I want to keep doing it.

A thought breaks through my trance – my current life-style isn't exactly conducive to frequent dive trips – but I push it away.

Andrew gets his buoyancy quicker than usual, although I see Hugh snicker when Pippa grabs Andrew's hand and yanks him back down. Sometimes I think scuba-diving is like being on the moon – with a jacket full of air on, you can't really control any of your movements. And everyone looks hilarious when they try, like stumbling toddlers just learning to swim.

I've got the hang of it after yesterday and can scuba like Hugh does, with my arms crossed in front of me, each hand grabbing my opposite elbow. Yesterday, Hugh was the only non-instructor to dive in this position, and when I try it today, I pick it up quicker than I thought I would. Keeping my arms crossed in front of me helps direct my body, so if I tilt my arms up, I go up, and if I tilt them down, I go down. The only thing I can't get the hang of is stopping in front of something and remaining still. My breath lifts my body up and down, and I'm always afraid I'll sink low enough that I'll hit the coral, which is a *big* no-no – divers should not disturb coral at any cost.

This morning, I get my camera out immediately. I am on a mission. As soon as we get in sight of the reef, our group disperses to look around. We've swum into a semicircle of coral, and Vanessa hangs out at the open-ing of the structure so she can keep eyes on all of us at the same time. Miguel is swimming around, point-ing out interesting fish. I beeline for the staghorn coral, where butterfly wrasse like to hang out.

The reef is just as breathtaking today as it was yesterday. Coral doesn't grow uniformly, it builds and layers on each other, creating nooks and crannies teeming with life. Everywhere I look I see a different species of fish. Some fish have huge, flapping dorsal fins, some have spots, or stripes, or patches just above their eyes. I'm starting to feel like underwater is technicolour, and everything else is black and white. As I kick forward slowly, the coral fissures below me and I spot the dark green ribbon of an eel as it streaks through the rocky crevice.

I drift a couple of feet further, until I'm hovering over a flat bed of coral. Staghorn coral make up about 25 per cent of the Great Barrier Reef's ground cover. They come in many sizes, shapes and colours. All of them branch out, some resemble elk antlers, some are small and look like miniature forests, and some branch high into the sea, swaying in the current, and look more like pointy sticks.

I hover over a bright blue structure of staghorn branching up towards the surface. There are hundreds of fish darting around, most of which swim away as I get closer, but after I pause, doing my best to hover without kicking too much, the fish return.

I start snapping pictures as fast as I can. I don't see a butterfly wrasse, but I'm hoping I can comb through the pictures later and find one. It's hard to focus on one fish at a time when they are all moving. *I bet Millie could do it*, I think. As soon as she crosses my mind, my thoughts snowball.

Why did I think I could do this? What if I don't find the fish? Will it be because it doesn't exist or because

I'm bad at this? Will this be the last adventurous thing I ever do?

My lapse in confidence causes me to lose focus and I almost kick the coral beneath me. Frightened, I swim away from the reef, backpedalling towards Vanessa. From there, I watch as the divers continue to explore. I feel defeated, floating in the ether, untethered, like I could drift off into the ocean, letting the current carry me further out to sea.

After a beat, Hugh comes to join us. Annoyance prickles my spine. I needed a moment alone and here he is, encroaching, always the ever-present buddy. I try focusing instead on the magic of seeing the reef structure from far away. It's massive and dynamic. There are schools of fish swimming and floating both above the reef and closer to the ocean floor. I notice Hugh moving out of the corner of my eye and turn to find his shoulders shaking with laughter.

I follow his eyes, and see Andrew, who is floating two feet above where he should be, not exactly cause for laughter. I look back at Hugh, who's still locked in on Andrew, so focused that he doesn't even see me looking at him. Then, I see it. There are bubbles, big bubbles, escaping from the bottom of Andrew's suit. He's farting. And he's not letting a little one slip out, he's really passing gas. I know it's childish, but I can't help it, I fall into giggles too. Both of us use way more of our air than we should laughing about farts.

We're still giggling when Vanessa darts forward in excitement. She points to a fish hovering a few inches above the sandy bottom. It has a skirt-like flap that encircles its body, and it's pushing away the water beneath it to move. It's almost translucent and is moving very slowly. When I focus, I spot its eyes, and suddenly I can't look away. They are huge, with giant black pupils that seem to see straight through me. I breathe in and out of my regulator, transfixed.

Vanessa looks back to make sure Hugh and I are paying attention and then pokes her finger at the fish. Instantly, it flushes a darker colour, more the colour of grey stone than the bright white sand, and begins to flutter its skirt and swim towards the reef. It looks like a cross between a squid and an octopus. It's large, about the size of a pizza, and a bit oval-shaped. I'm transfixed by its movements, we all are, and we watch as it swims towards the safety of the reef, soon blending in completely with its surroundings.

Chapter 14

Six dives to go

Before I know it, we're back on the boat, Miguel strapping in the air tanks to prepare for Aaron to rev up the engine. We're headed to Wonder Reef next. We'll dive there twice. Millie wrote in her notes that the last butterfly wrasse sighting there was in 2016, so I don't have high hopes. Wonder Reef sits on the outer edge of the reef structures, and a major current brings in plankton and organic debris in from the ocean, making it the most biodiverse of all the reefs on our schedule.

Everyone's content but tired, all of us wrapped in towels. We are huddled together in the captain's room, all wanting to be outside, but also wanting some protection from the wind coming off the waves.

We're moving to another entry point to drop anchor before going on our afternoon dive and eating lunch. Tonight is our night dive, which is scheduled for seven thirty, right when the sun goes down. Pippa wheedles Aaron until he promises he'll point out some constellations tonight if it's clear enough.

As soon as the boat picks up speed, fragments of music start to blare over the ship's speakers. The volume picks up until it's blasting and when the chorus blares through the speakers everyone starts to sing along to 'Island in the Sun'. Vanessa pops her head out of the cabin and cheers.

'Let's dance!' she cries, swaying her hips in time with the music. Pippa squeals and joins in immediately, tugging Andrew behind her. Before I know it, we're all crowded on the ship's deck, shouting the lyrics, limbs flailing wildly in the air. Even Natalie seems to be letting loose, she's doing a hula move with her hands and rocking her hips back and forth.

'Escape (The Piña Colada Song)' comes on next, and everyone yells out the words. Vanessa puts on hit after hit, and every time the song switches Hugh's face lights up in recognition. Between the sound of the waves and the wind, at some points we can hardly hear the music over our own off-key singing. I raise my face up to the sun during a chorus of 'More Than a Feeling' and sing it so loud my voice cracks.

Pippa attempts a viral TikTok dance and whacks Derek in the face accidentally, making me cackle with laughter. He takes the hit in his stride and playfully starts to dance alongside her. Vanessa teaches Miguel the steps to the start of a swing dance. Hugh is sillier when he dances than I imagined. He moves his feet like he's doing an agility drill and punches the air with his fists. I'm having so much fun that I don't want to stop, but singing at the top of my lungs in salty air is drying out my throat by the second. I'm about to sit down when Miguel grabs my hand and pulls me in close before spinning me out towards the railing. Laughing, I let him pull me back in, and when our torsos meet, he lowers mine into a dip. Pippa hoots.

When the next song comes on, I sit down on the bench, exhausted.

Hugh plops down next to me and runs a hand through his damp hair, causing it to stick out in all directions. When it's wet it's noticeably darker, and he looks more brooding than normal. But his eyes are playful when he turns to me and says, 'That was fun.'

I nod. 'I didn't know how much I needed that.'

Both of us turn to look at the rest of the group: Vanessa, Miguel, Derek, Natalie, Andrew, and Pippa, who are all still rocking out to 'All Star' by Smash Mouth.

'We must have eaten a lotta beans last night, don't you think?'

It takes me a minute to process what he's saying. His eyes are glinting with mischief, and he nods his head ever so slightly in Andrew's direction. He's still dancing with Pippa, and we catch him in a moment where he's wiggling his butt. Then I remember the stream of air escaping his stinger suit on our dive earlier. I burst out laughing, so hard that I snort and then immediately clap my hand over my mouth.

'What's so funny?' Pippa asks, she and Andrew losing steam and collapsing down next to us. I blush harder.

Hugh claps his hand over my knee and gently squeezes, a warning for me to be quiet, which makes trying not to laugh even harder

'Nothing,' Hugh says, his face impassive. Tears are springing into my eyes from holding giggles back.

'OK,' says Pippa, but she gives me a questioning look. Her eyes dart to where Hugh's large hand is resting on my thigh and suddenly it feels like my leg is aflame.

I tense up and Hugh takes his hand off my knee and stretches it across the top of the seats. I can feel the heat coming off his skin, but we aren't touching. I wonder what it would feel like if he relaxed his arm over my shoulders and pulled me in close, but he doesn't. He remains stretched and comfortable. My thoughts flit to my dream world, just Hugh and I in our miniscule room, doing whatever it is we want to do.

We jostle over a big wave and his arms falls. I place a hand on his thigh to steady myself. I feel as if I've been electrocuted in the best way. I glance at him through the tumble of movement and he's staring at me, eyes blazing. For a moment, it feels like we're the only two people in the world. As the boat rights itself, we stop touching each other. I fold my hands in my lap and Hugh does the same. We scoot a centimetre apart. I feel like neither of us are breathing. Hugh clears his throat.

'About twenty minutes until we drop anchor for the afternoon dive,' Aaron announces, startling me so badly that I jump an inch off my seat, Hugh stifling a chuckle from the seat next to me.

I drag myself downstairs to review Millie's notes one more time. I try to think of ways to change up my strategy, maybe I need to spend longer monitoring under the coral instead of hovering over it, or maybe I need to expand where I'm searching to more than just staghorn . . . I reread her notes for the third time. She's meticulous and clear, but I can hardly concentrate. I'm not sure what game Hugh is playing anymore, whether he's purposefully trying to distract me from the reason I'm here, but whatever he's doing, it's working.

I am in the middle of strategising how to stop Hugh from getting in my head, or at least how to get him out of my head while we're diving, when Miguel steps directly into my line of sight to ask if I want to do the night dive. I had been staring at Natalie and Hugh, who are talking at the far end of the boat. Natalie has on such a skimpy bikini that I wonder how she manages to keep it covering the right bits when she pulls her stinger suit on. She's laughing at Hugh and places a hand gently on his bicep. Something stirs in my belly. I can't tell if it's anxiety or jealousy, but whatever it is, I don't like it.

'Millie?' Miguel asks again, following my gaze towards Hugh. Both of us watch Natalie toss her head back and laugh. 'Night dive?' he prompts, mercifully not addressing the conversation we are both watching. 'You really should go, you won't want to miss it.' He's holding a clipboard with our names on it, marking who is signing up for the dive so he can enter it into the dive logs.

I hesitate.

'I'll protect you!' Miguel says, flashing the papers at me one more time.

I nod. 'I guess,' I answer reluctantly. I can't *not* go, not while I'm on an all-expenses paid Great Barrier Reef trip. That would be criminal. But night diving is terrifying, and I've only done it once before, with Millie, who made me go. I was scared the entire time. The ocean is so *dark*. You can't see anything around you. I felt like I was inches away from a shark or an eel (they have surprisingly strong and dangerous jaws) at every moment.

I want to ask if Hugh is going. Miguel will most likely be assigned to Derek again. I don't want to dive if he isn't. He's knowledgeable and good at diving, and he did manage to come between me and a shark. Plus, I'm worried that the other girls won't want to go, and I don't want to be partners with Andrew, who can't control his buoyancy, or Derek, who gets so easily distracted. I watch as Miguel approaches Hugh and Natalie. When Hugh nods excitedly, my shoulders relax with relief.

Pippa walks over to me, her eyes flitting to Hugh and back again. 'Gosh, you have *all* the fun!' she laments dramatically.

'What are you talking about now?' I look pointedly towards the ocean, hoping to direct her attention away from Hugh.

Unsurprisingly, it doesn't work. 'Miguel and Hugh! Hotties! I knew there would be a hot American on this boat and turns out there's a hot Colombian and Australian too! It's like an international *Love Island*.'

'Natalie is hot,' I agree glumly.

'No dummy,' Pippa swats at my arm playfully. 'You!'

I stare at her blankly.

'Don't play that game with me. Your hair is brilliant. Those curls are to die for. And your cheekbones! It's no wonder Miguel and Hugh are falling all over you.'

'They are not.'

She ignores me. 'Which one are you gonna pick? When I came over here you were watching Hugh like a shark!'

'Ugh.' I shudder. 'Too soon.'

'OK fine, a lioness. Now fill me in.'

'There is *nothing* to fill you in on,' I say definitively, making it as clear as possible that whatever she is putting on the table should come off it.

'You had a cheeky moment over there before.' Pippa raises one eyebrow at me.

'Pippa, be serious. I'm here for work,' I say, although my voice lacks conviction.

'You know what they say,' she reminds me. 'All work and no play . . .'

'Hugh thinks he knows *everything*, and he's stubborn. Plus, he's trying to sabotage me.'

Pippa raises an eyebrow again.

'I'm serious!' I say. 'The only reason he is paying me any attention is because I'm trying to find this fish, and he's trying to prove it's extinct. He's trying to get in my head on purpose.'

'For starters, you can't say you don't like someone just because they don't agree with you. And give yourself more credit. Hugh could be into you just because you're hot and brilliant, and not because of some dumb fish.'

'Mhm,' I grunt.

'He's not that bad, you know. Andrew quite likes him. And he's cute.'

'We've known him for, like, one day. And he's not that cute.'

Pippa smirks. 'Millie, you have the same eyes as the rest of us.'

What is with these Commonwealth people and their smirking?

'Incoming,' Pippa says under her breath. Hugh is walking towards us, leaving Natalie standing by the railing, talking to Miguel.

'Ladies,' Hugh says, looking right at me.

'I'm gonna grab my water,' Pippa says, with a glint in her eye.

I try to glare at her as she walks away – I know she's trying to play matchmaker – but she avoids my gaze.

'Just me and you then,' Hugh says, sitting down next to me.

'Yep.' Absent-mindedly, I twirl an escaped curl around my finger.

'You having a good holiday? You know, apart from your sister . . .'

A seagull's caw pierces the air just as a breeze ruffles across the deck. 'How could I not be?' I ask him. 'We're in paradise.'

Hugh nods. 'It'll end too quickly.'

'You're telling me. At least you live here.'

'Well, I don't live here, I live in Sydney. It's not as close as you'd think.'

'I know but . . .' I trail off, looking wistfully at the horizon.

'It's a lot closer than Columbus,' Hugh agrees.

'Something everyone seems dying to point out to me lately.'

Hugh laughs. 'The commenters on our articles can be a real pain in the arse.'

'I know,' I agree.

'So . . .' He trails off and gestures at the ocean. 'What's your favourite colour?'

'My favourite colour?' I burst out laughing.

'Never mind.' He blushes, leaning away from me slightly.

My breath hitches in my chest.

'No, no, I liked it,' I say quickly. Hugh shoots me a look, narrowing his brilliant blue eyes. 'My favourite colour is blue, but you could have gone with a more normal get-to-know-you question . . . like . . . tell me about your family?'

Hugh grunts. 'I don't see the difference, but I guess we could talk about that.'

'OK,' I prompt. 'You start.'

'I have a brother named Shaggy, we're really close.'

'Shaggy?' I ask, howling with laughter.

'You are impossible to talk to,' Hugh says, but I can tell he's trying not to smile. 'That's not his real name, it's just a nickname that stuck.'

'So does your mom call you Scooby?' I tease, ignoring the last bit of what he said. 'And by your mom, I mean Daphne. Or is she more of a Velma?'

'She doesn't call me Scooby, thank you very much. And her name is Gracie.'

'OK, OK,' I say, my giggles subsiding. 'Well, as you know I have one sister, and we are also really close. We live near my parents too, so we see them quite a bit.'

157

Our next dive approaches too quickly. Hugh's only just started to explain how much of his childhood he spent looking after his little brother. Both of us seem to put our siblings first, even at the expense of our own best interests. When I met him, I thought we would never be able to agree on anything, that I would never be able to tolerate being around him. But I'm starting to feel like I may have been completely wrong.

Chapter 15

After our conversation is interrupted, Hugh and I buddy up quickly for the afternoon dive. Everything goes according to plan. I relish the feeling of jumping in, when every other sound melts away, and it's just me and the open ocean. It's also nice to get off the small confines of the boat.

Wonder Reef was spectacular, vibrant and teeming with life. Everywhere I looked there were flashes of colour and whirls of movement. But I didn't see anything specifically of note, and I didn't see a single butterfly wrasse. Instead of being disappointed, I try to use the hour underwater to make me feel more comfortable, mentally preparing myself the entire time for entering the sea later, under the cover of night.

As we set up for lunch, I go through my pictures of the staghorn coral from our four dives so far. I have taken about a hundred and fifty. There are only two that show promising hints of what could be a butterfly wrasse, but I can't tell for sure, which means it won't be conclusive enough proof. Identifying fish means you have to see their unique characteristics clearly, and butterfly wrasse are the easiest to identify by the extra fin they have on their underbelly. Neither of the photos captures an underbelly. I just have one fish face that has purple scales behind it and one tail that's purple with a yellow stripe. Both could be butterfly wrasse, but they could also be something else entirely.

Discouraged, I follow Andrew and Pippa downstairs to take a break and eat lunch. The crew has outdone themselves again. I spot a quinoa salad studded with bright vegetables and platters of fruit. Pippa fills her plate with a sample of each. I spot a container of Oreos in the corner, which fills me with excitement. I pack my plate, avoiding the cookies for now, and balance my tray as I scale the ladders upstairs. I head to the platform to eat in the sun, with the breeze ruffling my curls. I can't even begin to imagine how wild my hair looks. I took it out of my braids in my attempt to shower last night and couldn't wrangle it back into one, so now it's alternating between a messy bun and cascading in a heap down my back.

Right now, I can tell it's frizzing around my face, so I tie it behind my neck while I eat. Just as I start to dig in, Hugh appears from the side of the boat.

'Do you mind? The captain's room is discussing the royal drama.' Hugh rolls his eyes.

I pat the seat next to me, inviting Hugh to sit down.

'Like British royal family drama?' I clarify.

Hugh nods. 'If I hear another word about it, I swear I'll feed myself to a shark.'

'OK,' I agree, laughing, 'no royal talk. But I don't want any shark talk either.'

'Done.' Hugh sighs, relaxing into a seat next to me. He places an Oreo on my plate. My eyes widen in surprise. 'I saw you eyeing them.' He shrugs. He has one on his plate too.

Both of us are silent as we tuck in hungrily. Scuba-diving is more of a workout than I anticipated. It's been a long time since I was so ravenous. After a couple of minutes, we both slow down and exchange smiles.

'The food is way better than I expected,' Hugh says happily.

'Me too. I thought all we were going to have was lunchables.'

'Lunchables?' Hugh asks, cocking his head at me.

I laugh and explain the concept of pre-packaged slices of meat and cheese and some sort of cracker. Hugh listens, his mouth grimacing in disgust.

'They're actually not so bad,' I say, defending myself. 'My mom used to get them for Mi—' I pause in panic right before I was about to say 'Millie and me'. 'My mom used to get them for my school lunch,' I say, forcing out the first word I can think of that starts with a 'm' sound.

Hugh seems satisfied with the explanation, but then starts asking me a lot of questions about my upbringing. It's fun to feel like he thinks I'm interesting, but growing up in the suburbs of Ohio isn't exactly riveting, which makes answering his deluge of questions difficult. He's shocked that classrooms only taught American history until high school, and he's surprised they trusted our parents to pack our lunches, especially considering what my mother was sending us to school with. 'No fruit or vegetables!' Hugh keeps lamenting. 'Not even an apple!'

Eventually, he lets up, and both of us head downstairs into the cabin to load up our plates with seconds.

We settle back into our seats, staring down plates of quinoa, pineapple salsa and a delicious mix of cauliflower and farro. I pick up my camera and look at the only two photos that may contain the tail end or the face of a butterfly wrasse.

'What's that?' Hugh grunts through a mouthful of salad.

'You don't want to know,' I tease, holding the camera out of his reach.

'Did you see one?' He grabs at the camera, his previous decorum gone.

'I don't know,' I confess. I keep the camera out of his reach, but lean in to show him the photos. Our shoulders graze when he scoots closer to me for a better look. Neither of us move to keep them apart. Hugh stares intently at the camera screen.

'What do you think? And be honest.' I give him a serious look, and he returns my gaze with one just as serious. His eyes are a deeper blue. I make a mental note to stop thinking about how often they change colour.

'I don't know,' he says hesitantly.

'Are you just saying that because you don't want me to find one?'

'No, Millie, honest.' He crosses his heart with his fingers in a gesture that reminds me of children. It's so endearing that it softens the blow of his answer.

'It's not enough, is it?'

'I'm afraid I don't think so.'

A pit forms in my stomach.

'We still have a lot more dives to go,' he says, his voice soft and reassuring.

'You shouldn't be the one comforting me about this.' I try to sound nonchalant, but my voice comes out flat and glum. 'I bet you're thrilled.'

'No,' Hugh corrects me. 'Although I have to confess, I don't know why you're so hell-bent on finding this fish. You can prove corals can rebound another way. You can emphasise the pollution problem another way.'

'I could, but people can identify with a fish; fish are less abstract than coral.'

Hugh nods thoughtfully. 'OK, but coral bleaching is often one of the easiest ways to make people understand what a crisis global warming is because something literally *changes colour*. Take what happened in Florida, for example. One hot summer and boom, all the coral turned black – and died.'

'But most people don't even know that coral are animals. They don't even know what dead versus bleached coral looks like! They don't even know zooxanthellae!'

'Millie, hardly anybody knows zooxanthellae. They can learn. And that's beside the point.'

We're seated so close. I feel more heat under the scrutiny of his gaze than I do from the blazing sun. 'Why do *you* care so much whether or not this fish exists anyways?' I ask.

'Well.' Hugh sighs and leans back. 'Because I really don't think it does. I think coral bleaching killed it, and I think it's important to acknowledge that. We have to make people see that sometimes there is no coming back from the decisions we've made. We can't turn back time.'

'I think I'm going to prove you wrong.'

'We can agree to disagree.'

'Fine.'

'Fine.'

I don't want to keep thinking about the wrasse, so I change the subject. 'If,' I say, leaning back and closing my eyes against the bright sunlight, 'you could have had anything for lunch, what would you have?'

'Every day for lunch or like just today?'

I crack an eye open. 'Hmmm . . . what about both?'

'Okay,' Hugh leans forward. 'Today, fish and chips. I couldn't eat it every day, but we've been working hard out here and, man, does that sound good. For every day . . . a salad maybe or a grain bowl. Something light.'

'Something light?' I tease. 'You sound like you're on the cover of a women's magazine.'

'Well, you said every day. I can't be eating a hamburger for lunch every day. What would you eat?'

I pause, mulling it over. 'Today, I would eat a BLT on an everything bagel. Every day . . . I guess a salad,' I mumble the last bit.

'A salad?' Hugh howls. 'You hypocrite!'

'Oh, come on, it was weirder when you said it.'

Our conversation continues as we clear our plates, sneak a couple more Oreos and reapply sunscreen. Casually, Hugh hands me the sunscreen bottle and asks, 'When you're done making fun of me, can you get my back?'

'Wait!' he says, when I'm centimetres away from placing my sunscreened palms onto his shoulder blades. 'I didn't hand you the sunscreen you brought, did I?'

'Hugh Harris, I swear to God, do you want me to help you or not?'

'Fine,' he says, with a chuckle.

Tentatively, I spread sunscreen over his tanned, muscular shoulders. I rub into his neck, and down to the hem of his swimsuit. This is the most we've touched, and I ache to think of a way to fill the silence. I feel jittery all over, like I just drank six cups of coffee.

'Want me to get you?' he asks.

My mouth is so dry I can only nod in response. His hands are strong and so large that they cover most of my back without even moving. In slow circles, he massages the lotion across my shoulder blades, slides a hand underneath the strap of my swimsuit, and works his way down my back to the hemline of my bottoms. With a single finger, he rubs sunscreen right up against the line of my swimsuit.

I feel so weak at the knees that I grab the table to steady myself as soon as Hugh turns to head upstairs. When I meet him back on deck, he dives back into our back and forth without a second thought. I feel like my head is filled with cotton. We get comfortable, both of us reclined. I listen to Hugh explain to me why coral bleaching is, actually, the *best* example of climate change, and my eyes slowly start to close. The rocking of the boat is lulling me to sleep. The sun is beating down relentlessly. My last thought before I fall asleep is that his accent is melodious, it's like listening to a song.

I wake up with a start, confused. My copy of *The Marinist* is no longer in my hand, and my head is on a chest. A strong, tanned, hard-as-rock chest, that somehow has just enough give and warmth to be comfortable. It smells like coconut sunscreen and a touch of man's deodorant. Just as I'm nestling back into it to keep sleeping, I realise what I'm doing and bolt upright. I sit up straight into the edge of the hammock, and my head crashes into Pippa's bum.

'Oi!' she shouts, scrambling upright, causing the hammock to swing erratically back and forth.

Hugh grumbles and opens his eyes. 'What's the matter?' he asks, sleepily.

'I fell asleep,' I respond breathlessly. I scramble up and stand on the deck, grabbing the rails.

'OK,' says Hugh. He flops his forearm back over his eyes.

Pippa grunts and nestles back into the hammock to continue her nap.

I stare out at the horizon. *I can't believe I just fell asleep on his chest. I cannot keep fraternising with the enemy like this!*

I am not this person. I am not someone who lets a hot guy get in the way of her goals. In the past, hot guy distractions have been Millie's vibe. She's bungled a test after a night out, she's shown up late for a family dinner with a handsome random man in tow. But I have never let myself get that carried away, and I am not about to start now.

I promised myself I would take this time to think! Not get swept up in some dumb boat fantasy with someone I will never see again. I glance back at Hugh, who seems to have already fallen back to sleep. He makes it so easy for me to forget why I'm here. I could be going back over the photos I took; I could be interviewing Miguel or Vanessa about potential sightings. I could be reviewing Millie's notes.

I am usually more in control than this. I am always planning. I am steady and reliable. I am the sister and the daughter who is always in the place she needs to be, even when I don't want to.

Growing up, Millie was always the loudest and the most exciting. She had the most polarising opinions; she glowed the brightest in every room. She looked better in clothes. She was, and still is, habitually late, but the energy she brings into a room makes up for it every time.

Everyone has to find their own space in a family – where they fit, where they find a niche of comfortability, where they add value or feel loved. I found mine being everything Millie wasn't. It felt so natural at first: I would be early everywhere, I always kept my room neat as a pin. Those were easy compliments to get from my parents – Millie's room was so messy but Andi's, Andi's was perfect. I loved that praise.

Somewhere along the way finding my space snowballed into creating my personality around it. I always remember birthdays, but I'm never the first person invited to a birthday party. I can talk knowledgeably about a lot of subjects, but I never have a hot take that makes people gasp in salacious delight. When we get in family disagreements over dinner, even when I think everyone else is being pig-headed, I keep my mouth shut and nod with a tight smile. Nobody ever seems to notice that I don't really agree with what they are saying. Not like Millie, whose face is as expressive as an eighteen-month-old baby that just learned how to say no. I am Millie's perfect foil. That's why we are best friends.

I look over at Hugh, whose arm is still draped over his face. His abs are glistening in the sun. He looks like a Greek god except for his hair drying in a wild poof on top of his head. I know he is the kind of guy Millie would go for. Well, usually – in this specific case she hates him, but he does look like a lot of her past boyfriends.

Is this why I like Hugh so much? Because I'm so fully trying to be Millie? Why does it feel so good? I don't even want to admit it to myself, but the voice in my head asks quietly, *Why does it feel more like me?*

I try to remind myself of all the things he does that irk me. He's condescending, he's stubborn and . . . and . . . I run out of steam. The list of things I hate about Hugh is getting shorter by the day.

Chapter 16

Five dives to go

Shortly after I wake up, Vanessa and Miguel start readying our gear for the night dive. The sun is slowly starting to edge towards the horizon. Our dive is scheduled for right after the sun goes down. With the complete absence of any artificial light, the reef goes dark in a matter of minutes. I try and forget about the feel of Hugh's chest under my cheek, and instead pull back up the photos of the butterfly wrasse, trying to strategise how to give myself a better chance at spotting one tomorrow.

I'm lost in thought when Pippa bounces off the hammock and comes to stand next to me.

'Aren't we lucky?' she says, gesturing out at the ocean. 'I can't wait to dive again tomorrow. And again, after that!'

'We really are,' I agree. 'It's amazing how much scuba can open you up to what's underwater. It's like a whole new world.'

'I couldn't agree more,' says Andrew, sidling up next to me. 'How often did you say you get to do this?'

'Not as much as you'd think, actually. It's been ages.' *Does Andrew know Ohio isn't near an ocean?* I think.

'But isn't this a work trip? Aren't you looking for something?'

I nod. 'I am looking for a fish, but sadly, my lab didn't subsidise it.'

'Because they know you won't find it,' Hugh grumbles, appearing so close behind me that I jump.

'Don't you have better things to do than bother me?' I ask. 'Last time I checked you were "working" too, but all you seem to do is nap.'

Andrew laughs. 'Right, the marine biologist rivalry.'

'Exactly,' says Hugh.

'So, what do you do, Andrew?' I ask, pivoting the topic away from the butterfly wrasse. Andrew explains that he works on corporate strategy for a whole foods conglomerate. Despite the dryness of his job title, he has so much enthusiasm for it that I find myself bobbing my head along to his explanation of how shipping lines and currency exchanges affect egg prices at the grocery store.

'Sweetheart,' Pippa says eventually, laying a hand on Andrew's shoulder, 'you're gonna bore them to tears.'

'You're not boring us!' I say quickly, shooting Pippa a 'be nice' look. But Andrew laughs it off and says he probably should go get a glass of water. Hugh goes with him.

'I love him to pieces,' Pippa says once they're out of earshot, 'but he can really carry on about that job.'

I shrug my shoulders. 'It would be nice to have a job you love.'

'You don't love yours?' she asks.

'Not even a little.' I realise my mistake as I watch the surprise bloom on Pippa's face. She opens her mouth like she's about to ask who in their right mind wouldn't love being a marine biologist.

'I mean,' I backtrack furiously, 'it's an expression. I don't love it a little, I love it a lot!'

She looks at me quizzically, but an errant strand of her hair whips in the wind and snags her lip, distracting her enough that the moment passes.

'Wait,' I say, redirecting us to the beginning of our conversation. 'Did you say you're not diving again until tomorrow?'

Pippa nods vigorously. 'Oh, I can't be bothered with night diving, are you kidding me!' She shudders as if she's already imagining things touching her in the pitch-black ocean.

'So, Andrew will be without a partner . . .' I say, casting a glance over at Hugh, who's chatting with Natalie and Derek.

'Yeah,' Pippa says. 'He really wants to see that bloody octopus.'

Before I can overthink it, I lean back away from the railing and motion to Hugh. 'Buddies for the night dive?' I mouth. I already had one shark encounter. I can't take my chances on having someone else as a buddy, I need someone I can trust. Someone who I'm already comfortable with.

Hugh winks at me.

Pippa interrupts her musings on why jellyfish are scarier than sharks to give me a meaningful look.

'What?' I ask, feigning innocence.

'Oh, you know what I'm talking about, Millie,' she replies sweetly. 'Oh, Hugh?' She whispers under her breath in a fake American accent. 'He's the worst. We're just friends . . . not even friends really.' She carries on, mimicking what I had said to her before.

I swat at her, rolling my eyes, but her American accent is atrocious and I can't help but laugh. I wait until I regain my composure before saying, 'There is nothing going on. I am working.'

Pippa rolls her eyes. 'Working?' she asks. 'Seriously? That is such codswallop.'

'*Codswallop?*'

'You know what I mean. Nonsense!'

'No, it's not!' I argue. 'I have stuff riding on this trip. It's important to me and I promised myself I would make the most of it. I only asked Hugh because he's the best diver here.'

'If you say so,' Pippa replies, but I can tell by her face she doesn't believe a word coming out of my mouth.

Vanessa lugs an air tank by us, Miguel following close behind with another. Miguel and I make eye contact as he passes, and he stares at me a beat longer than usual. 'You're going to be great,' he says encouragingly. This does not escape Pippa, who elbows me as we scoot to the captain's room to get out of their way.

Thankfully, everyone's already seated, so I'm spared Pippa's commentary on Miguel. Hugh and I are next to each other in our usual spots. We're not touching but we're close. I can feel the heat coming off his skin – like he absorbed the sun and now he's radiating the heat back out. At some point during my conversation with Pippa, he's wet his hair and ran a hand through it, because now it looks nicely mussed and doesn't resemble a haystack as much as it did before. Natalie and Derek are seated to the left of us with his camera equipment between them. I fight the urge to groan when I see it. I'm already jittery enough about the idea of a night dive, the last thing

I want is to be waiting for Derek while a shark sniffs around. I hope Vanessa tells him he can't bring it.

Andrew and Pippa are nestled together opposite Hugh and me, looking every bit the lovebirds they were when the trip started. I'll miss them when this is over, and I wonder if they'll want to stay in touch. Then I remember that Andi hasn't met Andrew and Pippa, Millie has.

'I can't wait to bring this bad boy back out there,' Derek says to no one in particular, patting the camera that sits in between him and Natalie. 'I hope we see a shark tonight.' He grins. 'The guys at work will love it.'

No one responds to Derek – I chalk this up to the fact that he sounds like the Texan frat boy he is.

'I didn't know you were supposed to bring your camera on night dives,' I say finally. It's a lie, but I'm hoping someone (Vanessa) jumps on it and tells Derek that he has to leave his camera behind. I also hate awkward silences. I am, to a fault, reliably polite.

'Oh yeah,' Derek says with a grin. 'I mean, in Texas you can do anything you want.'

'Hmm.'

'They even give you more air in Texas,' Derek whispers, his eyes glinting.

'But you're not supposed to fill up tanks more than regulation,' I remind him.

'If you pay enough, you can do whatever you want.'

I feel Hugh stiffen beside me.

'That sounds super safe,' I say, a tight smile on my face.

The air seems to crackle with tension. Even Pippa and Andrew have quieted.

'It's my choice,' Derek says defiantly, 'and isn't everybody all up in arms about "choice" these days?'

White-hot rage courses through me at his dismissive mention of the right to choose. I force myself to take a deep breath. The ocean is not the place for politics, I remind myself. I need to stay calm before this dive, I cannot afford to jump underwater with my heart already beating out of my ears.

Derek looks at me smugly, knowing he's riled me up. Before I can open my mouth to respond, Hugh interjects.

'I'm not sure if you can just "choose" to break the law, mate. Those rules are in place for the safety of dive instructors too. It's not cool to pay more and expect them to compromise their own safety.'

Derek opens and closes his mouth twice, looking exactly like a fish, before he excuses himself to go prep his camera, clearly at a loss for words.

Only when he leaves does Hugh finally relax his ramrod posture.

'Thanks,' I whisper.

'He was being a right dick,' Hugh whispers back. 'But for the record, it's now the second time I've rescued you.'

'I didn't know I needed rescuing.'

'Well,' he muses, 'I guess you've bitten my head off plenty. Maybe I should have let you do it to someone else for a change. But you seemed to be floundering so I think that counts as a second point in my favour.'

'I didn't know we were keeping score,' I murmur.

'As long as I'm winning, we're always keeping score.' Hugh crosses his arms in front of his chest and grins.

Despite how annoyed I am at Derek, I can't keep my lips from curling up into a smile.

As time marches towards the night dive my anxiety grows. We are supposed to start our descent in a little over an hour. When Pippa starts joking about us all going on the night dive to our deaths, I snap at her. I apologise as soon as the words leave my mouth, but I definitely don't feel like myself. My anxiety is getting to me. I vow to spend the remainder of the evening, at least before the night dive, by myself.

Alone in the cabin, I lie down on the small twin bed. Everyone else is upstairs, chatting or reading or asking Aaron more questions about his life before he was a captain – he dived commercially to harvest sea cucumbers, which is something I would find very cool if I wasn't totally stressed. I toss and turn, a ball of nerves. I wish I knew how Millie was doing. I wish I had proof of the wrasse already. I'm glad it's a foregone conclusion that I won't see them tonight. They're not as active at night, and I don't have a camera that takes night photos.

I turn on my side and pick at the peeling paint in the corner of the room. Maybe I should just opt out of the night dive. There's no reason for me to do it. I'm anxious and I need some rest. If I don't do the dive, I'll be better prepared for tomorrow. That settles it, I think. No night dive for me.

I arrive at this conclusion just when Hugh knocks softly on the door.

'Millie?' he asks.

'Come in.' I stare at the ceiling.

'Are you OK?' Hugh says finally, sitting down on the bunk bed below and across from me. I know he's looking up at me, but I can't bring myself to meet his eyes.

'Yeah, just tired.'

'You'll find the wrasse tomorrow,' he says after a pause.

'You really think so?'

'I do.'

Somehow Hugh being so encouraging about something he doesn't want to happen just makes me feel worse.

'Hugh, I don't think I'm gonna do the night dive . . . If you want to ask Andrew to partner . . .'

'Andrew?' Hugh sputters. 'You want me to partner with Andrew on a night dive? Even during the daytime, he can't tell the ocean floor from the sky!'

'Shh!' I hiss, but despite my mood, he gets a laugh out of me. Hugh's right, Andrew will have a harder time controlling his buoyancy in the dark, which is a recipe for disaster.

'Why don't you want to go?'

'I don't know I'm just . . .' I trail off. I'm scared. I'm sad. I'm disappointed. I practically just explained to Pippa how much I need to *focus*. None of which I really want to get into with Hugh.

Hugh drops his voice lower and says, 'The ocean in the dark freaks me out too.'

'It does?' I can't bear to look at him.

'Yeah, it does. I've done a lot of night dives and they don't get easier. But I'll be next to you the whole time.'

'But it's so *dark*,' I whisper.

Hugh stands up, his head almost brushing the ceiling, and steps closer to my bunk. 'Hey,' he says softly, 'have you ever seen anyone doing a night dive? Like, have you ever been on a boat while people go underwater?'

I shake my head.

'Well . . .' He pauses, and I turn to look at him. We're as close as we've been to each other, his face mere inches from mine. 'You're just going to have to believe me then,' he continues, 'but from the boat, you can see all of us really easily. We'll each have a flashlight, and they're so bright that Aaron and Pippa will be able to track us, no problem. So if that makes you feel better, you don't need to be as nervous. You have people you trust looking after you.'

'I do trust Pippa,' I admit.

'Exactly,' Hugh says. 'And Aaron knows his Tripadvisor ratings will really plummet if they lose somebody. He'll have your back.'

The tension in my chest begins to ease. I give Hugh a half-hearted smile. 'OK,' I say in a small voice, 'I guess I'll go.'

'There we go.' He grins. 'I knew you wouldn't let me down, wrasse girl!'

'Wrasse girl?' I exclaim. 'That's my nickname now? That nickname sucks!'

'I can see how it's not the most appealing of nicknames. But you are obsessed with them . . . I could call you wrassie instead?'

'Hugh,' I say in a falsely menacing tone, 'I do not like either of those.'

Hugh steps back from the bunk as I climb down to the floor.

'Seeing as it's three to one,' he says, tapping a finger on his chin, his eyes sparkling, 'I'm fairly sure I can call you whatever I want.'

'That is not fair,' I say, 'technically I would have stood up for myself with Derek. And I would have gone on the night dive! Eventually . . . I think . . . I just needed a minute.'

'OK, how about this? If you go on the night dive, I'll never call you wrassie again.'

'Or wrasse girl,' I counter.

'Deal.'

'Deal.' I realise I'm smiling, something I thought would be impossible before the night dive. 'Thank you, Hugh,' I say, a few seconds later. 'You're not as bad as I thought.'

'What?'

'Don't make me repeat myself,' I whine, shucking off my cover-up and tossing it onto the bed. I know when we get upstairs we will immediately have to change into our stinger suits.

'Millie,' Hugh says, a few seconds later, the playfulness gone from his voice. 'Before we go upstairs, I have to tell you something.'

My heart stops. This sounds bad. I freeze. *Natalie. Did Natalie say something?* His voice is heavy, like he's about to tell me something serious. *I knew I should have stopped him from talking to her.*

'What is it?' My voice is squeaky and high-pitched.

Hugh takes a deep breath and starts speaking quickly. 'I know I was just the one convincing you to go on the night dive, but the ocean at night kind of creeps me out.

Everything I said was as much for me as it was for you,'
he says, breathless as he finishes his sentence. 'There,
I said it. I just thought you should know because . . .
because you'll be my buddy. And we'll both be scared.'

I don't realise I'm holding my breath until I have to
pull in a lungful of air to sigh with relief. I'm so tempted
to reach for his hand that mine twitches at my side. I
place it on the wooden frame of the bed instead.

Hugh is waiting for me to say something, his eyes wide.

'Thank you for telling me,' I smile softly, 'but I can't
believe you just convinced *me* to be your buddy, you
already had to save me from a shark!'

'What was I thinking?' Hugh says sarcastically, throwing his hands up in fake frustration. But he laughs, half-
heartedly, and I know we both feel relieved after being
honest with each other.

'That you wanted to spend more time with me,' I say.
'Let's go get ready, we'll be fine, I think.'

'I'm not so sure about that,' Hugh groans, but he follows me upstairs anyway. Instead of thinking about the
night dive, another thought is crowding my headspace –
Hugh's face when he's worried how someone will react,
like a little-boy version of himself, with his eyes wide
and his nose scrunched, might be the most captivating
thing I've seen yet.

Chapter 17

Our group gathers on the deck to watch the sunset. Everyone gets ready for the night dive quietly, as if spellbound by the glowing orange and red of dusk. It feels like the ocean creatures have fallen asleep and we need to respect them, like we would if we were camping in a deep secluded forest and didn't want to wake the baby deer.

The only people who feel no need to lower their voices are Miguel and Vanessa as they bossily hand out flashlights, instructing us on how to turn them off and on. Only once everyone has demonstrated their flashlights work does Vanessa pull Derek to the side, instructing him under her breath that he cannot bring his camera.

'What!' he exclaims.

'We need everyone to focus—' Vanessa stays firm '—and that's easier when there is no extra equipment.'

'But—' Derek starts to argue.

Vanessa cuts him off swiftly. 'No buts. The rules are for your safety. Either you dive without your camera, or you don't dive at all.'

Derek looks angrier than I've ever seen him, but he keeps his mouth shut.

Vanessa turns her attention back to the rest of us. We're all seated at the rear of the boat, buzzing with nervous energy. 'Never turn the flashlights off,' she repeats, over and over again 'not until we are back on the boat.'

I nod vigorously. Turning my flashlight off is the last thing I plan on doing. Miguel steps around Natalie, who is consoling Derek, to get closer to me.

'Hey,' he says, kneeling down with the bench so we are eye level. 'You ready?'

I gulp. 'Yep.'

Miguel smiles at me like we're sharing a secret. 'Everyone is always nervous for these, but you'll be great down there. I've got your back.'

I let out a deep breath. 'Thanks, Miguel. That makes me feel better.'

It's colder with the sun down, and I start to shiver when I strap on my BCD. Hugh sits down next to me, and I crave his heat but he looks preoccupied and I don't want to disturb him, so I resist the urge to scoot closer. When we do the buddy checks, he avoids looking in my eyes. I purposefully take longer than necessary to pressure test the straps and check his air pressure, trying to meet his gaze to reassure him that everything will be fine, but his eyes are glued to the floor of the boat. It's only when I start to visibly shiver that he breaks his silence.

'You're cold,' he says, placing a hand on top of mine. The gesture is jarringly intimate. The warmth from his hand feels divine. I feel myself relax towards him, like I'm slowly melting in his direction.

'And you're nervous?' I whisper, venturing a guess as to why he seems so withdrawn into a shell.

Almost imperceptibly, Hugh nods.

I squeeze his hands. 'It'll be great,' I say, both to myself and to him.

He squeezes mine back and attempts to smile, but it doesn't reach his eyes.

Miguel and Vanessa hustle us into the water.

We descend into pitch-black. It's hard to believe this is where we were diving just two hours ago. In the darkness, it's impossible to see anything. The water feels warmer than the cool night air. I remember learning that water gains and loses heat much more slowly than land. The resurgence of knowledge I thought was lost momentarily lifts my confidence, and I descend lower, finding my buoyancy, hovering three feet off the ground, waiting for Vanessa to give direction.

With flashlights, we can see pretty well. We're hovered over white sand, and I spot a sea cucumber in my peripherals. We're momentarily stalled waiting for Andrew to equalise and find his buoyancy. I look at Hugh to see if he's laughing, but I can't see his face in the darkness. I try to remember what Hugh explained about our flashlights, how Aaron and Pippa will be looking after us from the boat, but the pitch-dark is all-consuming. I sift through facts in my brain, seeing if I can remember anything from Principles of Oceanography, my favourite class freshman year, the one that set me up to get a degree in marine biology. If I can focus on facts, maybe I'll be less spooked by how much of my surroundings I can't see.

We had a whole unit on pelagic communities, the bodies of fish that live in the open ocean and not near the shore or the sea floor. I found their migratory patterns spellbinding. Some tuna complete migratory journeys that are 5,000 miles long, and they do it when they're only one year old. For a moment, I let myself wonder what my life would be like if I had decided to follow in Millie's footsteps. Instead of tweaking slide decks in a cubicle, I could be thinking about marine life. Maybe, I think, maybe I would have met Hugh on my own, not through the lens of Millie's disdain, or through a veil of pretending to be her. Maybe I would have gotten myself published in *The Marinist*.

Vanessa's roving flashlight interrupts my thoughts. Andrew has gained his buoyancy. It's time to move.

We follow Vanessa blindly, kicking towards her flashlight, dutifully pointing our army of beams at the ground. One of the hardest things about diving at night is that it's shockingly easy to blind your fellow divers. A flashlight to the face compromises your vision instantly. But, because you can't see hand signals, flashlights are the only way to communicate. You have to use your flashlight to signal to others, to ask how much air they have in their tank, and to tell them you're OK. You're supposed to point your flashlight at your own hand to make it visible, but sometimes the ocean's currents move the flashlight and point the beam in a different direction. It's a tricky business.

Miguel turns on a special flashlight that lights up the bioluminescence of the reef. I am struck to find that once again, a fact resurfaces from the depths of my brain. Corals absorb harmful rays from the sun and turn them back into pink, purple and green bioluminescence. All of us are still as we watch the reef light up under Miguel's blacklight. It's as if we're at an underwater rave – every coral is lighting up a different colour. There's blue, and green, purple, yellow, pink. Like someone passed out different coloured glowsticks.

We start moving again, slowly. My gaze strays from Vanessa's beam and into the black abyss beyond. Past the light of my flashlight, I imagine an army of sharks, sitting and waiting for me to get separated from the group. Sometimes I cast the beam of my flashlight out into the distance to make sure nothing is lurking there, but I have yet to see anything in the pitch-black open ocean.

I see Vanessa's flashlight moving in a fast circle, which means 'PAY ATTENTION'. Then, she pivots the beam into the dark, dark blue. A pair of pale eyes reflects back – a shark.

I tense and grab for Hugh's hand. Even more so than usual, he has remained the ever-present buddy, not straying from my side. We swam the entire dive up to this point almost perfectly in sync, which is hard to do in the dark.

When we move forward, we each keep one arm outstretched, flashlights pointing at the ground, our other hands tightly intertwined with each other. Everyone has stopped moving except Andrew, who has started floating towards the surface. Miguel shoots up a hand and grabs him, pulling him down towards the rest of us. We watch as Vanessa's flashlight traces the shark's movements. It's large and grey, a lot bigger than the one Hugh and I saw before. Its mouth is open menacingly. It swims towards us slowly and then veers in the opposite direction, disappearing into the darkness. Even though I can't hear it, it feels as though everyone has sighed a collective sigh of relief.

Hugh and I keep our fingers interlocked as we continue in a slow circle around the reef. Suddenly Vanessa's flashlight is zigzagging again, this time over a rocky crevice. Our fingers unravel when we see what Vanessa has spotted – an octopus. We all jockey for space to watch it swim over the coral. It dances over the rocks, perfectly blending in. Its tentacles reach and pull more gracefully than I've ever seen anything move. It's pulsing a dusty brown, with soft edges and hooded eyes. It's the same octopus I had told Andrew about. I glance in his direction, knowing how badly he was hoping to see one. He has covered his mouth with both hands in excitement. I feel a swell of happiness that his dream has come true. The octopus is mesmerising, and we all watch it slowly melt away in between two rocks, its body perfectly pliable.

I yearn to grab Hugh's hand as soon as we start swimming again, but I force myself to keep my hands locked in front of me, one arm folded over the other. *Our hand hold meant nothing*, I tell myself. *Hugh knows I'm scared and is just being nice. Hugh is scared himself. Even Miguel and Andrew grabbed for each other's hands when we saw the shark.* A thought ripples through me with such clarity it sends a chill down my spine despite the warmth trapped in my stinger suit. I told Pippa I can't afford any distraction, and I meant it. But the truth is, if I keep letting Hugh distract me, if I keep falling for his eyes, and his accent, and his pockets of pure vulnerability . . . if I keep letting him know me, then in three days my heart will be seriously messed up. I cannot let my rebound be a man in Australia who only likes me because he thinks I'm my sister. It will destroy any ounce of self-esteem I have left.

'We saw an octopus!' Andrew hollers as soon as we surface. Pippa is waiting for us at the railing. 'And a shark!'

'Bloody hell,' she says, her face paling in the moonlight. 'Terrifying.'

'It was BRILLIANT!!' Andrew excitedly yanks off his fins and scales the ladder.

Hugh and I are both treading water. He's grinning from ear to ear, which I'm betting looks like excitement, but I suspect is secretly relief. 'Right, you go,' he says in that gravelly accent.

'Are you sure you don't want to be out of this water already?' I tease.

Hugh narrows his eyes at me, but I see a hint of a smile play across his lips. Stubbornly, he waves a hand towards the ladder. I climb up, more aware with every rung that he is watching my backside as I scale my way onto the boat.

I turn to help Hugh up the ladder, and he clasps his fingertips around mine.

'Thanks, wrassie,' he says, as he hauls himself all the way onto the deck. Our faces are close enough that I can count the beads of water lingering on his eyelashes. My breath catches in my chest.

'You can't call me that, remember?'

'I guess I'll have to think of something better, then.' Hugh winks at me before turning to unzip his BCD and offload his scuba gear.

I sink onto the bench slowly, shirking off my fins and handing Miguel my vest and my air tank.

'What did you think?' he asks excitedly.

'It was amazing,' I breathe. 'Thank you, you know, for the pep talk before. I needed it.'

'Everyone's nervous for that one,' he says. 'Andrew is lucky, that's the first time I've seen an octopus on one of these dives.'

I bob my head in agreement. 'We're all lucky.'

'We sure are,' Miguel says, as he stows my equipment away. 'Go get warm,' he adds warmly, shooing me to the front of the cabin with a good-natured grin. I haven't given him enough credit for balancing his flirtation with his job, I think, as I meander towards the front of the boat.

Pippa comes up to me with a dry towel in hand.

'Thanks.' I wrap myself up and catch a glimpse of Hugh out of the corner of my eye. He's wrapped in a towel as well, sitting next to Aaron.

'So, how was your dive together?' she asks, nodding towards Hugh. 'You looked pretty cosy coming out of the water.'

I shrug my shoulders and she raises an eyebrow at me. 'Come on, Millie. We're on a boat in the middle of nowhere without Wi-Fi, for God's sake. Nothing is as interesting as this budding romance. And stop staying you don't want to be distracted!' She playfully punches me in the arm.

'Ugh,' I groan. 'Pippa, I'm not purposefully trying to be coy. I just . . .'

'It's soooo obvious you guys like each other.'

'Yeah, but . . . that's the thing. I, like, can't like him. I mean I shouldn't . . . I mean . . .' *I can't fall for some-*

one who thinks I'm my sister. How would I ever explain to Millie that I destroyed her professional reputation for a fling?

Pippa's eyes widen. 'Why shouldn't you? Are you . . .' Now it's her turn to trail off. I can practically see the wheels in her brain turning. 'You're not already bloody with someone?'

'That would be less complicated than my current situation . . . And no, actually. I broke up with my boyfriend a couple of months ago.' My shoulders slump, it might have been a few months but it feels like a lifetime. It's also incredibly confusing to blur my own life with Millie's, I'm starting to feel like Andi doesn't even exist.

'And you don't want to rush into things,' Pippa supplies.

It's easier for me to let her believe that's the reason, even though not even the half of it. 'Exactly,' I agree with Pippa.

'That's understandable,' she says warmly, not catching on that I'm not telling the full story. 'But it would be a shame to miss the perfect rebound opportunity.'

'Right,' I say half-heartedly.

I excuse myself to rinse off. On the way, I almost thwack my head into the door frame because I'm so distracted by my conversation with Pippa. I duck around the dining table on autopilot, steadying my hand on the vinyl bench as the boat rocks with the waves. *Would it be crazy to tell Pippa about the whole pretending to be Millie thing?* I'm thinking, as I ease into our tiny cabin.

I notice that, for once, Hugh's stuff is spilling out of his duffel, and I'm relieved he isn't as neat as I thought he was. My belongings have been dumped entirely across the twin mattress.

I shimmy out of my bikini and grab for my towel, mentally preparing to have to crouch under lukewarm water and not feel like I've washed all the conditioner out of my hair. I'm moving slowly, still running a pros and cons list for whether or not I should tell Pippa. Pros: I won't be in this alone and she gives good advice. Cons: I don't actually know if I can trust her, and if I blow this, Millie will kill me.

Lost in thought, I'm still wrapping my towel around my body when I open the door to head to the shower.

The boat lurches just as I step out of my room and I fall directly on top of Hugh, somehow managing to dislodge my half-wrapped towel in the process.

Before I even process that I'm completely losing my balance, my brain only focuses on how *strong* Hugh is. Like some primal instinct in me is thinking, *This man could save me from a mountain lion*. His skin is smooth and pulled taut across his abs, which ripple up his body. My face lands right in the crook of his neck and he smells so *clean*, like cedar and grass and the ocean. My hands grab for the skin on his back, clutching around his broad shoulders involuntarily, pulling my body towards his. I forget that I'm dirty. I forget I need to shower. Instead, I think, *Why are we not in our bedroom?* I hear Hugh's sharp intake of breath and all I can think is that I want to keep making him breathe that way.

Hugh loses his footing as the boat sways, pulling me out of my thoughts and into the present moment. He grabs for the nearest railing, saving us both from a tumble to the floor. As we hang in the balance, precariously supported by the strength of Hugh's dazzling forearm, my brain is thinking *oh no, oh no*, and my body is thinking *oh yes*. Our bodies melt together – Hugh is damp and I'm sticky with seawater. I want to be touching every part of his body, but there's a towel around his waist. My arms are wrapped around him, my towel flailing in one hand like a flag of surrender.

His hips shift beneath me, and I feel a bulge between his thighs. My nipples tighten against his chest. His breath hitches again and so does mine. For a moment we are both breathless. I wonder how I can manoeuvre off his towel and simultaneously get us closer to the privacy of our bedroom. I want to bite the inside of his neck, right above his shoulder. I want to taste him so badly that I feel a tug in between my legs, right in the heat of my belly, that pulls me towards him.

The boat lurches again, and Hugh grunts as he hoists us to a standing position. The momentum pulls my face from the crook of his neck, and our eyes meet. His eyes are narrowed and piercingly blue, his mouth open in a perfect 'o', the muscles in his cheek twitch.

'Millie,' he breathes.

Alarm bells sound off in my brain. My heart pounds in my chest. *Millie*. Hugh is staring at me, eyes full of desire. *Millie*.

I stumble backwards, my sister's name crashing through my consciousness. *Millie* is what's at stake, *Millie* is what's important here. *What am I thinking?*

The hallway is so narrow that I've backed myself fully up against it. We're still only inches from each other. 'I'm so sorry,' I stammer breathlessly, turning away from his torso as fast as I can, quickly wrapping myself in my towel. I gulp in air, trying to slow my racing heart. When I glance back up at Hugh, he's eyeing me cautiously.

He opens his mouth to say something, but before he can, I speak: 'I didn't mean to.' The words tumble out of my mouth. 'I've gotta, um, go shower.'

Hugh's cheeks colour red. 'Oh . . . OK . . . I didn't mean to . . .'

I shake my head dumbly. 'You didn't do anything. It was an – it was an accident.'

'Yeah.' Hugh nods, he isn't meeting my gaze anymore.

'We're fine,' I say, more to myself than to him.

Hugh meets my eyes this time. 'Yep,' he agrees, but his voice has lost any trace of emotion.

He retreats towards our room, and I want so badly to touch him again. My hands twitch, pulled by an invisible string to reach up and place a thumb on Hugh's bottom lip, to run my fingers through his damp hair. My hips want to find his.

My brain cuts through my body's noise. *You can't do this to Millie!* it screams. I feel like I've been lit on fire.

I stumble to the shower, staying under the water as long as I can before it feels impolite to the rest of the people who need to use the miniscule bathroom. I still don't feel like I've scrubbed the Hugh off my skin.

The way his chest felt, so firm and strong, the way our hips locked together immediately. I feel like I just drank three cups of coffee, and yet my throat still feels dry.

I'm nervous to climb above deck. After our collision I feel vulnerable and terrified, and the shower did nothing to still my beating heart. I throw on an oversized T-shirt over a pair of baggy jean shorts, hoping to cover myself up as much as possible. I pile my hair up. When I step out onto the cabin and onto the deck Hugh looks up. For a moment, our eyes lock.

It's going to be a long night, I think, as I gingerly make my way over to my usual spot. There is not enough room in that crowded cabin for the tension between us.

Chapter 18

Four dives to go

Hugh raises his eyes to meet mine when I sit down. My heart skips a beat. I hold my breath as I wait for what he'll say.

'Well, look who decided to show up with clothes on,' he says.

I turn the colour of a tomato but manage an eye roll to at least give a semblance of not caring. 'Shut up,' I hiss, but I let out a sigh of relief that he seems willing to go back to our normal back-and-forth. Maybe we can pretend like that never happened.

I feign interest in the group conversation. Everyone is chatting excitedly about the shark. Andrew is already exaggerating the story, saying he could have reached out and touched it as it swam by. Most of us have showered by now, and we're all waiting for the dinner call.

Pippa has had enough of Andrew's antics and she soon changes the subject, chatting about the day they have planned in Cairns for when we return. There are rules for how quickly you can fly after diving, so most everyone is staying in Cairns for at least twenty-four hours after the trip. The ascent into altitude on an airplane after being under sea level can make people sick – it's called 'the bends', and the bends can be really dangerous. All divers I know are really wary of it.

Every time we descend and ascend in the water, we do it really slowly, with Vanessa and Miguel, and our little BCD computers, telling us how much time we need to depressurise. This helps the nitrogen release slower in our bodies, but with each dive, our bodies absorb more nitrogen, so the more dives you've done in a twenty-four-hour period, the more time you need before flying. Otherwise, when you go up to altitude in a plane, nitrogen gets dumped too quickly into your bloodstream.

The rule of thumb is to wait twenty-four hours after a single dive, more time if you've dived more than once. But the US Navy says you can wait only six hours, so there's not an exact guideline. It seems like everyone has followed the 24-hour rule of thumb based on their plans.

Natalie and Derek have booked a food and wine tour in the Tablelands, about an hour inland from Cairns, for the afternoon we return. Pippa has booked her and Andrew on a waterfall hiking tour, which she pressures us to join.

'They're definitely going to have space,' she's saying. 'And you can book it from the marina! It's supposed to leave from the docks around two-ish and will get us back by six.' She twirls a curl around her finger. 'Come with us! It'll be cool!'

'Anyone could come with us,' Natalie suggests. She glances at me then at Hugh.

Hugh stiffens. 'I'm not sure what I'll do yet,' he says casually. He glances over at me, but I keep my eyes focused on the horizon. I can't risk being with Hugh when we're back in service, when he could so easily google my sister and realise that there are slight differences between her and me. What if he finds her LinkedIn page and asks me about a specific job, what if he finds a recent photo and asks me why my eyes are greener, my nose rounder, my hair frizzier?

'I've been meaning to ask you, Millie,' Natalie says, emphasising 'Millie' so heavily that my stomach drops.

'Dinner!' I hear Vanessa call, interrupting Natalie mid-sentence.

Thank God, I think as the group immediately starts to mobilise.

'Great! I'm starving!' Pippa jumps up and heads straight to the stairs. I follow behind her quickly, pretending I didn't hear Natalie's question.

I squeeze next to Pippa in the booth and pick at my food – tonight's dinner is rice bowls with marinated tofu – but my appetite has vanished. It doesn't feel nice to avoid Natalie, and I know I'm being paranoid, but I can't tell if she is malicious or curious. She seems to ask Hugh a lot of questions, I've spotted them talking at least twice each day. And while I'm juggling pretending to be somebody else, the less questions the better.

The conversation hums around me. Vanessa is asking people what else they are hoping to see on the reef. Andrew wants to see a manta ray now that he's crossed octopus off his list. Pippa's excited to see Fitzroy Island. As the boat lurches through another swell, and my plate comes sliding towards my lap, I can't blame her. After a full day of diving tomorrow, I think I'll be ready to rest my sea legs for a little too – and get off this *tiny* boat.

I don't contribute to the conversation. Instead, I stare at my plate, feeling like I'm at a crossroads. I either come up with a plan for what to say whenever Natalie explicitly calls me out for going by two different names, that is, if she even remembers, or I can come clean. If I hadn't messaged Hugh from our joint Instagram account, then I could have said my middle name was Millie. But it's too late, I've already told him my middle name was Andi. I could say the airline used my middle name accidentally, and I heard my last name called so I went to the counter, but that excuse seems flimsy, especially on an international flight where they have my passport.

I glance over at Hugh. He's chatting with Miguel. Miguel sees me looking and smiles in my direction, his dark lashes fluttering against his cheek. He is cute. And so much less messy. Maybe Pippa was right when she encouraged me to go for Miguel at the beginning of the trip. If I had, I wouldn't have to worry about this Millie mess at all. But for some reason I can't explain, Miguel feels firmly stuck in friend territory.

I smile hollowly back at Miguel while my brain churns through scenarios. If I'm going to come clean to Hugh, it should be tonight. That way I won't have lied to him for a long time, and if he's no longer interested in me because I'm not the person I said I was, then at least I'll know sooner.

As soon as I decide this is the best course of action, I wonder what I'm thinking, jeopardising Millie's career because of some stupid crush. But then I remember how Hugh's body felt against mine, and my thoughts circle once again.

Similar to last night, we play another round of Hook Line Sinker after dinner. Pippa beats Andrew this time, much to everyone's delight. She rubs it in his face smugly, even though he's a very gracious loser.

Pippa wears Aaron down until he agrees to point out constellations to us, and we crowd on the platform, huddling together while Aaron points out Orion and Aquarius. He thinks he can see Venus winking in the distance, but I'm not so sure. Everyone laughs at Aaron's attempt to retell a Greek myth associated with one of the constellations, which he punctuates freely with colourful slang. Eventually, the group dwindles. There's a chorus of 'thank yous' to Aaron and the rest of the crew. Miguel claps people on the back as he takes his leave. Our group of nine is starting to feel closer now, more intimate than I was expecting. Pippa and Andrew head to bed. Natalie resigns herself to another face mask after she lays it on thick for Hugh to come with them on their Tablelands tour. She keeps referencing the thing they 'need to talk about' and every time she does, I feel my pulse start to race. I'm relieved when she and Derek go to bed.

'You were quiet at dinner,' Hugh says once we're alone.

'Yeah,' I say, relaxing into the sturdy planking of the boat. I watch the empty hammock sway above me. I focus on my breathing, in and out, and on the stars and the sound of the ocean waves hitting the hull. I try everything to distract myself from the thoughts swirling in my head. 'I've got a lot on my mind.'

'If it's about earlier . . .'

'It's not,' I lie. 'That was . . .' I'm at a loss for words. *That was electrifying, terrifying, hopelessly sexy, something I want to happen again, something*

I can't let happen again . . . 'Um,' I hesitate. If there is ever a moment to tell Hugh the truth, it's now. I try to formulate how to explain it. *I've been pretending to be my sister* sounds a little psychotic.

'If it isn't about before, is it about your sister?'

I am wondering how he read my mind when it clicks. *Millie's surgery.* The surgery I've conveniently forgotten about all day because I've been distracted and having fun and only thinking about myself.

Hugh takes my guilty silence as an affirmative and scoots closer to me, wrapping a large arm around my shoulders. 'Hey,' he says, his voice low. There is so much to that word, *hey.* I feel cared for, and seen, and valued all at once. There is no ask for anything physical, there is only *Hey, I see that you are sad. I am here.*

I sink into his chest, grateful to have him next to me, unable to think straight.

'Do you want to talk about it?'

'No,' I murmur. I know there's nothing I can do from out here and I know this is where Millie wants me to be, but it feels wrong to be enjoying myself so fully while she undergoes a terrifying procedure, and I hate not knowing how it turned out. It feels like I made a bargain with the universe where I got to go do *this* and I have to find the butterfly wrasse in order to earn it.

We sit in companionable silence. The heavy heat of Hugh's arm hovers on the fringe of my thoughts. He runs his fingertips gently up and down my skin. It feels like this is the emotional version of what happened earlier, and now that we've crossed two bridges, there's no going back. We're into each other. Or at least, one of us is into the other and the other thinks they're into someone called Millie.

I like Hugh. I really like Hugh. He seems like a good person despite his know-it-all tendencies. I can't keep lying to him.

Just as I'm about to open my mouth, Hugh speaks first. 'Tell me what your sister is like.'

'Umm,' I hesitate. It makes the most sense to give Millie my actual job, so I go for it. 'She works in business. Operations for a cereal company. Pretty run-of-the-mill.'

'Hmm,' Hugh grunts. 'And you guys are close?'

'Depends on what you mean by close,' I say, biding time as I figure out if I should continue describing myself or if I should switch to actually explain Millie and maybe cut down on the lies a little.

'I like knowing things about you,' Hugh says softly. In that moment I decide to describe myself, who I really think I am. It's vulnerable serving yourself up on a platter to someone and knowing they will judge you with total honesty. I'm glad he's not facing me as I try to describe myself through my sister's eyes.

'Andi's great,' I say, testing the waters, wondering if he knows me well enough to hear the lie in my voice. If he does, he doesn't say anything. 'You always know what you're getting with her. She's nice and reliable. She never lets people down.'

'She sounds like I would like her.'

'I think you would,' I answer honestly, 'I hope.' There's a hint of regret in my voice. I clear my throat in an effort to hide it.

'Does she look like you?'

'Yes.' I describe Millie this time. 'Skinnier thighs and shinier hair, but she looks like me.'

'I like your hair. And I like your th—' Hugh stops himself.

'What?' I ask, wanting so badly to hear him say that he likes my thighs. My voice is a whisper loaded with desire.

It's Hugh's turn to cough, and he does, changing the subject after. 'I know you're not quite on the market. I know what happened earlier caught us both off guard.' He elbows me when he says it, but his voice is husky.

'Mhm.'

'But if you were . . .' I know that he's turned to face me. A lump rises in my throat. I know that if I turn my head to his, we'll be close, nose to nose, exactly like my dream. I know I won't be able to resist kissing him. I know that I should. I know that Millie's most hated work associate is off-limits. But as I'm thinking all these things, I'm also feeling a magnetic pull to turn towards Hugh, to press my lips to his, to taste his skin, to smell his hair, to run my hands all over his chest.

The magnetic pull wins. I flip onto my side. Our noses almost touch.

'Millie,' he whispers, gravelly and low. I ignore my sister's name this time. When I look into his eyes, I know he's seeing *me*.

I feel desire making the tangy sea air even thicker, like there could be steam rising off both of us. And then, slowly, but all at once, he kisses me.

It feels like a lightning strike from my head to my toes. Hugh's tongue gently parts my lips. His hands find their way to the small of my back and the nape of my neck. He pulls me closer to him, and suddenly we're touching everywhere. I feel like a live wire. Every sensation that isn't Hugh dims.

I kiss him back hungrily, like I'm finally getting a drink of water after being stranded at sea. Now that I've started, I don't know if I'll ever be able to stop. I reach my hand inside his shirt and up to his shoulder blades, pressing my chest to his, and I feel his muscles tighten.

He breaks our kiss to take a deep breath of air, and as he pulls back, I wonder if I've ever seen a sight so beautiful than Hugh Harris, with a deep suntan and wind-ruffled hair. A pulse of desire ripples through me, and I feel heat building between my legs.

I've never had such a raw physical attraction to anybody before. My heart is racing. I am aching for his touch. My nipples are hard. Our lips collide again, and he bites my bottom lip. My hips tilt towards his, and he reaches a hand around my ass and pulls me closer to him. When he kisses my neck, both of us are practically panting.

Now that I've tasted him, I want him so badly, focus be dammed. I start to raise my leg, to wrap my thigh around his, bringing us as close together as possible, just like my dream, when his hand slides from my ass towards my breast.

My chest arcs towards him with desire, like my body is on autopilot.

Stop. A little voice in my brain. *It's not too late. This is not what you are here to do!*

I freeze, and Hugh notices. His hand stills, his fingers centimetres away from their target. They're just barely caressing the bottom of my breast. I want his hands all over me. My nipple tightens. I want to tell him to continue so badly. I want to bite his bottom lip, I want to roll on top of him. I want him inside me.

Instead, I take in a lungful of the ocean air before I say the words I don't want to say, but I know I should. 'Hugh,' I whisper. 'We have to stop.' Hugh's hand is still hovering over me. 'We're in the middle of the boat.'

Hugh doesn't say anything.

'Someone could come up here any minute.'

He rolls onto his back, still quiet. I know he's thinking what we both know – everyone else is asleep.

'We just . . . we shouldn't . . .' I say finally, mimicking his posture and rolling away from him.

We both lie next to each other and stare up at the sky, our chests heaving with breath.

'I'm sorry,' I whisper.

Hugh reaches over and squeezes my hand. 'Don't say that.' A minute or two passes. We stare up at the stars, blazing bright and clear above the ocean. Finally, he clears his throat. 'So, tell me about you. What did you want to be when you grew up?'

A giggle escapes my throat. 'That's what you want to talk about?'

'Well, yeah. You didn't come up with anything better. Hey, why are you always laughing at my questions?'

'Because you ask things like "What's your favourite colour?" and "What do you want to be when you grow up?" and I feel like I'm in elementary school.'

'Well, what did you want to be when you grew up? A mom? A wife? The president?'

'Hmmm, I think if you asked six-year-old me, Madam President. But unfortunately, that ship has sailed.'

'OK, so if Madam President is off the table, what about a mom or a wife?'

'Women can be much more than that you know,' I say, giving him a stern look.

I watch the profile of his face and see his cheeks scrunch with a smile. 'Touché,' he says.

I think about my answer. 'I don't want to get married as much as I want to be confident in my partner. I don't care about marriage itself, but a lasting commitment with someone is something I really want. If I had that, I would love kids.'

Hugh is silent, staring up at the night sky.

'What about you?'

He sighs. 'I want that too, I think. I'm worried I'll be really bad at it, if I'm honest. My mom and dad weren't so great at the marriage thing . . .'

'That doesn't mean you won't be.'

'I'm not good at being in love.' Hugh's voice sounds thicker than it did a moment before. I wait for him to continue. 'I'm not good at saying it,' he says finally, 'I can act on it, but I can't tell someone. It's hard for me. I feel so . . . naked. The only person I told was Sophia, my ex and that —' He cuts himself off.

We both listen to the sound of the waves slapping the side of the boat. Everyone else has long since gone to bed. It feels like we are the only two people left in the world.

'I'm not good at it either,' I admit finally. Something about the stars, or the reassurance of the thump of the waves, or the smell of Hugh's body wash, or maybe just being in the middle of a huge ocean, miles from home, masquerading as someone else, makes me feel like being completely honest. 'In fact, I'm terrible at it,' I say in a small voice.

'What makes you say that?'

'It's just . . . I think I let things with my ex drag on for too long.' I shift some weight from one shoulder to the other. 'It ended up that everybody got hurt.' We're both on our backs, gazing at the stars. I hardly listened when Aaron pointed out the constellations earlier, and now I wish I had, just to have anything else to talk about.

'What happened?' Hugh asks, interrupting my thoughts.

'I don't know . . . well . . . I do know . . .' Hugh waits for me to continue. 'He proposed,' I confess. 'And I knew right then and there it wasn't what I wanted. And I said no.'

'Woah.'

'Yeah, it was terrible. I felt awful. It was my fault, I was the one who changed, I was the one who all of a sudden wanted something different . . .'

'He got down on one knee and you said no?' Hugh asks, his voice raw with disbelief.

'Yeah,' I whisper. 'We were at an Italian restaurant. He had planned a big party with our friends the next day. We had to cancel it.'

'That's terrible,' he breathes. 'Had you talked about it before? Did you know it was coming?'

I shake my head. 'No, I thought we still had time . . . but apparently he had been planning it for ages. Our friends . . . his friends, were so excited for us. Everyone was so disappointed with my answer, it felt like I lost a lot more than him.'

'Millie, I'm so sorry.'

'Thanks, it sucked. It felt like no one understood. My parents were disappointed. Our friends thought Zach needed more support, after all, he was the one who got rejected, so no one really checked in on me. It was the wake-up call I needed, I think, but it was really bad.'

'It sounds like it was terrible.'

'There are some silver linings, I guess . . . I'm here, that's one.'

'And you're not the only one who's glad you're here.'

'Yeah. It didn't feel like a good thing when I broke up with him, but it's starting to feel better each day.'

'Sometimes it takes time.' Hugh pauses like he's about to say something, so I stay silent and wait. The boat creaks back and forth. 'Sophia and I were really serious. I thought we were going to get married. My mom and my brother loved her. I was going to propose. And then she fell in love with her Italian tutor and told me she was moving to Italy.'

'What!' I exclaim. 'That's crazy . . . Hugh, I'm so sorry.'

Out of nowhere, Hugh starts laughing. 'It's ridiculous, actually. I felt like I was in a movie. It's taken me a good year, but now I can at least laugh about it.'

I start laughing too, more out of relief than anything else, glad he seems to have come to terms with what happened to him.

'Her Italian tutor,' he says, between laughs, 'how cliché!'

'How cliché,' I agree.

'I'm worried,' he said at last once our giggles had died down. 'I'm worried that I'll never find the one. I thought it was her, but I was so wrong. I don't know how I'll trust my judgement again. Now I feel like I'll have to start dating and everyone I date will remind me that my last relationship, no matter how it ended, was the best I'll ever have. Like that was all the happiness I'll ever deserve.'

'I don't think that's true.' I shift to face him. 'But I feel the exact same way.' It was the first time I had ever heard someone describe my own fears so articulately. 'Like the universe gave me something good and just because it didn't work out doesn't mean I'm entitled to anything better.'

'Exactly. And even if I get past that, I don't know how I'll trust people again.'

'You can trust me,' I say, before thinking about the statement I just made. If I want Hugh to trust me, I need to tell him the truth tonight. It might already be too late. I need to tell him the truth now.

Lying on our sides, Hugh and I stare at each other. Tenderly, he caresses my cheek with his thumb.

'I wish you didn't live so far away,' he whispers, so softly that I almost don't hear him.

'Me too,' I whisper back, my voice cracking. 'Look,' I say, 'I haven't been . . .' the words *I haven't been honest with you* are on the tip of my tongue, but I can't bring myself to say them. I can't risk jeopardising

Millie's one chance at these fish just because I have a crush on some guy (who she happens to hate). I would be giving Hugh so much ammo to take Millie down professionally – it's definitely a career-ending move to send your little sister on a work trip without telling your boss. Especially when said sister doesn't have the proper credentials.

I untangle myself from Hugh's arms. 'I've just had a lot going on lately,' I say finally. 'I'm worried I'm losing my ability to focus on the reason I'm here.'

'I'm not helping you focus?' He pulls a face and I crack a smile.

'Not really.'

'I like that about you,' he says after a beat. 'Your ambition.'

'Yeah,' I mumble. 'I don't actually have too much of that.'

'You know you don't give yourself enough credit. You're all the way out here looking for it, for starters. And, you're not on a research vessel, you're spending your own money to do it.'

I shrug.

'I mean it. I don't know why you can't see it. You are fearlessly pursuing something you don't even know exists. That's objectively pretty cool. And you're quick-witted. And I can make you laugh, which does wonders for my ego.'

I can't bring myself to look at him. I can't forget that he doesn't want me to succeed. I can't forget that he has no idea who I actually am. I can feel his eyes on me. He thinks I am a person who loves adventure and does night dives and has sacrificed my whole life to do something good for the world. There is no way he would like me if he knew I spent every weekday in a cubicle and every weekend rotating through the same breweries with a bunch of other couples that were exactly like Zach and me. He wouldn't look twice at me if he saw me in my natural habitat – boring, quiet, steady Andi.

I will never be enough for someone like Hugh – so passionate and exciting and full of pure ambition. An even more terrifying thought crosses my mind.

Millie would be enough for Hugh. If Millie could overlook how much they disagree, they might even be *perfect* for each other. I hate thinking about it, but the thought draws me in anyway. It's like looking at a car accident. I can't look away. Scenes unfold in my mind's eye, playing out in slow motion.

Millie and Hugh meeting, bonding over hating people who use toxic sunscreen, charting a course to sail around the world, stopping in Sydney and Los Angeles, dropping anchor in Maine and Newfoundland. Never mind that Millie doesn't even know how to sail, I can see it all.

'Look, Millie,' Hugh says, interrupting my thoughts. 'I know I've gotten in the way of your . . . focus . . . but I genuinely do want you to have a fair shake at finding the wrasse.'

'Since when do you care about giving me a fair shake?' I tease. The boat rocks us closer together. He flips on his back. Absent-mindedly, I nestle back into the crook of his shoulder.

'I could be giving you a fair shake right now, but someone said we shouldn't.'

I cackle 'Sounds like someone has good judgement,' I reply, swatting at his bicep. 'Really though . . .'

'Well, it'll be good for me to know when I publish that there was a recent expedition to find the wrasse, and it still hasn't been found.'

Alarm bells go off in my head. 'When you publish what?'

'I have a paper coming out in February. I'm actually going to Boston in April to present it.'

The mention of Hugh coming to Boston makes my heart race with excitement. Boston is a two-hour flight from Columbus, which means in four months he will basically be in my backyard. I shake the thought out of my head and force myself to focus on the issue at hand. 'And that relates to the wrasse how?'

'It actually is about the extinction of the wrasse.' Hugh at least has the decency to start to mumble.

'You have written an entire paper on the extinction of the fish I'm all the way out here to find?' My voice is rising. I forget that this fight is Millie's fight – suddenly, I'm all in.

'We have to keep publishing to get promoted,' Hugh says by way of explanation. 'You know that. Even if *we* have to pay to do it,' he grumbles.

'You have a promotion riding on this?' I exclaim. I launch myself off the platform like it's made of lava. 'This is unbelievable.'

'Woah, Millie. What is going on? You knew I didn't believe the wrasse existed.'

'I didn't know you had a promotion depending on me not finding it!' I retort. 'No wonder you're doing all of . . .' I gesture at Hugh wildly with my hands. 'All of this!'

'All of what?'

'Don't act all innocent,' I say, half-heartedly lowering my voice in case the crew can hear us from their mid-level bunk room. 'You've been pulling the seduction act on me practically since we arrived! All that ridiculous teasing! Making the others think we're flirting!'

'Me seducing you? You accosted me in a towel! You were naked!'

'That was an accident,' I say through clenched teeth.

'Like I'm supposed to believe that. You like me, Millie. I can feel it, just like I know you can.'

'You know, Hugh, I wish I could say you were right, but unfortunately it's hard to like someone when they change personalities every five minutes.'

'I don't know what you're talking about.'

'First you're combative, then you're rude, stand-offish, and stuck-up,' I say, counting with my fingers, 'and then you're nice, and helpful, and caring and thoughtful. I don't even know who you are!'

'Millie, we've been over this. Being rude to each other was our thing. I thought we were flirting. I *am* nice and helpful. And yeah, I've been hitting on you, but it's because I think you're cute. You're easy to talk to. I feel like I can trust you. So what if professionally we don't exactly match up. It's not like I'm out to sabotage you.'

'I'm not that cute!' I say angrily. 'You know what, forget it. I don't expect you to understand. I'm going to bed, and if you don't mind, I would like a minute in the room alone.' I turn on a heel and walk towards the stairs, resisting the urge to look behind me.

'Millie, I can't believe you think I would sabotage you like that!' Hugh calls. I hear an edge of frustration in his voice.

I can't believe I let Hugh Harris get in my head. I have four more dives. I am not going to waste them.

Chapter 19

'Wake up!' shouts Pippa, knocking on our door. Groggily, I rub my eyes. I had been so upset when I went to bed the night before that I had forgotten to set an alarm.

'Millie!' Pippa shouts, rousing me from my thoughts. 'We're diving soon.'

Diving. We are diving. I'm on a boat in the middle of the ocean. In a room with Hugh Harris, who conveniently didn't tell me he has a promotion riding on the butterfly wrasse being extinct.

'I'm up,' I grumble. I'm getting scarily good at responding to Millie's name.

Millie. I can't wait to talk to her. In less than three days I'll be back in service and able to get an update from my family. Please, universe, I think, as I swing my legs over the top bunk, let her be OK.

Hugh's bunk is empty. I swear at him under my breath for not waking me up. The coffee is probably all gone, and he probably feels proud of himself for beating me to the hot water.

I find my swimsuit – an old, navy string bikini, and shimmy into it in the bathroom. I run a toothbrush over my teeth and secure my knotty hair into a messy bun. I can feel puffiness around my eyes from crying the night before. I can't wait to be off this boat, even if it's just to jump in the water.

I head upstairs towards the sound of voices and find the deck abuzz with activity. Miguel and Vanessa are filling our oxygen tanks at the back of the boat. We're headed to Queen's Point Reef today. I checked Millie's notes yesterday – the last butterfly wrasse was seen on Queen's Point in 2016. This site is shallower than the other ones we've been to, so it's a few degrees warmer. Butterfly wrasse prefer reefs with more depth. *If you've gotten here, you've already done so many dives!* she scribbled in the margins. *Miss you xoxo!*

Aaron is poring over a map in his captain's chair. Everyone else is milling about the deck. Natalie, Derek and Hugh are standing together, chatting. Natalie looks more animated than I've ever seen her, Hugh looks unsure, standing with his arms crossed over his chest. They all turn to look at me.

Natalie motions me over, but I pretend not to see, instead making a beeline for Pippa. It will be a small miracle if I can get through this day without talking to Hugh, but I'm certainly going to try.

'Thank you for waking me up,' I say to Pippa.

'Long night?'

I nod, yawning.

'I could tell,' she says under her breath, nodding in the direction of Natalie, Derek and Hugh. 'Did something happen between you two?'

'There is no us two,' I say with finality. My voice is tense. Hurt crosses Pippa's face at my tone. 'Sorry,' I say quickly. 'I don't want to talk about it.'

'It's OK,' she says, patting my arm. 'Sunscreen?' She holds out the bottle like an olive branch.

While I lather myself up, I ask Pippa if she'll be my dive partner this morning. I ask in front of Andrew on purpose, hoping if either of them is reluctant about separating I'll notice.

'Does that mean I'd get to be with Hugh?' Andrew asks brightly. Pippa rolls her eyes. 'I mean,' he backpedals, 'how could you tear me away from Pippa, a perfect angel, light of my life?'

I chuckle. Leave it to Andrew to make me laugh when I didn't even feel like I could smile.

'He's ridiculous,' she says, turning to me. 'You don't think Hugh will care?'

'It's not my problem if he does.'

'All right then. Who's gonna tell him?'

'I will,' I say defiantly.

She nods in Hugh's direction. He's broken off from Natalie and is standing alone, facing the ocean.

'I was going to tell him later,' I say, feeling a pit of dread form in my stomach. I hate confrontation, even when I think the other person deserves a talking-to.

'Later is now, babes,' Pippa says.

I roll my eyes, but I know she's right. I make my way over to Hugh.

'Morning,' he says softly.

'Hi.'

'I'm sorry about last night, I didn't think—'

'It's fine,' I interject, cutting him off. 'I knew you didn't want me to find the wrasse. I don't know why I was so surprised to hear you had a promotion riding on it. I just came over to tell you I'm gonna be Pippa's buddy this morning.'

Hugh's jaw goes slack. His eyes shift to a greyish blue. 'You are?' he asks.

My heart beats faster and my chest starts to ache. 'Yes,' I reply, forcing myself to keep my resolve. 'I think it would be best to be with someone who's not opposed to me achieving my goals.'

Hugh opens and closes his mouth. Finally, he says, 'If that's what you think is best . . .'

'I do.'

'OK.'

'OK.' I walk away. *Take that, Hugh Harris*, I think. I try to set my shoulders defiantly, but part of me feels like I just made a mistake.

We were a well-oiled machine yesterday, but swapping partners has taken a toll on our rhythm. I'm usually seated between Hugh and Andrew, and this time I have to get up and switch with Andrew, which proves harder than I expected because I'm already strapped into my air tank, which is extremely heavy. Miguel barely catches me in time when I lose my balance, and I fall into his chest.

'Oof,' he grunts, as he regains his footing and helps lower me down to the bench. Since I've been Hugh's partner, I haven't seen much of Miguel, but he's all smiles this morning, excited for the warmer water.

After my slip he's attentive to me and Pippa, chatting with us about our trip so far, wondering what we're most excited to tell our families. Pippa's enthusiastic and charming, as usual, but I'm having trouble focusing. I'm ready to be in the water, where it's quiet.

When Miguel gets up, Pippa does a cursory buddy check and is nowhere near as thorough as Hugh. I glance down the bench towards him, wondering if he's missing me too, but he's deep in conversation with Andrew. I perform a quick buddy check on Pippa and we both jump into the water. I'm starting to feel less clumsy as I enter. I make a mental note to ask Miguel to teach me the head-first entrance next time we dive. I feel calmer as soon as we're bobbing on the surface. Derek is bringing along his camera but I hardly care, I'm just anxious to go.

We're back to descending on mooring lines, hand over hand, slowly making our way to the bottom of the ocean. The water shimmers in the morning light. I relish the familiar woosh in my ears. I'm stuck behind Hugh, who is stuck behind Andrew and moving excruciatingly slowly, and my hand keeps bumping into his. He looks at me and for a moment I think I can see hurt on his face through his mask. *You should be sad*, I think. I hope Hugh regrets keeping me in the dark about his paper. Our bodies shift as a swell of a wave passes over us. I turn away from Hugh. As much as I want him to be sad, I don't want to have to witness it.

We cover more ground than we ever have this morning. It's calming, the constant swimming, and Derek is better about taking pictures as we move, which allows us to keep our pace up. I keep track of Pippa, who seems to have completely forgotten she's also supposed to keep track of me. She's a quick swimmer and stays right on Vanessa's heels. I have no time to turn around and check and see how Andrew and Hugh are faring. I figure it's better for me not to pay Hugh too much attention.

There are more currents eddying in the water today. I drift through a warm patch only to be hit by a blast of cool water. With the currents come more schools of fish — we swim through a shoal of damselfish, hundreds of silver scales, their bodies about the size of my hands, each one marked with a telltale gold circle on its tail. The fish are unbothered by us and flit so close to our faces and bodies that I could reach out and touch them if I wanted.

We scuba through two large stretches of reef and turn around, ready to make our way back. Just like Millie's notes said they would be, these reefs are shallower, closer to the surface. They sparkle in the sunlight and teem with life. Even the fish seem extra glittery here, the sun glinting off their scales as they dance around rocks.

Vanessa slows on our return trip, seemingly happy with the pace we've set so far, and our group breaks up a little to explore the hidden crevices around the reef. Pippa and I notice a large colony of pink and red starfish, all studded with white spots and spines. We watch them unstick and stick their arms and legs up for a while before turning to look for something new.

I find a cluster of staghorn coral and hover over it. Pippa is entranced by an anemone that is home to two clownfish right next to me, so luckily, she stays by my side as I take pictures of the coral beneath my flippers. I see hundreds of little fish darting around the coral, but none look like the butterfly wrasse. They look like a rainbow of zigzags, black, yellow, blue and orange. When Pippa starts to swim away, towards where Vanessa is tapping her carabiner on her air tank (a signal for all of us to pay attention), I give up and follow her.

Vanessa has spotted a sea turtle, and it's swimming in the direction of the boat, so our group starts to follow a respectful distance behind it. It flaps its flippers leisurely, sometimes surfacing up into the waves and diving back down. It doesn't seem bothered by our presence at all. It's fascinating to watch it swim against the deep, infinitely blue backdrop of the ocean. Derek's camera never leaves his face. I bet he's taken a hundred pictures. Eventually, the turtle veers off to the right. Vanessa continues to lead us straight ahead until we pass the second reef and arrive back at the mooring line. Hugh is behind me for the ascent this time, and I watch as he helps Andrew figure out how to ascend without popping up too fast.

When we break through to the surface, Hugh's mouth is in a thin line. He usually looks so happy after dives that I feel my heart tug in my chest. My first thought is that I hope Andrew wasn't too exhausting of a buddy – watching him struggle with his buoyancy is one thing, being a partner in his troubles is another. My second thought is that I shouldn't care. Thinking about Hugh no longer needs to be on my priority list.

As we bob in the current waiting for Vanessa and Miguel to lower down the bucket for us to drop our fins into, everyone starts to chat about the sea turtle. Hugh stays silent. So do I. We are the first to clamber up the ladder, and we wordlessly put away our equipment. I try not to remember how ironic it is that I am mad at him for keeping secrets.

Hugh clears his throat next to me. 'So how was your dive?' he asks.

'Fine,' I say, my voice taut. 'Yours?'

'Fine. So, you liked Pippa as a buddy then?'

'Yep.'

Hugh's shoulders slump, but he doesn't say anything else. I watch him walk away from the bench. I should be happier after just watching a sea turtle swim majestically over the Great Barrier Reef. I should feel triumphant after sticking Hugh with someone less experienced. Instead, I just feel confused. Revenge, however small, isn't as sweet as I expected.

Chapter 20

Three dives to go

Hugh knocks on the door to our cabin while I'm in the middle of pulling a shirt over my head.

'One second,' I call out. I pull down the T-shirt. 'OK, come in.'

Hugh squeezes into the cabin beside me. 'A lot more modesty than yesterday,' he quips darkly, 'things have certainly changed.'

'Look.' I spin around, hands on my hips. 'First of all, can you stop referencing our little accident as a seduction ploy. I wasn't exactly staking out your shower and planning to jump you in the hallway. Secondly, how did you not expect me to be upset about your paper?'

'I honestly felt like you knew that was where I stood.' Hugh runs a hand through his hair. 'I didn't mean to upset you,' he says quietly. 'I thought we were having a good time together.'

'We were,' I say, emphasising the past tense. I don't want to be in this tiny room with him. It smells like his cologne, which makes me want to wrap my arms around him, but my head wants to rip him to pieces. The tension inside me makes me want to explode.

'And now it's just ruined? For the rest of the trip?'

'I mean . . .' I trail off. I shrug my shoulders. 'I have to focus on finding this fish.'

'I could help you do that,' Hugh says, his voice bordering on pleading.

'I don't know how or why you would.' I cross my arms over my chest. 'Entertaining this at all was a bad idea.'

Hugh's eyelashes flutter. 'Got it,' he says quietly.

'Excuse me.' I sidestep him and exit our room, suddenly desperate for some fresh air.

I fidget restlessly until I eventually doze off on the platform in the sun, with Pippa swaying on the hammock above me. Our next dive is in a couple of hours, then we'll eat lunch and prep for our final late afternoon dive. I know I should be doing everything I can, reviewing Millie's notes or looking at the pictures I've taken so far, but I can't bring myself to look at my camera. I know I won't find what I'm looking for. Instead, I drift in and out of sleep as the boat gently rocks back and forth.

I am just about to drop back to sleep when I hear the words 'butterfly wrasse'. For a moment, I'm not sure if I'm already dreaming. I open my eyes a crack to figure out where the conversation is coming from. It's Vanessa's voice talking about the wrasse, but I can't see her from my vantage point. I'm about to get up when I realise why – Vanessa is in the crew's cabin, the one whose windows point out onto the platform. I'm right next to her, just on the other side of the glass. Whoever is inside can probably see me, but I'm not sure if they know I can hear.

I close my eyes and lie perfectly still.

'Haven't seen one,' I hear Vanessa say.

'You're sure?' asks Hugh.

That dirty bastard, I think. He's interviewing them for his paper. He's getting proof that the wrasse doesn't exist from the people who dive here for a living. I feel like some-one's reached into my chest and grabbed my heart . . . first-hand proof of the wrasse's extinction is the last thing Millie needs. I'm seconds away from getting up and storming into the room myself, just to point out the hypocrisy of Hugh saying earlier that he would 'help me' find the wrasse, when I hear him ask something else. I make out the words 'where would you look?' before I slightly shift my body and press my ear closer to the window.

'If the last place they were seen was Norman Reef, then I would try that,' Vanessa says.

'What are the odds we could do our afternoon dive there?' Hugh asks. We have two more dives today, a midday and a late afternoon.

'I can ask Aaron . . .' There's a pause. I remain as still as possible. 'Wasn't Millie the one looking for the butterfly wrasse?'

'I'm just trying to be helpful.'

The fist around my heart relaxes. Seconds later, I hear Vanessa call out to Aaron to come down into their room.

'Norman for the late afternoon dive?' he asks. I can picture him poking at a map.

I hear footsteps coming around the platform and close my eyes, pretending to be asleep. For a second, I think it must be Andrew, because I hear Pippa shift in the hammock above me.

I crack open one eye ever so slightly.

Hugh is seated right next to me, staring at me. He clears his throat when he sees me opening one eye.

Pippa climbs out of the hammock. 'I'll let you two catch up,' she says, making her way into the shade of the captain's room.

I stare at my feet. *I should thank Millie for making me get a pedicure before this*, I think.

'You're not very good at pretending to be asleep,' Hugh says.

'I wasn't pretending. You woke me up,' I reply, although my voice comes out a little higher than normal, exposing my lie. 'You didn't have to do that,' I mumble.

'Do what?'

'Ask Vanessa and Aaron where to find the butterfly wrasse.'

'Yes, I did.'

I pull myself out of my reclined position and sit up straight. 'No, you didn't. You don't have to prove to me that you want to help me. It's too late.' *Why is staying angry at Hugh so hard?* I think, watching the sun catch on the perfect slope of his nose.

'It's never too late,' Hugh says matter-of-factly. 'And I am not just doing it for you.'

'Really?' I raise my eyebrows. 'Because I feel like you lied to me, then you tried to downplay it, then you realised,' I drop my voice to a whisper, 'Andrew wasn't as good a buddy as I was, and now you're trying to make up for it by helping me find the wrasse.'

'Did you ever think that maybe I like to do things by the book, with integrity, and that means giving you the best shot at finding the butterfly wrasse even if that means proving me wrong?'

I pick at the hem of my T-shirt. 'No.'

'Well then. And—' Hugh drops his voice low, '—yes, you are a better buddy than Andrew, and I was hoping you would consider trading back.'

I fight off a smile. 'I'm still mad at you,' I say under my breath.

'Andrew,' Hugh calls, getting to his feet, 'we gotta talk, buddy.'

'Looks good,' I say, testing Hugh's regulator and double-checking the pressure in his air tank. I gently pull on the straps of his BCD. 'You're all set.'

'Now I get to do you.' Hugh's voice is low as he runs his fingers up and down the zipper of my BCD. A shiver runs up my spine. I try not to focus on how *right* it feels that Hugh is back to being my buddy. I try instead to manifest spotting the butterfly wrasse through positive thinking. *I can do this*, I repeat over and over in my head.

Pippa had laughed when I apologised for abandoning her so quickly to be dive buddies with Hugh again.

'I knew you two would work it out,' she said, waving it off with one hand.

'We haven't worked anything out,' I retorted back stubbornly.

She smirked at me.

Now she's bickering with Andrew about how much weight he needs on his weight belt, convinced that he needs more to stop him from constantly floating upwards. Hugh must overhear them too because he starts to chuckle under his breath.

'Let's do this?' he asks, holding out a hand to help me off the bench.

We approach the edge of the boat, and Hugh assumes his normal backwards, head-first somersault position. I stand awkwardly next to him, waiting to take a big step into the water.

'Want to try getting in the fun way?'

I hesitate with indecision.

'No,' I decide, 'not today. I have bigger fish to fry than gathering the courage to jump in head first.'

Hugh nods. 'See you in there then,' and backflips off the boat.

I take a wide step into the water, letting it rush into my ears, quieting the world around me.

We repeat the dive we did in the morning because Vanessa and Miguel said the visibility was some of the best they'd ever seen. The water is still crystal clear, with almost no current, barely any sand swirls up from the sea floor. Diving somewhere familiar is refreshing. I feel less disoriented and more like I know what I'm doing. With the absence of the current, the ocean is quieter, fewer shoals of fish rush by. I recognise a few landmarks – the sharp rise in the ocean floor as we get closer to the reef, the slow curve to the right of the first large coral structure.

I stop to hover over a staghorn coral cluster, and Hugh hovers right next to me. To my surprise, he pulls out an underwater camera too and gives me a thumbs-up. Together we snap pictures. He slowly makes his way towards another, smaller group of bright blue staghorn corals and continues to take photos.

If this is what it feels like to be on a research expedition with a team of scientists dedicated to a common goal, I want to go on one. I feel invigorated by the common sense of purpose Hugh and I are sharing, even if our end goals are somewhat different. It feels so nice to not be in this all alone.

We're interrupted by Miguel shepherding us along to the second tangle of reef. As we make our way there, we see a giant manta ray pass underneath us, gently cruising across the sandy bottom. It's sleek and grey, flapping its wings like an ocean butterfly. Our group turns and follows it for about twenty-five feet until Miguel gives us the signal to turn around. We're all spellbound.

I thought the shock of diving would wear off, that with each dive things would seem less spectacular, but somehow it doesn't. With every dive there is more to see, another crevice captivates me, a colour I've never seen before saturates my view, a new fish piques my curiosity.

No butterfly wrasse are spotted, but we do catch sight of another lobster. Hugh and I poke at a couple of clown-fish protecting their anemone. Vanessa finds another coral whose petals disappear as we swim by it, and we take turns watching the purple tendrils appear and retract. Andrew thinks he sees something, and calls us all over, but it turns out he just saw a clump of algae in the crevice of a rock.

On our way back we swim right past a school of angel-fish, their fins glinting in the sunlight as they swish past.

I feel a low trembling of anxiety that I will never be content in a cubicle in Columbus again.

Chapter 21

Two dives to go

Lunch sets the group on a trajectory towards a siesta. We only have one more dive today and it's not for another three hours. Natalie and Derek have camped out in the sun of the platform. The wind has picked up and is ripping through the captain's room, making it hard to find any peace and quiet on the benches. I retreat downstairs to take a nap on my bunk bed. My skin needs to be out of the sun, at least for a little while.

Before I head downstairs, I see Natalie and Hugh talking, and when Hugh glances at me during their conversation I feel my gut clench. *Natalie has no reason to dig up the first-class debacle now*, I remind myself, but I still end up lying on my twin mattress staring at the paint-peeled ceiling, unable to sleep.

I dug myself in too deep by expecting Hugh to be perfectly honest with me and getting angry with him when he wasn't. And then he doubled down on 'having integrity' and actually tried to help me find the wrasse. I could never let him find out I wasn't Millie. He would never forgive me. And I would rather live with never seeing him again, but knowing that he liked me, than having to tell him the truth.

I must drift off at some point because I wake up groggily to creaking on the bunk bed below me.

'Hugh?' I call out softly.

'Ugh,' Hugh grunts. 'These beds are so tiny.'

I grunt in affirmation.

'Since Derek and Natalie took our usual spot, I figured I would come see if this worked.'

'It's not the same.'

'Not at all,' he agrees.

I stare at the ceiling. 'How was your chat with Natalie?' I finally get up the nerve to ask.

He doesn't respond.

'Hugh?' I prompt. My heart rate starts to pick up. I feel sweat dampening my inner elbows. *Oh no.*

Hugh coughs.

I want to peer over and look down at him, but I'm frozen with fear.

Finally, he speaks. 'Yeah, about that . . .' His voice sounds off. I can't put my finger on it.

'What is it?'

After he doesn't respond right away, I gather my courage and peer over the bed. Hugh is hunched over his mattress, his knees pulled up towards his belly.

'I think I'm feeling kinda seasick.' He looks up at me, his face noticeably paler. His eyes have gone a light icy blue.

'Oh God,' I reply, first feeling relief and then worry. 'Is there anything I can do?' I ask, but Hugh's already halfway out the door.

'I gotta—' He takes a gulp of air '—go upstairs.'

I follow Hugh upstairs right away, clambering out of my top bunk and scampering up the ladders behind him, but I reach the deck only to find him already reaching for a mask and snorkel.

'Care to join?' he asks, all but sprinting off the boat.

'What—' I begin to ask but he interrupts me.

'I gotta go swim for a bit,' he says, as he takes a running start and dives into the water.

Vanessa is standing next to the bucket of snorkels and shrugs. 'Being in the water helps seasickness.'

I scan the boat to see if anyone else is swimming, and see Miguel pointedly looking the other way, clearly trying to stay as far from potential seasickness as possible.

I stand awkwardly by the railing, watching Hugh surface and duck under waves, steadily kicking further from the boat and closer to the reef. The top of the reef is barely visible, a foot or two under the surface about thirty yards from the boat. After a minute, Vanessa nudges me with her shoulder.

'Do you want to go?' she asks impatiently. 'If you go, then I don't have to. But I don't want him out there alone – it's getting a little choppy.'

It's the least I can do after Hugh recharted our dives. 'I guess.' I shrug.

I grab a snorkel from the bucket, spit in the lens, and swish it out with water. Then, I follow Hugh. I try to take a running start like he did, but I chicken out and slip in feet first, nice and slow. The ocean is cool, especially without our stinger suits, and I take a few strokes towards Hugh to warm up. He's already diving down with his snorkel to check out the reef and surfacing back up like a seal.

'Are you feeling better?' I ask, when I reach him and we're both above water.

He nods happily. 'Much.'

'You're a good swimmer,' I observe. Even though we've been scuba-diving together for days, it's hard to tell how comfortable people are in the water without a life jacket strapped to their chest keeping them afloat.

'You're not so bad yourself,' Hugh replies. Although his gaze is directed at my body, and we're treading water so close to each other that I think he's talking about something else entirely.

I blush. 'I'm pretty sure there's more interesting things than me to look at around here.'

'I'll be the judge of that.' Hugh grins, and dives down again.

Access to the reef from a snorkeller's vantage point is totally different. Some parts of the reef are so close to the surface that there isn't even room for us to swim over them. We are awestruck at the view, the late-afternoon sunlight streaming over the rocks and the coral.

There's kelp-like grass reaching for the surface and slimy rocks covered in barnacled algae. Sunlight catches on the slime left from snails that move slowly across the rocks. Curlicues of coral send their fluffy spikes towards the ocean's surface; they remind me of layers of feather boas.

I'm just as fascinated with the coral as I am with the fish, and there seem to be more fish up here, closer to the sun. They're smaller, and a lot of them have a silvery sheen, which glints in the sunlight as they dart around our bodies. For a moment I wish I'd brought my camera, but then Hugh grabs my hand and directs my pointer finger towards a crevice. He's spotted something.

Together we take turns diving down to gaze at a reclusive lionfish. Lionfish are not native to the Great Barrier Reef, they're invasive and detrimental to the native fish species, but there is no denying they're beautiful – every single one of their spines is perfectly striped reddish brown and white. The lionfish we're looking at is mesmerising, but we keep our distance – both of us know they're poisonous. After a while we tire and flip on our backs to rest, snorkels in hand.

Hugh's free hand grabs mine. I feel my entire body jolt with energy. My thoughts race. *What am I doing? How have I forgiven him so quickly?* But we have to keep holding hands so we don't drift apart on the waves. I don't have a choice but to enjoy our bodies knocking together gently, both of us staring up at the sky. We float over a crest that is so big it flips both of us onto our backs, and suddenly our limbs are intertwined. The saltwater makes us both float easily. Our faces are inches from each other.

I can see each individual drop of water flecking his face. One catches on his impossibly long eyelashes. His eyes are bright aqua, the same colour as the water, and I'm close enough to count the gold flecks around his irises. His face is mesmerising. I bite my bottom lip, suddenly self-conscious that he's looking at me as closely as I'm looking at him.

As if we're in slow motion, he brings a thumb to my bottom lip and frees it from my teeth.

'Are you cold?' he asks.

I realise I'm shaking, but I'm not cold. 'No,' I breathe.

Hugh runs his thumb over my lip and down onto my chin. Slowly, he wraps his fingers around the back of my neck. My entire body flushes with pleasure. Looking into his eyes is so powerful I feel like I could explode, so instead I focus on his shoulders, which are rising just inches above the water, and I watch as the tendons of muscle that wrap around his neck flex. I remember how it felt to have my face tucked into the crook of his neck and I yearn for it. The muscle in his jaw pulses.

I can't. I shouldn't. Not again . . . not when I need clear boundaries. But what was I thinking, kissing him for the first time in the dark? And now . . . he's lit up like a Greek god. How am I supposed to resist?

But you're lying to him, the other voice in my head reminds me.

'Millie,' Hugh breathes, 'how can you pretend like you don't feel this?'

I stare at him. 'I . . . I . . .' My voice catches. There are so many things I want to say that I can't bring myself to. *How did we get here? How did we get from sniping at each other's grammar to breathless in the ocean?* 'I thought we were supposed to hate each other,' I say dumbly, my thoughts jumbled and my words not making much sense.

'Maybe,' Hugh says, his voice low. 'But I don't hate you. I hate how we are sharing an impossibly tiny room that now smells entirely of your shampoo, but that you're sleeping as far away from me as possible. I hate how you beat up on your curls when you're worried about something.' He looks at my hand, which is tugging on an errant curl. I gulp.

'I hate how you always know just what to say to get under my skin and how determined you are to find a fish I don't want to be found, but I don't hate you.'

232

'Don't you when-Harry-met-Sally me,' I say, although my words lack conviction. Our faces are still inches apart. Our bodies bob up and down with the waves. If I leaned in two more inches, I could taste him again.

'When-Harry-met-Sally you?' His eyebrows knit together in confusion, forming a wrinkle. I want to smooth it out with the pad of my finger.

'You know . . . that movie . . . when he lists all the things he loves about her and makes her love him too.' I can hardly form a sentence, I'm so distracted by the proximity of Hugh's jawline.

Hugh shakes his head back and forth. 'But I said all the things I hate about you.' A lopsided grin forms on his face. He pauses, then says with a smile, 'So it worked in the movie?'

I am frozen with indecision. Somewhere in the back of my brain, my body is making me kick to stay afloat. I open my mouth to speak, but I don't know what to say. *It did work* in the movie. And it's working on me.

'Millie,' Hugh says again, his voice deeper, thick with emotion. 'Honestly, you've always intimidated me.'

'Me?' I scoff. Then I remember he's really talking about Millie, and she can be quite intimidating.

'But meeting you in person . . . you're . . . you're different. Softer . . .'

Under the water, Hugh runs his hand down my thigh and slowly pulls me closer. Somewhere in the recesses of my brain I'm aware that there's time to break the spell, but I can't manage to do it. I can't force my body to move, my attraction is too strong.

I cave into his gentle pull and suddenly our bodies are touching everywhere. A sigh escapes my lips. Hugh takes a deep breath. Ninety per cent of my brain is in an electrified heaven. Ten per cent knows this is wrong. *He thinks I'm my sister*. The ninety per cent takes over.

Hugh's hands caress my hips and the back of my head, his fingers gently pulling at my hair. Our faces are almost touching. Slowly, our lips meet, furtively grazing each other. Suddenly, we're plunged into a long, fervent kiss, both of us hungry. Our tongues are greedy, searching for the depths of one another. Our hips lock together and move in unison against each other. I bring both of my hands around the back of his head and finally get to dig my fingers into his hair. I feel him hardening through his swimsuit. I am wet in more ways than one.

I'm surprised to remember how he feels so viscerally, even though we just kissed yesterday, I feel like I'm having the best kind of déjà vu.

Hugh runs his fingers underneath the seam of my swimsuit and tugs at the string. I return the favour, slipping my thumb down the front of his waistband. He slips his hand over the front of my bikini and palms my breast, his finger caressing my nipple. I gasp. *More*, I think. *I want more.*

Our breathing becomes laboured, both of us focused on each other and not enough on staying afloat. A wave crashes over the top of our heads and drenches us, bringing the moment to a crashing halt.

We separate underwater, both of us pulling ourselves to the surface to take in gulps of air.

Hugh looks at me with a glint in his eye and inclines his head towards the boat. 'How do you feel about going somewhere a little—'

He's interrupted by another wave that surges around us.

'Less choppy?' I supply, once we've both caught our breath again. He nods, a wicked grin spreading across his face. 'Race you to our room,' I say, diving under and kicking as hard as my fins will let me.

Hugh is fast to follow, grabbing for my ankle with his fingers and barely missing, his fingertips dragging along my foot, the touch enough to make me want to wrap my legs around him all over again.

We reach the side of the boat at the same time, breathless. I reach up for the ladder rungs and Hugh trails his fingertips up my inner thigh under the cover of the water.

'How was it?' Pippa asks, her head popping over the railing.

Hugh's fingertips disappear. I wipe the smile off my face as fast as I can, but my heart thunders in my chest.

'Fine!' I say, hauling myself onto the deck. I try to readjust my swimsuit as nonchalantly as possible. I can't tell from Pippa's face whether anyone saw us making out in the water.

Hugh reaches the deck moments after me, his abs rippling as he stands up. I feel like the wind got knocked out of me all over again.

'I think I might go in,' Pippa muses, 'or is it too choppy?'

'It's not so bad,' I say, edging towards the stairs to my room. Pippa eyes me, but before she can say anything,

Hugh announces that he's going to go grab his phone. He walks downstairs calmly, like nothing happened. And every cell in my body strains to meet him in our room.

'I'm going to go get cleaned up,' I say, leaving Pippa in my wake. I force myself to walk excruciatingly slowly, hoping no one notices how much of a hurry I'm in to follow Hugh.

By the time I'm down the narrow steps, I'm racing towards our room. Only once I'm inside and have shut the door behind me, do I get to fully take in Hugh standing, his head slightly bent against the celling, staring at me with the most wolfish grin I have ever seen. The boat creaks loudly.

'Perfect,' he says, 'if that keeps happening, you can be as loud as you want.' He steps towards me and gently pulls at the tie of my bikini. The back comes undone. He unties the string around my neck next. I reach for his shorts, but he places one hand over mine.

'In case you haven't noticed,' he murmurs, his lips right next to my ear, 'there's only room for one at a time in here.'

I open my mouth to protest, but he covers my lips with his as he unties each side of my swimsuit bottoms. They fall to the floor and he lowers me onto his twin mattress. The smell of him on the sheets makes my hips arch with desire.

He thumbs my nipple with one hand and slips his other hand in between my legs. He kisses my neck, his lips fluttering over my collarbone. I'm ready for him already. He teases the edge of my lips with his finger, his thumb stroking my clit.

'Hugh,' I gasp. I reach for him, to pull him closer towards me, to feel his lips on mine, but he resists, swirling his tongue around my nipple instead. He slides a finger inside me and pleasure courses through me. I thrust my hips with him, wanting more of him, deeper in me. Another finger joins the first. I whimper.

His thumb keeps circling while his mouth kisses lower and lower. He swirls his tongue over my belly button. I see stars against the wooden frame of the bunk bed.

Suddenly, his mouth replaces his thumb, his tongue kissing the bundle of nerves with so much intensity my toes curl. His fingers maintain a steady rhythm, driving me deeper, and his other hand circles my nipple again. He teases me with pressure in so many places I already feel like I could burst.

'Hugh,' I gasp again.

Everything stops. His fingers still, he raises his head of shaggy blond hair.

'Millie,' he breathes. Then he sucks on me again, before raising his head once more. 'You taste.' Another lick, this one slower, more teasing. 'Incredible.' Then his fingers are in me again, pumping faster and faster. My hips are moving of their own accord, grinding against his face, his hand. I'm on the verge of climax, the pleasure too intense, when Hugh does something with his tongue that I've never felt before. A moan escapes my lips as I shatter around his fingers, my hips bucking up towards his face, my hands grabbing the sheets next to me. He doesn't stop until I've stopped shaking, my body relaxing into the mattress.

His head appears from between my legs, a lazy grin spreading across his face.

My brain starts to process my surroundings again, the creaking sway of the boat, the wood frame inches above my head. As the sensations ebb, a thought crystallises, repeating in my brain.

Millie, you taste incredible. Millie. Millie. I gulp in a breath of air. Dread settles over me like sand settling on the ocean floor. *How did I let it get this far? I can't keep lying to him. I can't jeopardise Millie's career this way.*

'Millie,' Hugh says, and my knees clamp together on their own accord. I scramble away from him, peeling myself off the bed.

'I should go shower,' I manage to mumble, the words hard to get out. His smile disappears. He bites his bottom lip.

'Already?' he asks, disappointment echoing in his voice.

'Yes, I . . .' I trail off, I don't know what to say. I pull a towel around my body, suddenly hyper-aware of my own nakedness. At the hurt look on Hugh's face, my heart feels like it's breaking into a million pieces. 'It's not you.'

'Was that not . . .' He trails off.

'It was,' I say, but my voice is tinged with worry. Everything Hugh just did to my body, to my senses, to my mind, proved to me something I didn't want to admit. That I really like Hugh, maybe even more than I've ever liked anyone. And that Hugh thinks I'm my sister. Which means . . . 'But I think it was a mistake . . . I think maybe we're better off as friends,' I force myself to say.

'Friends . . .' He repeats, his eyes glazed over, turning darker with every second.

I don't want to think about it, so I turn towards the door. I can't meet Hugh's eyes. My gaze flits over the stuff scattered across my bed and I see the journal Millie made for me. I remember the real reason I'm here – the reason I keep conveniently forgetting about, and Hugh keeps distracting me from.

I am here to do something for my sister. I am pretending to be her, but that doesn't mean that I'm no longer *me*. I am not someone who lets a random fling distract her for a job. No matter how deep in my bones I want to do to Hugh what he just did to me, no matter how badly I ache for it to happen again, no matter how much my body knows, although my brain can't admit it, that I've never felt a desire so strong for anyone else, I can't let my feelings keep clouding my vision.

Clutching my towel around my waist, I slip out of our room. I make a promise to myself for what feels like the thousandth time: if I can't tell Hugh the truth, which I can't, then no more letting him distract me.

Chapter 22

'Are you sure this is a good idea?' Pippa asks Miguel, squinting out at the horizon. Storm clouds have bunched together in the distance, forming a menacing line of grey.

'It's better underwater,' Miguel says brightly. 'Less chance to be seasick.' He gives me a sideways glance with a grin. I nod at him, affirming that I too do not want to be trapped on the boat with people who are sick. We haven't talked much over the last day. He's spent a lot of time with Derek and Natalie, talking about God knows what.

'OK,' says Pippa, although she clearly doesn't believe it. She shimmies into her stinger suit and straps on her BCD. I follow suit. Hugh and I have hardly spoken since I left the room earlier, but neither of us found another buddy. We do our buddy check silently. Hugh completes his quicker than ever but still manages to be very thorough. I squirm with discomfort when he triple-checks my regulator. Being so close to him is excruciating.

The group launches themselves into the water quickly, Derek even forgoing his camera, all of us thinking we either wanted to be inside or underwater when the rain hits.

We're at Norman Reef, the place where the butter-fly wrasse were last spotted. After Hugh and I climbed aboard, Aaron pulled anchor and we deviated from our schedule, sailing thirty minutes to Norman, which also happened to bring us thirty minutes closer to the incoming storm. As we start to descend, rain begins to pelt the surface of the water. The waves pick up so heavily that it's hard to grab the mooring line. With each swell, we are raised up and out of the ocean, our hands grabbing a rope that is pulled tight between the ocean floor and the boat. The ocean is murky, sand and dirt swirling around us. But everything subsides as soon as we're ten feet under. I'm so relieved to finally descend that for a moment I forget about what happened earlier only to immediately remember again, turning hot despite the water.

Thankfully, Norman Reef is deeper than the other reefs we've been diving, which proves to be a challenge for Andrew's buoyancy but helps separate us from whatever is happening on the surface. I try to tune out my thoughts as best I can, falling into a meditative state, kicking gently over coral and keeping an eye out for a flick of purple or yellow that could be a butterfly wrasse.

But having Hugh at my elbow makes concentrating impossible. All I can think about is how he made me feel. I have to resist the urge to grab onto his elbow. Hugh pulls out his camera as we hover over some staghorn coral.

He is still trying to find the butterfly wrasse, even after what happened earlier. The thought makes my heart hurt. It would be easier if Hugh was a horrible person, if he really was just out to stop me from finding what I was searching for. But the nicer he is, the worse I feel, the more I remember that I am the one keeping secrets and telling lies.

I turn away from Hugh taking photos. I can't take it anymore.

When we surface, the storm has blown through. It was an uneventful dive, one that felt more like a way to escape the storm, and possible seasickness, than to actually see marine life.

Hugh tries to catch my eye as we wait for our turn to ascend the ladder onto the boat, and I can't bring myself to look at him. I know he is hurt and angry – that his eyes would be a dark grey-blue, and it would do me in.

We hardly look at each other the rest of the evening. Everyone gathers on the side of the boat to watch the sun slowly dip into the water. It would usually stir my soul to watch something so beautiful, but I feel hollow and confused.

I avoid Hugh at dinner and sit at the opposite end of the booth. When everyone takes a beer up to the captain's room to celebrate our last full day of dives, I head to the cabin. I change and start to get ready for bed so I don't have to wrangle into my pyjamas while he watches. I can't face him. Especially not after he convinced Vanessa and Aaron to try Norman Reef, and even that didn't work.

The butterfly wrasse doesn't exist. I feel sure of it. I want to be angry at Millie for sending me on a wild goose chase, but I'm so worried about her well-being that it staves off my anger a little longer.

'Ahem.' Hugh clears his throat as he steps into our room. I jump, not prepared for anyone to come in. I had forgotten to lock the door.

'Sorry,' I say quickly, 'I'm just finishing up in here. I'll get out of your way.' I duck by Hugh and step towards the door, but he steps to the side and blocks my way out.

'Millie,' he says, his voice low. 'What are you doing?'

'I'm going upstairs,' I say weakly, nodding towards the door.

'No, what are you doing to *this*?' He gestures to himself and back to me again.

I look up at him. 'What do you mean?' I force out.

Hugh looks like he's about to roll his beautiful eyes, and then he sighs and sits down on his bed.

Something about his weariness stills me, and I sit down across from him.

'You know that we have something, the two of us. I know it's only been three days . . . and, well, some Instagram conversations . . .' He levels his gaze at me. 'You know I'm not good at talking about stuff like this, so me addressing this is something.' He laughs harshly. 'My therapist would call it growth.'

I force myself not to react that Hugh just mentioned his therapist. There is nothing more attractive than a man taking care of his mental health. *Why did I have to lie to him?* I think.

'But you're pushing me away.' He can't sit up straight under the bunk beds, so he's hunched over, looking at me.

'You don't understand.' I fiddle with my hands.

'I do,' says Hugh. 'I see what's going on. You're finding every reason to turn this down, to make me into a bad guy, because you aren't ready to see yourself as worthy of someone good.'

My chest tightens. I don't want to listen to Hugh telling me all the ways my confidence could be improved. I've been hearing that for my entire life.

'And I get it,' He continues, 'I was that way after Sophia. I couldn't imagine myself deserving anyone with half a brain. But, Millie, you're making this so much harder than it needs to be. You are smart, and savvy, and witty, and opinionated. You are ruthlessly sexy. Why can't you see that? Why can't you let your guard down?'

Normally I would be thrilled Hugh said I was ruthlessly sexy. Instead, I feel stupid and exposed. 'What is this?' I say, through gritted teeth. 'Hugh, you live in Australia. I live in Ohio, for crying out loud. This can't *be* anything! It's not a big deal, OK?'

'It could be something if we want it to be,' Hugh counters evenly, but then he stops himself. 'But if you don't feel the same way . . .'

I falter. I cross and uncross my legs. Hugh looks down at his feet. I know what I have to say, but I don't want to say it. I know I can't keep letting this play out. It won't end up going anywhere, and it's distracting me from what I need to focus on. I think of Millie. I think of Millie undergoing surgery, of all the things she has to go through while I get to lounge around on a boat.

'I don't,' I force out. 'I don't feel the same way.' Hugh's face starts to crumple, and I bolt. Hurting him was bad enough, I can't take watching it. I duck out of the room and into the bathroom, where I can cry in peace.

'Millie?' Pippa knocks softly on the bathroom door a couple minutes later. 'Is that you in there? I'm so sorry but I really need the loo.'

I squeeze myself out of the bathroom and let Pippa inside. She takes one look at my red eyes and says, 'Oh no.'

I sniffle.

'Don't go anywhere,' she says, ducking into the bathroom, 'I'll be right back.'

Pippa leads me to her room with the energy of a mom dealing with her high school daughter's first crisis. 'Why don't you sit down?' she says, offering up her bed. Her room is hardly bigger than ours but sports a double bed instead of twin bunks. I can tell which corner is Pippa's instantly, due to the array of brightly coloured scarf-like clothing items spilling out from a suitcase. 'I told Andrew we needed the room. Girl emergency.'

I feel a surge of gratitude towards both of them.

'Tell me everything,' Pippa commands, perching on the edge of the bed next to me.

I do.

Chapter 23

One dive (and one day trip) left

It takes me over an hour to explain to Pippa everything that's taken place over the past two weeks. Although fifteen minutes of it consisted strictly of Pippa gasping dramatically at everything I said.

Andrew only pops his head in once to ask if we need wine, to which Pippa responds, 'I trained you so well,' before she calls after him 'and yes please! See if they have rosé!'

My sister finding out she had the BRCA gene? Pippa gasped with such a deep breath she practically choked.

Revealing that Millie asked me to go on her behalf and that I wasn't really Millie, I was Andi, her non-marine-biologist younger sister? Pippa launched herself off the bed in disbelief.

Once wine was in hand, our conversation took a detour when I tried to explain to Pippa who Millie really was. When I told her about the time Millie tried to prank our mother by updating her phone to autocorrect all her texts to my dad with salacious phrases, Pippa giggled so hard she got hiccups.

The mixture of her laughter and the wine lifted my spirits, and I got off the bed to recreate Natalie's interaction with me at the airport, which I completed by using one of Pippa's bikini tops as a stand-in for Natalie's glamorous scarf.

'She's like a movie star,' Pippa sighed, 'you'd actually quite like her.'

'She's going to out me!'

Pippa gripped her rosé tightly. 'She wouldn't dare.'

Hugh having a promotion riding on me *not* finding the fish I am looking for? Pippa sat back and furrowed her brow in anger.

'But there's one more thing,' I said. 'We kind of like . . .' I trailed off, but Pippa looked at me knowingly.

'You got some,' she gasped. 'In these *tiny* rooms?'

'Well, technically *we* didn't, but I did.' I squealed, downing another gulp of my wine.

'Tell me everything,' she demanded.

I didn't give her all the details, but I gave enough for her jaw to drop open, especially when I described the toe-curling bits. 'Pippa, he was amazing.'

'God bless whoever taught him how to do that,' she said, lifting her hands in a prayer gesture towards the ceiling.

I didn't need to explain how much I've fallen for Hugh – Pippa knows. But I did explain why I couldn't bring myself to be honest with him – his past, and our argument, how much it killed me to have to tell him I didn't feel the same way. That I couldn't bear to betray Millie.

When I said, 'I know it's crazy to feel like this about someone after three days,' Pippa fell straight back onto her pillows and said, 'This is like something in a film,' in such a heartfelt voice I thought she was going to start crying.

And then she sat straight up and said, 'Well, we'd just better figure out a way to get you two to the last act.' She downs the last sip of her wine before she continues.

'First of all,' Pippa says, ticking off items on her fingers, 'I'll keep an eye on Natalie. If she brings up anything about you being fishy . . .' Pippa pauses and winks at me. 'Get it?'

I nod, rolling my eyes.

'If she brings up anything, I'll shut it down immediately. Cool?'

'That would be great.' I heave a sigh of relief. I should have told Pippa sooner. She rocks.

'Secondly,' she continues, 'you're going to find this fish. We have one more dive. It's meant to be, I can feel it in my bones.' She reaches to give my hand a squeeze. 'Believe in yourself, babes,' she says brightly. 'No one else is going to do it for you. Well, except me. I believe in you too.'

She doesn't wait for me to respond before continuing. 'Thirdly, and most importantly, is your situation with Hugh. I know you don't want to admit it, but he did hit the nail on the head with the confidence stuff. Who cares if you're not your sister? You're YOU. He. Likes. YOU. Show up as who you are and be proud of it. Don't let your insecurities get in the way. You should tell him the truth.'

'But I've been lying, Pippa. In every conversation. I act like I'm a marine biologist, like I live this exciting life, like I'm someone who would be compatible with Hugh and I'm just . . . not.'

'But you are living an exciting life,' Pippa points out, 'and you can't use that as an excuse to lie to someone.'

'But what if he uses it against Millie?'

We run this conversation in circles until Andrew knocks on the door and sheepishly asks if he can get ready for bed. Reluctantly, I slink back to my room, but not before thanking Pippa profusely.

'You're the best, Pip,' I whisper as I hug her goodnight.

'Get some rest, and try not to get seduced again.' She winks. Then she giggles. '*Andi*,' she whispers so quietly I barely hear her. I swat at her arm. 'Shh!' I hiss, but it feels nice to hear someone call me by my actual name and I can hear her giggling as I walk back to my room.

The lights are off in the room, and Hugh is nowhere to be found. I climb onto my bed and curl up under the covers, the wine making me feel oddly detached.

I wake up what feels like every hour, my head spinning. I remind myself that even though Hugh was right about some things, it doesn't mean I have to tell him the truth. The guy lives in Australia. *Why would I put myself through an impossibly hard conversation with potentially disastrous consequences for something with no future?*

The last thing I remember before drifting off into a fitful sleep is that when Hugh comes in the room to go to bed, he whispers, 'Goodnight, Millie.'

I wake up to the rolling of the ship. We are already moving, undoubtedly heading towards Fitzroy Island. Suddenly, I can't wait to get off the boat and out of these cramped quarters. I scurry down from my bunk. Hugh is still asleep, his mouth slightly open, his perfect, plump bottom lip looking extremely kissable. A shiver runs down my spine as I remember where his lips were yesterday. I steal out of the room before he wakes up to find me looming over him like a lovesick puppy.

If I'm not going to have the guts to tell him, maybe I can get through today with minimal Hugh contact.

Then I have one more dive, and I'll be home free. I grab a coffee and sit on the platform, the breeze ruffling through my hair. Aaron is already gunning full speed towards a green mountain in the distance. It's the only land around, and the only land we've seen in days. I feel a burst of joy at the prospect of finally getting off the boat. Fitzroy Island, here we come.

Fitzroy Island is a lush green mound in the middle of the sparkling aquamarine of the Pacific Ocean. It looks small from far away, but the closer we get, the larger it looms over the horizon. As we approach land, everyone clusters on deck, craning their necks to watch the white sand get closer and closer. If I thought Cairns looked like paradise, Fitzroy is ten times as beautiful. There's one lone dock jutting out from the beach, rickety and wooden, and we are the only boat as far as the eye can see. The island looks so untouched and uninhabited that I'm beginning to wonder if there is even a turtle sanctuary.

Vanessa sets down her coffee and picks up her clipboard.

'We hike first,' she explains, 'then we take our trip to the turtle sanctuary, which is where we eat lunch, then we have a couple hours at the beach, then we're back on the boat in time for a late dinner. Cool?'

'Cool,' the group echoes.

Aaron lugs a large container upstairs, the bin where we all placed our shoes, and everyone grabs their sandals.

Pippa clears her throat. 'Is the hiking, um, hard?' she asks tentatively. She wriggles her toes, which are painted a bright pink. 'I only have flip-flops.'

'It's not really a hike.' Vanessa sighs, as if she wishes that weren't the case. 'We're just going to the top of the island.' She gestures towards the mountain in front of us.

Pippa's jaw drops.

Vanessa bursts out laughing. 'I'm joking! We'll be walking to the neighbouring beach. Then we'll take a van to the top of the mountain on our way to the turtle sanctuary.'

Everyone visibly relaxes, including Natalie, who takes the opportunity to pull out her phone and start waving it around in the air, trying to get signal. *Millie*, I think. I get up, ready to scramble downstairs and grab my phone. Just as I'm at the top of the stairs, Vanessa calls to Natalie, 'No use doing that. There's no service here.'

My heart sinks. I turn around and make my way back to the bench, settling down next to Pippa. She gives me a sympathetic look. 'I'm sorry. Just one more day, then you'll be able to talk to her. I'm sure she's fine,' she says, patting my knee gently.

'I'm just ready to be off this boat,' I complain.

Pippa nods in agreement.

'I take it you didn't have any big conversations last night?' she whispers.

I shake my head. 'Not yet.'

All of us have sea legs when we clamber onto the dock. Hugh is walking ten paces ahead of me, leading the way with Vanessa. He's hardly looked at me all morning, which is technically what I was hoping for, but every minute that ticks by with us ignoring each other feels like a stab in the gut.

251

Hugh is off balance, teetering a little with each step he takes. I feel like the ground is rolling beneath me even though I know the dock is stationary. Derek has to steady himself by grabbing onto the wooden posts of the pier. Miguel, bringing up the rear, chuckles. Pippa and Andrew look like wobbly toddlers as we make our way towards the sand.

We walk up a gently sloping beach straight towards a dirt path that disappears into a thick forest. If I wasn't so relieved to be on land, I would be spooked at how truly remote the island feels. Low mangroves and eucalyptus trees line the edge of the beach. As soon as we duck into the thicket, the air stops smelling like the ocean and instead smells like dirt. I take deep breaths of it, relishing a scent other than the tangy smell of seawater and sunscreen.

Vanessa leads us slowly through the low rainforest. The dirt path morphs into a wooden walkway. Birds call from branches just overheard and animals rustle through the bushes as we trudge forward. Occasionally, Vanessa points out the flora and fauna she recognises, directing our attention to a cockatoo with a bright yellow plume of feathers and a loud screeching squawk. We all fall silent as we watch a huge lizard – 'A yellow spotted monitor,' Vanessa informs us in a whisper – make its way through the bushes right next to the walkway. The air is humid and sticky, and I'm already starting to sweat.

Ahead of me, as Vanessa falls quiet, Natalie and Hugh begin to chat, their heads bending towards each other. Derek is busy taking pictures of the birds and the trees.

Pippa sees what I'm looking at and takes immediate action, elbowing her way past Andrew and Derek until she wedges herself in between Natalie and Hugh.

'Natalie,' she says loudly, 'I've been meaning to ask you about Texas, everyone in England is dying to go there.'

I remain at the back of the pack, lost in thought. I'm grateful to plod through the trees alone.

The wooden path winds around a corner and takes us deeper into a mangrove swamp. The giant exposed roots and dark water, so markedly different from the sparkling turquoise of the ocean, look exactly like the mangrove swamps of the Florida Keys.

I've only been there once – I was thirteen and Millie was fourteen and our parents agreed, after months of begging, to take us to Key Largo for spring break. That year, our trip to Florida was one of the only things we could agree on. We had grown apart since Millie started high school. She had new friends and liked boys whose names I had never heard of. I followed her around when she came home from school and desperately tried to hang out with her friends, usually only able to stick around for five minutes before Millie kicked me out, closing her bedroom door with a heavy seriousness because she and her friends needed to 'talk about stuff'.

But as soon as our parents agreed to the trip, Millie and I got closer. I still wasn't allowed to hang out with her and her friends, but something about me became interesting again. Key Largo was all we could talk about – Millie had just broken her arm playing soccer and even her injury couldn't dampen our excitement.

It was the first time Millie and I had ever been to Florida. Usually, our family drove two hours to Cleveland and rented a little cottage on Lake Erie for spring break – it was always freezing. But that year we got to drive twenty hours to see alligators and snorkel in the great blue expanse of the Atlantic Ocean.

On our drive down we stopped at an Everglades National Park outpost where you could hike through the mangroves, go kayaking, and even go cliff jumping near man-made waterfalls. We traipsed our way through the humid jungle, working up a sweat before we arrived at a series of small pools borne from an arrangement of large, exposed rocks. There was a clear pathway up to the top, where there was about a twenty-foot drop into the deepest pool. Our parents went to the kayak stand to confirm our rental, and Millie and I loitered near the edge of the water.

There was a group of teenage boys around our age racing up to the top and jumping off. I fidgeted awkwardly, staring at them and at the cliff, wishing Millie didn't have a broken arm so she could go first and tell me if it was fun.

Reading my mind, Millie nudged me with her elbow. 'Go try it,' she said, shrugging her shoulders, 'it looks like fun.'

The spotlight was so rarely on me in our family that I balked. 'But you can't go,' I pointed out, 'I would have to go alone.'

'So?' Millie said.

'All those boys are up there.'

'So?'

'Boys think you're cool, but they'll make fun of me.'

'What makes you think that?'

I shrugged my shoulders.

'Andi,' Millie said to me sternly, at age fourteen already able to sound exactly like our mother, 'if you think it would be fun, do it. You don't need me to babysit you, and you definitely don't need to care about *them*.' She glanced at the boys with disdain, slightly sticking up her nose.

Something about the way she said it made me feel like she would think I was a loser if I didn't go. I took a deep breath. I had never done anything without Millie before. She was always there, trying things first, making them look cool. I was comfortable following in her footsteps. But the jump looked so . . . fun. I kept staring.

Millie elbowed me again. 'Just try it,' she whispered. 'You'll love it, you'll see. It's OK that I won't be up there with you. I'm right here. Show 'em how it's done.'

I don't know what came over me, determination or fear of disappointing Millie, or both, but before our parents could get back, I took a deep breath and charged up the stairs, launching myself straight over the cliff and cannonballing into the water below. When I got to the surface, Millie flashed me a huge thumbs-up from the side of the pool. I was thrilled.

For the first time in months, I felt like she wasn't embarrassed about me. For the first time in months, I was proud of myself.

That trip was where our love of marine biology was born. Millie swam the whole time with her waterproof cast, awkwardly squeezing into life jackets and paddling with one arm, logging every fish she saw into a dive book.

That trip was where I realised I could do things on my own, without my sister. When I realised that when I did things that made Millie proud, usually I made myself proud too.

Millie hasn't stopped pushing me, although now she pushes me to try a new book club or sign up for an online class. But, I realise, somewhere between now and then, I seem to have stopped believing her. I started to feel like Millie was my younger sister instead of my older one. I cheered her on and encouraged her to take up space but forgot to do the same for myself. I forgot that I could shine just as brightly as she can. As much as I feel like it's her fault for taking up space, I let her do it. I forgot what it feels like to make myself proud and make her proud along the way.

Pippa is right, I can't keep holding myself back. I can't keep worrying about what other people think. If Florida was any indication, maybe being myself will work out. But no matter what happens, it's time to tell Hugh the truth. I picture broaching the topic with him, being more vulnerable than I ever have, admitting that I did something wrong, and I know that I will be proud of myself if I have the hard conversation. Millie would be proud of me too. There's just one last consideration needling at my subconscious.

I know Hugh well enough by now to know that he won't use this to sabotage Millie's career . . . right?

Chapter 24

We pop out of the cluster of mangroves and arrive at a deserted beach on the south side of the island. I make my way over to Hugh, but he avoids me, ducking into a conversation with Natalie again. We make eye contact just as he sits down next to her. He looks away, but not before his mouth flattens into a thin line. I grit my teeth with exasperation. I know he's hurt, but I don't know how to figure out what to do next if I can't even talk to him . . . How am I supposed to decide whether to tell him the truth?

We lounge around the beach and stick our feet in the water, only relaxing for twenty minutes before Vanessa ushers us along. We head down a different path towards a paved road where a large white van waits for us.

'Everyone in,' she says, ushering us into seats.

Our driver's name is Alana. She's either really excited to see people or she's really good at her job, because she gives us a warm, enthusiastic welcome as she drives us to the top of the mountain. She describes the history of Fitzroy Island, how it used to be a part of the mainland, how the trail we were on before and the road we are using now are relics from when the island was used as a lookout location during World War II. She chatters about the turtle sanctuary, how she and her team take a boat out from the mainland every morning, how they have no access to anything but a radio if they need to call for help.

When Andrew asks if she likes working in such a remote environment, she laughs. 'Sometimes I really want to be able to order a pizza for lunch,' she says, 'but there's nothing like being surrounded by nature.'

When we reach the peak, we climb out of the van and Alana herds us to a giant rock, where we have a panoramic view of the island. Crystal blue water stretches out in all directions. We can see both the beach where *Coral Sea Dreaming* is docked and the private cove we had walked to earlier. The turtle sanctuary is at the opposite end of the island, we can just make out the white roof of the building from our perch.

I scramble around the rock and go stand next to Hugh, but he's talking to Alana about turtles. He's listening to her intently, his sandy hair mussed from the wind that's rippling over the mountaintop. She's so passionate about it that there isn't a moment to cut in, and she talks non-stop until we are all back in the van and heading to the place she calls her office. Although every time she says 'office' she giggles, like she's part of an inside joke. I'm envious of her passion for her work, and I find myself daydreaming about the possibility of having a job where I was so removed from corporate America that I didn't even have the option to walk with Bella to get bubble tea.

When we arrive, Alana walks us through a series of outdoor tanks, each one bigger than the last, home to a vast array of sea turtles, some small and some massive.

The sanctuary rescues turtles from everywhere around the Great Barrier Reef, up to hundreds of miles away, responding to distress calls from boats or volunteers who see turtles in need of help. Their team nurses the turtles back to health and releases them back into the wild.

We cluster around a tank, home to a turtle named Sparkle, and listen to Alana explain Sparkle's journey to the centre and her expected release back into the wild. Hugh is standing next to Natalie during Alana's speech, and I can't seem to tear my eyes away from him.

I catch Pippa raising her eyebrows at me and stifling a laugh. I edge closer to her, and she elbows me in the ribs. 'If you talked to him,' she says, 'you wouldn't have to keep your distance.'

I roll my eyes, but I'm grateful to have at least someone to share my feelings with. 'I'm trying,' I say. 'He's avoiding me.'

'You know what I'm going to say.'

'I don't know what you're going to say,' I disagree.

'It's pretty hard to avoid someone when you're sharing a teeny bedroom . . . You know if you do have that conversation, you should also invite Hugh to come with us on our waterfall tour when we get back to Cairns, spend some proper time together away from the fish.'

'I don't know even know if I'm going on that tour,' I point out.

'Let's be real, Millie,' Pippa says sternly, her blonde hair swinging around her face. 'You have nothing better to do.'

Lunch is a simple picnic set up around fold-out tables at the sanctuary. Alana passes out pamphlets explaining where our money would go if we were to donate. I tuck mine into my back pocket. Contributing to a cause like this isn't a bad idea. I could gift a monthly contribution to Millie for Christmas.

Everyone tucks into lunch, but I hardly have any appetite. People take turns asking Alana questions about the sanctuary, and we all listen to her talk about it, fascinated by her life and her work. I notice that Hugh leaves a half-eaten sandwich on his plate too.

The rest of the afternoon passes by in a blur. We go to the beach, where Vanessa says we're free to spend the rest of the afternoon, and I spend close to an hour trying to approach Hugh and losing my courage. He's either talking to Andrew or he sees me coming and walks in the opposite direction. Miguel has started surfing the shallow waves breaking near the beach and keeps trying to get me to join him, hollering at me from his perch in the ocean.

It's only when Natalie walks up to Hugh and they start to chat, both of them standing ankle deep in the calm water, gazing out at the horizon, that I get the nerve to address him.

'Hugh, can I talk to you?' I say quickly, forcing the words out of my mouth before I lose my nerve.

Hugh looks at Natalie, who spins to face me. 'Perfect,' she says, 'just who I wanted to talk to.'

'Actually—' I squirm '—I was hoping to talk to Hugh . . . alone . . .'

'Oh.' Her face falls. 'OK. Hugh, talk to you later.'

'What's up?' Hugh asks once Natalie is out of earshot. His voice is tight.

We start walking along the beach, which eventually curves out of sight from our group.

'I . . . um . . .' I stutter out, unable to form a sentence. I was so focused on getting him alone that I didn't think through what I needed to say. 'I need to tell you something,' I say, as we round the corner and disappear from everyone's view.

Hugh's eyebrows knit together, and for a moment his eyes are unreadable. It feels unimaginable that we haven't spoken all day, when the past three days all we've done is chat. The ache in my heart is so pronounced that my hand flutters to my chest.

'Seriously, Millie?'

'What?'

'You were rude to Natalie and she's been wanting to talk to you.'

'No . . . can we not talk ab—'

'Oh, wait.' Hugh's glowering now, and he kicks at the sand. 'Don't tell me. You're jealous.' He spins to face me and stops walking. 'Is that it?'

We've reached the end of the beach, and Hugh turns to keep walking, climbing over a rock and into the forest. 'She has a boyfriend for God's sake,' he says, 'we're friends! And if you actually bothered to talk to her, you would know why!'

'Wait,' I say, feeling like everything is spinning out of control too quickly. 'That's not it. I'm . . . I'm dealing with a lot right now. I'm not usually this all over the place, I promise.'

Hugh stops. We're both in the trees now, just steps off the beach. 'You're ridiculous, you know that? You tell me you don't want me, and as soon as you see me with someone else, you do?'

'This isn't what this is about!' I cry.

'Really?' Hugh takes a step towards me. My heart is pounding in my chest. He lowers his face closer to mine. 'What is it then?' he asks, but his voice is softer, like the anger has drained out of it. His eyes have returned to their light blue. He raises his thumb gently to my bottom lip.

'Hugh,' I whisper.

He leans in to kiss me, and I raise my face to meet his. His hand palms the back of my head and the small of my back simultaneously, pulling our bodies together. My thoughts disappear from my head and are replaced by *more, more, more*, as I reach my hands into his hair.

Suddenly, he pulls away.

'What is it?' I gasp, short of breath. My head is clouded with desire for him. There are so many words I've left unsaid, but there's no way I can say them now.

'You drive me crazy,' he says.

My pulse is racing. 'Mmm,' I reply, 'I think you just like a challenge.'

He looks at me, and his gaze is so filled with longing that my swimsuit feels like it will disintegrate off my body. His eyes travel the length of my body, up my legs, lingering on my waist, my breasts, my neck. I can't stand the anticipation, and just as I'm about to step forward, he moves, closing the space between us and grabbing the backs of my legs, picking me up with a hand under each thigh and pressing me against a nearby tree. The heat from his pelvis radiates towards mine.

All I can think about is undoing the drawstring of his swimsuit.

'Hugh,' I pant, as he grazes my neck with his lips, his kisses searing my skin. He's reached his hands underneath my swimsuit, and his thumb is circling my nipple. I moan when he lifts my breast into his mouth. I feel him harden at the sound of my arousal, and when I reach down to feel him, he catches my hand and sucks gently on my thumb. I squirm with pleasure.

I'm even more turned on than I was the last time. The heady anticipation has been replaced by knowing what Hugh can do to me.

'Please,' I whisper. He places his hands under my thighs again and steps out of the clearing this time, laying me down on the white sand in between two large rocks.

His grip is so firm that for a second, I don't feel the sand at all, I'm waiting for it to touch my skin. Then I realise I've wrapped my legs around him so tightly that I haven't touched the ground. I relax, and he releases me from his hold, slipping a finger underneath my swimsuit.

He gasps at my wetness, and I whimper at the feeling of his finger inside me. His thumb circles my clit.

'What if they come around the corner?' I manage to ask. I'm panting with desire.

'They won't,' Hugh says. 'And they wouldn't be able to see us.'

Everything seems to grow fuzzy with Hugh's touch, I'm so swept up in desire I can't see straight. His other hand palms my breast again.

'You,' I manage to say, 'I want you.'

I grab for the strings on my swimsuit and untie them. He brings his head down slowly and kisses me right where I need it. I writhe with pleasure, driving my fingers into his hair. I can't feel my toes anymore. I can hardly feel the sand.

By the time Hugh steps out of his swimsuit, I'm on the brink. If I can't have him, I feel like I'll die.

He takes a moment. 'I want to savour you,' he says, before placing his thumb on my clit one more time.

'Hugh,' I whimper. He kisses me again, this time his tongue is intense, claiming my mouth like he could consume me entirely. I suck his bottom lip into my mouth.

His hardness pushes into me, and I feel like I could explode. I see stars, clinging to his back, my fingertips driving into the divot between his shoulders.

He is slow at first, exploring, and as he moves faster, I grow closer and closer to coming totally undone.

When he looks me in the eyes I lose it, unravelling into pleasure, and watching me, feeling me, makes him climax too, both of us collapsing into a panting heap.

We lie on the sand together for what feels like an hour, not saying anything. I don't open my mouth, worried I'll break the spell. Our fingertips trace lazy circles on each other, until we know it's time to head back. I never gather the courage to say anything. I don't want to ruin the moment, our moment, underneath a cloudless Australian sky.

We dip in the ocean to rinse off the sand before walking down the beach to meet the others. I can't meet Pippa's gaze because I'm afraid I'll betray myself immediately, but I can't keep a smile from playing across my lips. Hugh's hand brushes my ass casually as we approach the group, and I know without looking that he's trying not to smirk.

We make our way down the rickety dock. The ocean has gotten choppier as the afternoon progressed, and the boat is rocking up and down with the waves. Everyone struggles to find their balance at first.

Hugh's face pales as he sits down on a bench in the captain's room. He doesn't remain in his seat long enough for the rest of us to sit down. Almost instantly, he is on his feet and making his way towards the front of the boat. Miguel looks at me with a mixture of disgust and conspiratorial superiority. It instantly confirms what I was afraid of. Hugh is seasick, and Miguel is wondering why I've been spending so much time with a liability instead of spending time with him. He raises his eyebrows at me ever so slightly before slipping below deck, presumably to get as far away from Hugh as possible.

After ten minutes I find a glass of water and gently walk over to where Hugh is clutching the railing.

'Anything I can do?' I ask softly.

He turns, all the colour drained from his face. His eyes are a light icy-blue again.

'This is rough,' he says.

'Water?' I ask, searching for any way to help.

Hugh shakes his head no.

I rub his back, gently placing my hand in between his shoulder blades. His skin is warm to the touch. Even though he's sick, touching him is reassuring. Being near him I feel balanced, like I can breathe again.

'It'll be OK,' I whisper.

I help him get ready for bed, bringing him water and a plain piece of bread in case he feels like he can eat.

When I dip a washcloth in cool water and lay it across his forehead, his eyes flutter open.

'Millie,' he says. His voice is hoarse, but he's managing a wry smile.

'What do you need?' I grab his bedframe to steady myself as the boat lurches again.

'I'm sorry I'm taking away our night together.' Hugh chuckles in disbelief at the situation, his throat scratchy. He leans his head back into the pillow and takes a deep breath, like that comment took every ounce of energy he had left.

'We have the mainland,' I say, smiling.

'I was hoping you'd say that.' Hugh grins.

'But I need to talk to you about something.'

He nods. 'As you wish.'

'And I still don't understand how we would navigate the Sydney–Columbus problem.' I can't resist pointing it out. I'm hoping that if we agree this could never go anywhere, I wouldn't ever need to tell Hugh the truth.

'That doesn't matter,' he says. 'I'll see you in April anyway.' He squints at me. 'Right?' He's referring to the conference he's going to in April to present his paper, the paper on the extinction of the butterfly wrasse. I know Millie would kill me for agreeing to participate in the circulation of Hugh's research, especially at her expense, but I can't help but agree to see him. A two-hour flight is a lot closer than a twenty-four-hour travel day.

'If you want to, then yes.'

'It's settled then. I'll see you in Boston. We can figure it out then.'

'That doesn't settle anything,' I argue back softly.

'Sydney is better.' Hugh closes his eyes briefly and then opens them again. 'I hated when we were avoiding each other all day.'

'I hated it more.'

'We would figure it out, you know,' he says. His voice is sleepy.

'I can't leave my family,' I respond, my voice in a whisper. 'They need me.' Although as soon as the words are out of my mouth, I'm not sure if they need me or if I need them.

Hugh squeezes my hand gently when I take the washcloth away. I leave him in peace, trying and failing to find distraction upstairs. Eventually, I come back to our room. He's finally been able to drift off.

'Goodnight, Hugh Harris,' I whisper, as I climb up into my bunk.

Chapter 25

One dive left

Hugh groans from his spot on the tiny twin bed. He looks comical in it, his six-foot two frame stretched out across the mattress. One of his legs dangles off the side. He's somehow got more tanned with each passing day. He's come a long way since I only knew him as 'angry suntan man'. His calf muscle twitches as he rouses himself out of sleep.

'Feeling better?' I ask. I've already had a cup of coffee and changed into my swimsuit. Once the sun came up, I couldn't sleep. Today is my last chance to spot the wrasse. The waters are much calmer this morning, the boat hardly rocking at all.

'Much,' he says, although he still hasn't opened his eyes.

Colour has returned to his cheeks. He looks healthy again. Staring at him, I wish I could stay here, in this cabin, for hours. I want to tell him the truth. Then I want him to forgive me. I want to feel his lips on mine once more, his strong hands, the gentle pads of his fingers on my skin. I want to run my hands through his hair, down his back, feel him respond to my touch.

'Millie,' he moans, interrupting my thoughts, 'I can't get up. I'm tired.'

'I'm really glad you're feeling better,' I say, reaching down to pat him on the shoulder. When my fingers touch his skin, electricity zaps through me.

He cracks his eyes open. 'Thank you for taking care of me.' He smiles, and then it quickly turns into a grimace. He blushes, and I register that it's the first time I've seen him flush such a deep red.

'It was nothing.' I wave it off.

'Seriously.' Hugh looks at me intently. 'I owe you one.'

'No, you don't.'

'Am I remembering correctly that you still wanted to see me in Boston, even after the night I had?'

'Maybe,' I say coyly.

He punches the air triumphantly. 'And you have to talk to me about something.' He looks me in the eye. 'And I take it, now is not the time.'

I shake my head. 'They're prepping our dive,' I say, 'we have to get ready.'

'Already?' Hugh moans again, turning to his side. 'I'm exhausted.'

'I would say you can stay and rest, but I've got a wrasse to find, and I need my partner.'

I stride out the door, leaving him grumbling in my wake.

The group gets ready in record time.

'This will be our longest dive,' Vanessa announces. We all smile at each other, giddy with the prospect of the best dive of the trip. Nobody acknowledges that it's also our last.

Derek is lugging around his camera again. Andrew is practically shaking with excitement. Miguel is keeping his distance from Hugh, who managed to rouse himself from sleep and put on his stinger suit in time for Vanessa's briefing about the reef. When he climbed onto deck, Aaron clapped him on the back, congratulating him for 'sticking out a rough go last night'.

Pippa had glued herself to my side as soon as she woke up, waiting until we were drinking coffee alone on the deck to ask me if I had told Hugh.

'Did you see him last night?' I asked her. 'How was I supposed to tell him that while he was half delirious?'

'I didn't know if you told him when you two were off on your own!' she retorted.

'We were . . . busy.'

'Ooo!' Pippa hooted. 'I want all of those details. And tell him today! Then invite him on the waterfall tour with us. It'll be so fun. But I don't want any drama.' She raised her eyebrows at me. 'Deal?'

'Deal.'

Hugh and I sit down to strap in and perform our buddy checks next to Andrew and Pippa, who are chatting excitedly about the last items on their list they want to see – Andrew wants to see a glow worm, and Pippa wants to see an octopus since she missed one on our night dive.

We strap into our BCDs and perform our buddy checks. Yesterday feels like a lifetime ago, but every time Hugh touches me, I feel like I'm back in that moment, our lips inches apart, his breath tickling my cheeks. We make eye contact. His eyes are a peaceful blue today, a mix between aqua and the turquoise of the sky, like the deeper parts of the ocean.

'You guys seem like you're getting excited,' Pippa says innocently. I can hear her trying to hide the laughter in her voice.

'Yep,' I say, casting my eyes down at the floor of the boat and trying to hide the flush in my cheeks.

'Millie's gonna find that fish she's been looking for,' Pippa says, 'I can feel it.'

I groan.

When we hit the railing for our last entry, Hugh slips in backwards. I take a deep breath, staring at the ocean waves roiling beneath the boat, and follow, entering the same way Hugh did, head first.

My nerves only grow as we begin our descent. We go hand-over-hand down the mooring line and congregate at the bottom. There is a buzz of energy around our group this morning. A school of sweetlips fish lazily swim by us. Their mouths and tails are bright yellow, their bodies black and white striped. They are striking, and we all stop to stare. Vanessa taps her carabiner on her oxygen tank and forces us to move along.

'A lot to cover today,' she had told us on deck. 'No dawdling.'

We dutifully follow her, our fearless leader, towards the reef. The sweetlips fish disappear in our wake. We swim over another giant clam, ringed in neon purple barnacles. Colourful fish are hovering above it. One of them is purple. There is a yellow stripe down its back. Before I can see if it has an extra fin on its underbelly, it twitches its tail and swims away. I want to believe it was a butterfly wrasse, but I can't be sure.

The further we swim the more my anxiety rises. My breathing is picking up. I check my PSI. I'm taking in more oxygen than usual, unable to regulate my intake with my nerves spiking. Hugh notices, reaching for my hand, letting his fingertips brush mine.

I take out my digital camera and hold it in one hand, trying to manifest a butterfly wrasse appearing. Hugh notices and our eyes meet. He flashes me a thumbs-up. I try to ignore the fact that if I find these fish, he'll lose his promotion and his publication opportunity.

We follow Vanessa towards a looming coral structure. It's the most colourful one we've passed so far. The ocean floor is dotted with blues, pinks, purples and yellows. There are huge cracks and crevices with fish teeming in and out of them. I see the telltale flash of brown spots — a pufferfish darting between the rocks. I struggle to remain optimistic and enjoy the dive – it's one of the best we've been on, but I don't feel that familiar tug of excitement as the group passes over a brain coral with a large crab scuttling over the top.

Someone in the group spots a moray eel. I see a flash of its large dark-green mouth and I back up, away from the hole it's hiding in. Moray eels are dangerous. Their jaws are extremely strong. But their long sleek forest-green bodies are also hypnotically beautiful. Derek hovers to take a picture. We see another crab scuttle across the rock, claws waving in the air.

I station myself next to staghorn coral, camera out, and wait. I feel like every cell of my body is hoping. Familiar worries surface in my brain, that I'm not good enough, qualified enough to successfully do this for my sister. That I'm a fraud and a liar. I look over at Hugh, who is just as intently searching for the fish, and I feel guilt tug in my chest.

How will I come back empty-handed to Millie? How will I face myself, a failure, returning home to a job I hate?

I feel the commotion of the others swimming behind me. Miguel calls over the group to show them something else. I remain right where I am.

Time ticks by. I stare at the coral, wondering if I would have a better chance if I swam around it or stayed put. Hugh is swimming in gentle circles around the coral I'm hovering over, every now and then taking an interest in something else. I hear the clang of Vanessa's carabiner. *This can't be it. The trip can't be over.*

Tears sting my eyes as I turn to swim away, accepting defeat. I'm making my way to Vanessa when I realise I forgot to make sure Hugh was behind me.

I turn around to see Hugh hovering, motionless, in the spot I had just vacated. His attention is snapped to something, but I can't quite make out what it is. My heart starts beating faster.

I kick towards Hugh slowly, barely breathing. About two feet underneath his nose are three fish, little, no bigger than my palm. Bright, fluorescent purple, almost magenta. There is a yellow stripe down their backs. I'm terrified to look, but I cast my gaze towards their underbellies. Sure enough, there is a tiny fin moving back and forth, helping keep the fish stationary.

I don't even want to blink in case I miss them. I carefully manoeuvre until I'm right next to Hugh, who is spellbound, staring at the three little fish nosing around the staghorn coral. The butterfly wrasse. I finally found them. I have full tears running down my cheeks now, fogging up my mask. *This is it!* I think, forcing myself into action. I use every ounce of my concentration not to move, lest I scare the fish. I press the button on my camera.

Chapter 26

Just as I'm taking the photo, all the fish dart away from me. Impossibly quick, so quick that what happens doesn't register until I've turned around in confusion.

Hugh has backpedalled and is hovering right behind me.

I feel fury building in my brain like a pressure cooker. *He moved?! He scared away the FISH!* My brain goes a thousand miles a minute. *Did Hugh sabotage me on purpose?* He wouldn't dare . . . would he? But Hugh is turning around too, like he's just as confused as I am.

Over his shoulder, I see what really spooked the fish. A massive potato cod swims close by, with Vanessa and Derek trailing behind it. Vanessa must have tapped her carabiner to call attention to the cod. Potato cod can grow up to five feet long, this one is probably about that size, and are known for being inquisitive and playful, as well as for the potato-shaped markings on their skin. Most likely, the movement of the cod, Derek and Vanessa made the fish jumpy. I watch the cod as it passes, its mouth opening and closing in cartoon fashion.

Once it's passed Hugh turns back towards me. Slowly, he points at his chest, then his eyes, then towards the staghorn coral where the butterfly wrasse were. Then he flashes a thumbs-up, pats me on the back and swims away.

There's no longer any doubt in my mind that Hugh saw them too. *I found the butterfly wrasse. I did it!* My relief is so euphoric that I start to swim away from the coral. I'm ready to be back on the boat, speeding towards Cairns. The sooner I can tell Millie, the better.

But something tugs at my thoughts, and I remember I need a picture, which I'm not confident I have. My excitement ebbs. I turn back to the coral, watching and waiting for the butterfly wrasse to return. After a few beats, I notice the movement of other divers around me, but I don't look away. *Come on*, I think. I don't know if I've ever felt this desperate. *Please – just one fish.* There's no way that the picture I took earlier will turn out, the fish darted away too quickly. *I just need one clear picture*, I think. I feel so frustrated that tears start to form at the edges of my eyes.

I press my fingers down on the top of my goggles and blow forcefully out of my nose to clear my mask of water. I keep watching the coral. I focus on the millions of polyps dotting its surface like pores. I can't bear to think about the photograph on my camera that is undoubtedly blurry and completely unhelpful. Angelfish and cardinalfish and grunt swim by me. There are striped fish and spotted fish and neon fish and rainbow fish. There are no butterfly wrasse.

Miguel hovers nearby for long enough that I think he's spotted something, but just when I turn to see, he swims away. Eventually, I hear the familiar clang of a carabiner on Vanessa's oxygen tank. This time she's actually calling us back. I feel a pit of desperation in my stomach that is so heavy I feel like I will sink to the bottom and never come up again. I have failed Millie. No one will take my word as gospel truth that an entire fish species is still alive. Especially since I'm not even a marine biologist.

I let myself cry.

I don't stop crying until I am on the boat, my BCD shucked off, my weight belt littered on the floor, and my mask placed back in the communal equipment bucket. I feel silly crying in public without a snorkel to hide my tears, so I sniffle and head straight for the cabin to shower, hoping I can quell my tears by the time I'm done getting cleaned up.

'Millie.' Hugh's hand is on my shoulder. It's heavy and warm and stops me in my tracks. 'Millie, turn around.' His voice is gentle and commanding, and I find myself rotating to face him.

'Oh,' he says, when he sees my puffy, swollen face and bloodshot eyes. 'But you saw them.' He brings a thumb to my cheek and wipes away a tear. He sounds tired, but not angry.

'But I didn't get the photo.' My voice breaks.

'Millie,' Hugh says with a sigh. 'You just need a witness to corroborate that you saw them.'

'I don't see how that matters,' I say, my eyes brimming with tears again, threatening to spill over, 'when you are that witness.'

'Yeah,' says Hugh. He steadies himself against the railing and runs his other hand through his hair. 'But I'm not going to do that to you.' He sighs again.

'But—' I say.

'No buts,' he interrupts. 'All you need is a signed dive log from the two of us that a species was sighted. And we both saw those fish.'

Could that be true? I wonder. *Millie would know.* 'Are you sure?' I ask Hugh.

He nods. 'I'm sure. The witnesses have to be marine biologists, it can't just be anyone, but I've done it before for a buddy I work with when we both saw a rare species of turtle.'

I gulp. 'That's a big sacrifice for you,' I mumble.

'It's not a sacrifice when it's the truth,' he says simply, like it's the easiest logic in the world. Although his voice is a little huskier than normal.

'OK,' I whisper. I place a hand on his forearm. 'If you're sure?' I already feel my emotions clearing, my tears subsiding, making way for elated joy. I start to smile.

'I'm sure,' Hugh says, wrapping his arms around me in a hug. 'I'm happy for you, Millie. And honestly, I'm happy those little suckers made it.'

'Oh my God,' I whisper. I'm not sure if I say it in relief or because being pressed up against Hugh's chest feels terrifyingly right. I melt into his frame. He pulls away first and looks intently at my face. When he seems satisfied that I'm no longer at risk of falling into full sobs, he pulls me back into a hug.

The heat between us could sizzle the remaining water from our skin. His pecs press up against my chest and his forearms are heavy and strong around my shoulder blades. Even after being in the water, he still smells like Hugh. I breathe in deeply from the crook of his neck.

'Did you see it?' Pippa asks, poking her head from behind Hugh.

We break apart and I nod the affirmative to Pippa, my eyes still a little teary.

'I knew you could do it!' she cries, triumphant.

I grab onto the railing to steady myself. I didn't realise how much tension and fear I was holding onto until it was gone. I feel free.

'I can't wait to tell my sister.' I take a deep breath of the ocean air.

'She'll be excited for you?' Hugh asks.

'You have no idea.'

The boat ride back to Cairns takes upwards of three hours. I am blissed out, lying on the platform. Pippa sways in the hammock above me, chatting excitedly about the waterfall tour. I have yet to invite Hugh because I haven't had the talk with him. After finding the wrasse, my impersonation felt even more explicit. I also wanted to give him space to come to terms with whatever this means for his paper and his promotion. If he's disappointed or upset with me because of what I found, he hasn't let it show.

I watch Miguel dismantle the oxygen tanks for the last time, cracking up with Vanessa as he does it. His brown hair gleams in the sun and his smile is bigger than ever, like he's excited to be done with the trip too. If Hugh hadn't been on this trip, there's no denying that Miguel could have been fun.

Andrew is pacing the deck and talking animatedly to Derek about how excited he is to be on dry land. Every now and then I crack my eyes open and gaze at Hugh, who is lounging on the platform within reach of my fingertips. His eyes are closed, and his mouth is slightly open, his full bottom lip sticking out. I watch the rise and fall of his strong, tanned chest. I resist the urge to touch him, although with finding the butterfly wrasse off my plate, it's all I can think about.

Will I have to be honest with him tonight? Or should I let us just enjoy our last night together . . .

Pippa catches me staring at Hugh and snickers loud enough to disturb him. He mumbles something incoherent, raising his eyebrows at her. I glare at Pippa. She laughs and flips over in the hammock.

'We're nearing the harbour,' Aaron announces, prompting everyone to congregate, once again, in the captain's room. Hugh wakes up and trudges inside, following Pippa and me. One by one, we filter in and out of the downstairs cabins, repacking our stuff and preparing our exit.

Finally, we see Cairns.

I take a deep breath when the first building comes into view.

Being closer to land means being that much closer to cell service . . . and to finding out how Millie's surgery went. Natalie already has her cell phone out. She's waving it in the air, trying to get signal. Derek is fretting over his camera. Things feel like they are returning to normal, like the closer we get to land, the more I will feel like this never happened. Hugh and I sit together in our normal seats by Aaron's chair.

'This is weird,' Hugh says.

'Like the closer we get to land the more this feels like a fever dream?' I reply.

'Exactly.'

A shiver runs up my spine at how in sync we are after just five days. I slightly move my thigh so that our legs are touching. Hugh glances at me out of the corner of my eye, and I pretend not to notice. I drink in his stature and his smell – sunscreen and woodsy with a hint of fresh grass and male cologne.

Hugh places a hand on my thigh. 'Now that you're done focusing on finding that fish. And now that I'm feeling better,' he mumbles throatily, never taking his eyes off the horizon.

'I'm listening,' I whisper coyly.

Just then, Aaron abruptly cuts the motor, startling Hugh's hand off my knee. We've entered a no-wake zone. Andrew and Pippa turn their phones on, and they start to vibrate with what I'm sure is a deluge of calls and texts they missed while we were on the water.

'You gonna check on your sister?' Hugh asks, gesturing at the phone that still sits on airplane mode in my lap.

'I'm nervous.'

Hugh reaches over, swipes down on my phone screen, and toggles the button to turn off airplane mode. 'Better do it sooner than later.'

'Thank you,' I say. I mean it. I know he's right, and I didn't have the strength to do it myself. My hands are shaking.

My phone starts to vibrate, first slowly, every twenty seconds or so, and then furiously, like it could explode. My breathing shallows.

I watch as texts pour in from my mom, coming in random order.

She's in surgery.
We're waiting.
We had to go back to the hospital.
She's headed back.
Murphy is doing fine without you.
We're headed home!
What have you been feeding this dog?! He eats so much!
Millie says she loves you.
She's through surgery!
Honey, Millie has an infection. We're taking her back to the hospital.

And then . . .
A missed call from last night at 10.20 p.m.
A voicemail.
I press on the voicemail with shaky hands, fumbling to bring the phone up to my face. Hugh rests a reassuring hand on my knee, noticing that something may be wrong.

With the motor off, the air on the boat is still and silent. We are drifting lazily towards the dock. The voicemail from my mother starts blaring from my phone. I barely register that I must have accidentally hit the speakerphone button. I listen with a racing heart as my mom speaks.

'Andi? Shhh,' the voicemail breaks and turns fuzzy, then my mom's voice comes through crystal clear again.

'Paul, I'm leaving Andi a voicemail. Honey? Millie has a bad infection. We had to go back to the hospital. We're here now – we've been here about . . .' she pauses '. . . about sixteen hours. Millie's asleep. The doctors say this complicates the road to recovery.' She pauses again and clears her throat. 'I know you're not supposed to come home for another day, but do you think you could come home early?' Her voice gets further away from the phone. 'Paul, she needs to know,' she tells my dad sternly. 'I love you, sweetheart. Call me when you get this.'

I stop breathing. I don't feel like I'm in my body anymore. At some point in the voicemail, Hugh has taken his hand off my thigh. My heart slows. I barely register Pippa's eyes on mine, large and sympathetic. Even Aaron looks concerned.

Nobody speaks. There's a faint ringing in my ears. It drowns out the seagulls calling and the sound of the boat's motor.

'We'll be on land in five,' Aaron says softly. 'I'll radio for a taxi to take you to the airport.'

I nod my head. My mouth feels like it's filled with cotton. I can't seem to form any words with my lips. *My sister*, is all I can think. *My big sister*.

Tears pool in my eyelids and start cascading down my cheeks.

My head feels light and my knees feel weak. I place a hand on the bench next to me to steady myself. *My sister*. I feel blood draining from my face. My hands feel clammy. I breathe in through my nose. *Breathe*, I think. *Just make it to the airport*. I can see the dock in the distance. I lock my eyes on it. *There's nothing you can do from here*, I tell myself, but it doesn't make me feel any better.

I feel a tear land on my thigh in a heavy drop. I can't help but picture Millie in a hospital bed, alone, without me. Thinking about the beeping of machines makes my breath come faster, in shallower spurts. I wipe my nose with the back of my hand. *My big sister*.

Just then, Natalie's head snaps to attention. She smacks her palm on her forehead.

'Andi!' she exclaims. She covers her mouth immediately, as if she knew right away that was the wrong thing to say in the moment.

Instinctively, I swivel to look at her, responding to my name. Pippa turns to glare at Natalie, opening her mouth to interrupt her, but she's too late.

'I'm sorry,' she mumbles. 'I— that's just what they called you at the airport, it's been bothering me this whole time. You're Andi.' She starts to babble, more than I've ever heard her talk before.

My big sister is still echoing through my brain. I'm having trouble concentrating on what Natalie is saying. I'm not even sure if I care anymore.

'I kept wanting to ask you about it but . . .' Natalie's saying, 'I wanted to make sure I had your name right because I was hoping . . .' I tune her out again. The dock is closer now. All I care about is getting to Millie as fast as I can.

But Hugh's voice breaks through my daze. 'Wait . . . Is that true?' he asks from beside me, his voice low. 'I thought your mom was . . . so, you're not Millie, you're the . . . the other one?' Realisation dawns on his face slowly. 'If you're Andi . . .' He trails off.

I think about lying again, saying I switched names with my sister when we were little and I go by Millie, but even to my exhausted brain that story sounds flimsy, so instead I just nod. This is too much to process, all at once. I hear Aaron softly communicating with a cab driver, describing who he needs to wait for at the edge of the pier. Brown curly hair, average build.

'You're not Millie.' Hugh's voice is hard.

I nod again. 'No.' For a moment I wish I could just step into the ocean and let the waves pull me under. I don't feel strong enough to face this conversation. I don't feel strong enough to face whatever is waiting for me at home.

'So, you're not a marine biologist?'

I shake my head again.

'But you knew everything.' It comes out as a question and a statement.

'I studied it in college.'

'But you're good.'

'Thank you,' I whisper.

Hugh's face crumples as the information continues to sink in. His eyes are dark and stormy, his mouth settles into a grim line. He's created distance between us, scooting further from me on the bench, and our legs are no longer touching.

I open my mouth, but no words come out.

After a moment, Hugh lets out a sharp bark of a laugh. 'And you were angry with me because I didn't tell you about my paper,' he says, in a tone dripping with disdain.

For the second time in two minutes, my heart completely shatters.

Chapter 27

True to his word, Aaron tells me a cab is idling at the end
of the pier when we pull in.

Everyone's been quiet since my bad news, Natalie's
outburst and Hugh's revelation. Hugh stalked to the
front of the boat shortly after he realised I was Andi. I
couldn't bring myself to go after him. My legs felt like
jello. My heart was pounding, each beat thundering
Millie, Millie, Millie.

Pippa hustles me downstairs to grab my bags as the
crew is docking the boat. I give her a tearful hug goodbye,
promising to call.

'Tell me how Millie is,' she says, squeezing my arm
one last time.

I promise that I will.

I am the first one off, scrambling to disembark with
my luggage in tow. I wave and thank Aaron and Vanessa,
Miguel pulls me in for a quick hug. He touches my cheek
affectionately. 'Good luck,' he says, his accent thicker
than usual.

I break apart from Miguel and look to Hugh, searching for forgiveness in his eyes, but he is at the front of
the boat, unreadable and far away, all hard muscle and
tanned skin.

I pull my suitcase down the rickety wooden dock, not
even trying to avoid the little mounds of bird poop. Time

is crucial – if I rush to the airport and there is space on the flight, I can get out of Cairns tonight. When Aaron called the taxi, Pippa had the wherewithal to ask about the bends, making sure that if I were to make the flight, I wouldn't get sick. Vanessa and Aaron assured me that because yesterday we didn't dive, and this morning we only dived once, I should be OK to make the trip even though I'll be a couple hours short of the twelve-hour window. I hardly even care about nitrogen poisoning anymore, I just want to see my sister.

I'm yanking my luggage over a stuck-up wooden board when I hear flip-flops slapping the dock behind me.

'Hey,' Hugh breathes.

'I really have got to go,' I say. I can't turn around. I can't face him.

'I'm coming with you.'

I keep walking. 'You don't have to do that,' I say, but my steps falter.

'Pippa told me I was being a bloody idiot and that I shouldn't let you leave while we're in the middle of a fight. Especially given what's happening with your sister. And that you had good reasons for doing what you did.'

Despite all the emotions swirling in my head, a half-hearted chuckle forces its way out of my throat. 'Of course she did.'

'I don't understand why you did what you did, but I don't want to leave us this way. At least let me go with you to the airport. We can talk on the way.' Hugh grabs my luggage and starts carrying it. I feel a weight lift from my shoulders.

'OK,' I manage to squeak out before I start to cry.

Hugh puts my stuff in the trunk, and we climb into the back seat of the taxi. I can't get comfortable, I'm so nervous that there won't be space on the plane. I'm leaning forward, willing the driver to go faster.

I try to call my mom, desperate for answers, but it's the middle of the night and she doesn't pick up. The backs of my legs stick to the leather vinyl. I would usually dread getting on a fourteen-hour flight without a shower, but now it seems like the least of my problems.

'I'm sorry about Millie,' Hugh says, as the car pulls away from the kerb. His voice catches as he says Millie's name.

'I'm scared,' I whisper. My voice breaks on the last word.

Hugh squeezes my hand.

After a few minutes of silence, he clears his throat. 'Why didn't you tell me?' he asks quietly.

'I tried. I was going to earlier, on the beach, but then, you know . . . we got . . . distracted . . . and then I wanted to last night . . .'

'That's the thing you had to talk to me about? That you've been pretending to be someone else the entire time I've known you?'

I nod, staring at my lap.

'Who was I even talking to on Instagram?' I can tell he's trying his best to keep his anger at bay, but it's creeping into his voice.

I lay a tentative hand on his forearm. 'Me,' I confess, finally meeting his eyes. 'I was pretending to be Millie because you insulted my grammar. I proofread all of her stuff.' I sniffle. 'And then she had to get surgery, and she didn't want to miss her chance to find the wrasse. And now . . .' I trail off and start to cry, my voice breaking and tears welling up in my eyes.

Hugh wraps his arm around me protectively and pulls me into his chest. 'Shhh,' he repeats softly, stroking my hair. 'It'll be OK.'

'I'm so worried,' I cry, smearing snot across his shirt. 'And I'm sorry I have to go like this,' I say through sobs. 'I didn't mean for it to go this far.'

Hugh doesn't say anything. I pull myself out of his grip and look him in the eyes. They're brilliantly blue.

'I know why you have to go,' he says, reaching out to wipe a tear from my cheek. 'I understand.'

I cry harder.

The taxi pulls up at the airport and Hugh jumps out, beating me to the trunk to unload my luggage. When the driver leaves and we're alone on the kerb, both of us fall silent.

'I don't want to pretend like I'm OK with what you did,' Hugh says finally, kicking a pebble next to the road. 'But I want to hear your full explanation, and I know now isn't a good time to give it.'

If anything could have made me like Hugh more, that sentence was it. I wrap my arms around him, giving him a huge hug, nestling once more into his smell.

'Thank you,' I breathe. There are so many things I want to say to Hugh. Apologising seems impossible with so much emotion already clouding my mind. 'I'll miss you,' is what comes out of my mouth instead.

'I'll miss you too.' Hugh runs a hand through his hair. 'Maybe I can get that explanation in Boston?' he asks.

'OK,' I agree, relief flooding through me at the thought of seeing him in April. I can figure out how to explain everything by then. 'Boston.'

Hugh leans down and kisses me, swiftly and deeply. I melt into his arms, my emotions running so high that his kiss makes me want to cry. Knowing I have a date when I'll see him makes my trip back home a bit more bearable.

When we break apart, I turn and start to head into the airport. I take one last look at the giant green rolling mountains dominating the landscape behind me. I'm going to miss Australia. I'll miss the laid-back nature of the people that choose to live here. I'll miss the awe-inspiring natural beauty of the country, the way it feels like there is so much left to explore and discover. I'll miss the reef, with its colours, salty air and turquoise waters.

I'm almost to the doors, which are automatically sliding open and closed, sending a woosh of air conditioning towards me every time they shut, when I realise I didn't get Hugh to sign my dive log. I've been keeping a record in my dive journal of what fish I saw and when, and the entry for the last day has the butterfly wrasse and a place for a witness's signature.

I hesitate. If what Hugh said on the boat is true, then his signature is the proof I need for Millie. But the faster I get inside the airport, the better chance I have at getting a seat on the early plane. *I need to go in.* But I can't return home to Millie empty-handed.

'Hugh,' I shout, turning and sprinting towards him. He's at the far end of the walkway, and I have to run to catch up to him. 'My dive log.' I gasp for air. 'Can you sign it?'

I'm already pulling it out of my backpack by the time I see Hugh's face. His eyebrows are knit together, his eyes are dark.

I hand him the paper and he takes it gently. He glances at it and his eyebrows knit together. 'Seriously?' he asks in a small voice.

'Um,' I stammer, 'yes?' I squirm. 'I have to go.'

'Millie—' he says, before he clears his throat and corrects himself. 'I mean Andi. Andi, I can't.' He starts to hand the dive log back to me.

'But . . .' I falter. We're both holding onto the paper now. He's pushing it into my hands, but I'm refusing to take it. 'You said we were OK, that I would see you in Boston. How . . . how are you refusing to sign it? We saw the fish.' *This isn't happening*, I'm thinking. *He's not going back on his word already. He's not changing his mind about us already. He's not doing this to get back at me . . . is he?*

Hugh takes a step back, putting distance between us. 'Andi, I can't sign that.'

'What do you mean you can't?'

'I don't understand how you're asking me that. That is an official Global Marine Biology record log. And it's false. I can't sign it.'

'But we both saw the fish!' I say, exasperated. My voice is louder than I intended. I feel anger surging in my chest. My heart rate is rising again. *This can't be happening*.

'But you're not Millie. And it says Millie right there.' Hugh points at the paper. His jawline is more pronounced than usual, like he's clenching his perfect teeth.

I know I'm not Millie! I want to scream. I want to reach out and touch him, I want to shake him back and forth, erasing the anger from his face. I want to break down the wall I feel like he's building.

'But I'm doing this *for* Millie. I thought you understood that.'

He doesn't budge.

'Hugh, you can't be serious,' I say through a clenched jaw. I can feel him shutting me out. My chest tightens. My heart rate picks up. I don't know how we got here. *Weren't we just making plans to see each other in Boston?* I think. *How do I get back to that?*

'I don't know what to tell you, you're not a marine biologist. It wouldn't be ethical.' Hugh's expression hardens with frustration.

'I can't believe you,' I say, fighting back tears. 'This is it? You're just going to refuse to help me? After everything?'

'Look, I'm sorry.'

'You're sorry?' I sputter back.

'Andi, you can't make this my fault.' Hugh is incredulous. 'First you lie to me for days and now this? Asking me to sign something that's false?' He hesitates. 'I thought I was going to get over you lying. I thought with time we could move past it. But, Andi, this is too much. I don't see how you can't understand why I don't want to do what you're asking me to do.' And the way he says my name, with such finality, such resignation, completely does me in.

'I really do want the best for your sister,' he says, but he's already turning to leave.

'But,' I say, refusing to believe that this is how he will leave me, that a stupid falsified dive log will be his last straw, that he will really go without giving me the one thing that I'm desperate to do for my sister. I can't wrap my head around him walking away from me, from us, after the last five days we shared together.

But he does. He leaves without so much as a wave goodbye.

I am left standing on the kerb, watching helplessly as he gets into an Uber, my dive log fluttering uselessly in my hand.

Chapter 28

Life on land

I make it onto the earlier flight, probably because I sobbed to the gate agent incoherently until she rebooked me. I try to call my mom one more time, but she doesn't answer. I leave her a message with the details of my flight.

The plane hurtles into the night sky. The man next to me nods off, his head dropping towards his chest. I hug the window, pressed to the side of my seat. Only when the flight attendant asks me nicely what I would like to drink do I realise that I have just been sitting, staring out the window, for the better part of an hour.

'Um,' I fumble.

She rattles off options. 'We have water, soda, coffee, tea, wine—'

'Wine,' I interject. 'Red wine, please.'

She sets down a flimsy plastic cup and I take a big sip, the acidity tingling the back of my throat. I resist the urge to knock it all back at once. I stare at the screen in front of me some more. Nothing is playing. I watch the flight tracker blip, flickering in and out. I alternate between staring out the window and falling into fits of sleep. I'm too shocked to be angry, and I'm too numb to be sad. That will come later.

My mom picks me up from the airport, and we drive straight to the hospital where my dad is waiting for us. As soon as I breathe in the cold Columbus air, I want to turn around and go back to Australia. I miss it already. I feel like I'm being pulled back to it, even from this far away, and I don't think it's just because it's a balmy summer there and the icy dead of winter here.

My mom fills me in on the way. I learn that Millie's surgery had gone well, better than they hoped even, but things took a turn the second day she was back home. She had a bad fever and chills, which she dismissed as post-surgery exhaustion. Eventually, my Mom called the doctor, just to check and see if Millie's symptoms were normal. They ended up rushing to the hospital because the doctor thought it sounded like Millie had a blood infection, which she did. The infection overwhelmed her body, her blood pressure dropped so low that the only way to stabilise her was to keep her overnight and for a couple of days.

Mom retells it with a shaky voice.

'She'll be OK,' she says, and I don't know if she says it more for herself than for me.

'Thank God you called the doctor,' I say, gently placing a hand on her arm.

Mom starts to cry, which pulls me out of the reverie I've been living in for the past twenty hours. My flight to Dallas, my connection back to Columbus, I had remained perfectly stoic the entire time. I watched movies that I didn't pay attention to and could hardly remember the plot of. I read and reread the same chapters of my book. Now, sitting in my mom's old Toyota Highlander, I feel my veneer start to crack.

'I bet it was so scary, Mom,' I manage to say, although I'm starting to sniffle. I start to cry. She reaches over and squeezes my hand.

'She's doing better now. Her blood pressure is back to normal, and she only has a low-grade fever.'

I feel some of my terror start to ebb, but I know I won't feel relieved until I see Millie myself. 'That's good. Is she resting? Can I see her when we get there?'

'She might be asleep, but we can go in. Visiting hours are from nine to six and . . .' she pauses and checks her watch ' . . . we should arrive right at nine.'

I turn on my phone in the last ten minutes of our drive, expecting Hugh to have messaged me. He hasn't. I feel rejected and disappointed and hurt. I try to ignore my own feelings, but it's hard for me to wrap my head around the fact that he didn't text me to ask about Millie, or if I got home safe. *How could I have interpreted his feelings so incorrectly? Why did I believe he really cared about me?* I want to throw my phone out the window.

I stare at my phone, relief that Millie is OK giving way to anger. The one thing I really wanted to bring for my sister, the proof she's been searching for, the reason she sent me on this trip to begin with, Hugh took away from me. Feeling angry with him is better than giving in to the wave of sadness threatening to overwhelm me, so I lean into it, glowering out the window. I don't want to keep thinking: *What if? What if I was honest? What if I didn't ask Hugh to sign that stupid dive log? Would he still like me? Would I still feel like we had something I've never felt before with anyone?*

My mom hates silence, so she breaks it after about two minutes. 'I haven't even asked you about the trip. I'm sorry everything has been so hectic at home. And you had to come home early—' She breaks off mid-sentence, glancing over at me with wide eyes.

'Mom, it's fine,' I reassure her. 'I didn't have anything to stick around for anyway.'

She doesn't say anything for a moment, which is not her usual MO, and I know she can hear the underlying sadness in my answer.

'Did something happen?'

'It's a long story.'

'You didn't find the fish?'

As soon as she asks, it hits me that no one has asked until now. Not her, not my dad, not Millie, which must mean that Millie was really sick, otherwise she would be texting me herself or begging them to do it.

'I did actually,' I say, 'but I don't have any proof, so it doesn't count.'

My mom claps her hands together. 'Millie will be so happy! This is just the news she needs.'

'But, Mom,' I say, my voice bordering on a whine, 'she won't be happy. I didn't get any *proof*, my sightings are worthless.'

'Surely someone else saw it too?' she asks brightly.

I know she's hoping desperately for something to lift Millie's spirits, but her question feels like a dagger to my heart. I force myself to shake my head. 'It doesn't matter,' I mumble.

We pull into the hospital and park, making our way through a maze of garages and elevators and hallways until we meet up with my dad in the waiting room. He's pacing back and forth.

'Hi, pumpkin,' he says, greeting me with a bear hug. I surrender to his smell, which has been the same my whole life. For the first time since I landed, I don't feel trapped to be back in Columbus. I feel relieved.

'Millie doesn't quite look like herself,' he says, pulling back from our embrace and squinting at me. There are deep lines of worry across his forehead, and his hair looks like he hasn't combed it in days.

'OK,' I say. My voice echoes, sounding small in the hospital hallway.

'Well . . .' He pauses, checking his watch, which he's worn for as long as I can remember. It's gold and chipped around the edges. 'We're right on time. Visiting hours just started.'

I gulp. Now that I'm here, I am overcome with nerves. I drag my feet as I follow my dad towards Millie's room. There's a folder outside with her name on it. I try to wriggle behind my mom, but she sidesteps me, forcing me forward.

'She'll be so excited to see you,' Mom reminds me under her breath. She nudges me inside.

Everything smells like disinfectant. The tiles on the floor are scratched and beige coloured. Fluorescent lights flicker overhead.

'Hi, honey,' my dad says, pulling up a chair next to the bed. Millie's reclined underneath hospital blankets. Her skin is pale, and her cheeks look gaunt, like she's lost ten pounds since I've last seen her. Her chest is bandaged, and the gauze is visible under the neckline of her hospital gown. Her eyes are closed.

There are tubes hooked up to a machine that beeps next to her, fluids running into her arm from a bag next to the bed.

I choke back a sob. I'm not sure if I'm relieved that she's OK or terrified of the condition she seems to be in. Mom squeezes my hand.

'Millie,' she says, stepping closer to the bed and resting a hand on my sister's forearm. Millie stirs this time, awakening slowly, clearly disoriented.

Her eyes find mine right away.

'Hey, you,' she says. Her voice is weak and hoarse.

'An—' My dad gestures to an empty seat and I take it.

'So?' She coughs after she asks me, and my mom passes her a glass of water.

My parents exchange a confused glance, but I know exactly what she's asking about. 'I saw one,' I tell Millie, leaning closer to her. 'I don't exactly have proof yet, I still need to get the dive log signed, but they're alive, I promise.'

Millie rests her head back onto the pillow. 'I knew it,' she says. She starts to smile but her lips are chapped so she stops mid-grin, bringing a finger to her bottom lip. 'We'll figure out proof later. I may just have to go and get some myself.' She smiles again, smaller this time, and her eyes get caught in a blink, fluttering closed for a couple seconds before she opens them again.

'Sorry.' She yawns. 'This stuff makes me so tired.' She gestures at the IV stand next to the bed. 'Was it everything I promised?'

'Everything and more,' I reply.

I spend the next hour recounting my trip, making sure to eliminate any mention of Hugh. Millie awakens slowly, listening intently, her eyes glued to mine the entire time. All I do is talk about the dives, our instructors and the weather. I talk about Miguel, his flirting and his dancing. I explain how Vanessa always kept us in line. I know that Millie will freak out about Hugh if I tell her, so I keep that part of the trip to myself.

Millie asks a couple of questions about the reef conditions, the quality of the boat itself and the dive instructors, but mostly she stays silent, her eyes half closed, totally absorbed in my story.

'I love Pippa,' she says when I mimic Pippa's British accent. She wrinkles her nose when I describe Derek, and she gasps when I recount seeing the shark on the night dive. After an hour of talking non-stop, Millie yawns and the nurse gives our family a meaningful look.

I remain seated in the chair. I'm not ready to leave Millie's side, even though she's falling asleep. Her eyes are closed and her hand twitches next to her.

'She looks OK,' I whisper to my mom.

'She's better than yesterday. They should discharge her tomorrow.'

'They said she shouldn't go back to work for a couple weeks,' my dad says, 'she has to go home with IV antibiotics and visits from a home health nurse.'

'Oh no.' I know how important it was for Millie that no one at work knows about the surgery. 'What is she gonna tell them?'

'She has to tell them the truth,' my dad says grimly.

Millie groans from her bed, cracking one eye open. 'I haven't figured out what to do yet.'

I reach for her hand and squeeze it. 'They'll understand.'

'I wish I didn't have to tell them and you could go to work in my place. It seems to have served you well so far.'

I roll my eyes. 'I can't hold a candle to you, and you know that,' I reply.

'You seemed pretty good at doing it in Australia.' Millie shrugs her shoulders. 'Maybe no one will know that it's you underneath a lab coat.'

I laugh. 'Sure, Millie. I'll quit my job and do yours instead.' I'm laughing, but I start to picture going to Millie's place of work instead of my own and feel a twinge of jealousy followed by a surge of hope. *What if . . .*

'I'm gonna have to tell them, aren't I?' Millie says.

At that moment, the nurse bustles in, shooing us out of the room.

'We'll come back in the afternoon,' Mom promises Millie as we scurry out. We make our way back through the maze of hallways and into the parking garage. Mom makes multiple references to how badly I must want a shower, which I do, but she calls attention to it so many times that I check myself in the car mirror, wondering how awful I must look.

Now that I've seen Millie, all I can think about is seeing Murphy. I'm so excited my body is buzzing. But as we near the house, I realise I'm not sure if the idea of working in Millie's lab has something to do with my excitement.

She couldn't have been serious, I remind myself. Although there's a nagging voice in my brain again asking me: *Why not?*

Chapter 29

Murphy pees on the garage floor when he sees me, which makes me laugh and breaks my heart. How have I survived being away from him for so long? My mom sighs theatrically, but I don't care. I almost peed when I saw him too. I feel immense relief to wrap my arms around his shaggy body, to have my face covered in his sloppy kisses.

When we're inside, my dad starts laughing at how hard Murphy's tail is wagging. 'You'd think we tortured him all week!' he exclaims, picking up a glass before Murphy's tail knocks it off the coffee table.

I pet Murphy behind the ears. 'I missed you so much, buddy,' I whisper.

I shower and halfway unpack, throwing clothes in the laundry. When Millie gets home tomorrow, I want to stay at my parents' with her, so there's no point in schlepping my stuff back to my place, or confusing Murphy by bringing him home and making him leave again. There's just one problem with being at my parents' – I feel like I'm already regressing, turning into the person I was before I left to go on the trip. It's all starting to feel like a fever dream.

We go see Millie during afternoon visiting hours, where she tells me all about the episode I missed on *The Bachelor* (he's down to six contestants now and we hate two of them) and we strategise a way to tell her work what happened. Eventually, we compromise on a strategy: Millie agrees to tell her boss that she couldn't go on the trip but that she kept in touch with some divers who did go and is hoping to use some of their findings.

By the time we head home it's hard for me to remember that the last night of sleep I had was on a tiny boat in the middle of the Pacific Ocean.

But I remember Hugh. I remember everything about him. His smell, the way his lips taste, the way the hair on his forearm is so lightened from the sun that it practically glows. I remember how the name Millie sounds in his mouth and the way his eyes look when he's staring at the ocean. I remember how he made me feel – simultaneously like I was on the most exciting terrifying roller coaster of my life and also like I had finally found a place to call home.

I keep expecting time to take away the sting of not hearing from him, but with every passing hour it cuts me deeper. Pippa texts me to ask about my sister and the scrap of pride I have left is the only thing that keeps me from asking if Hugh ended up on the waterfall tour with them.

I miss Australia. I miss the accents and the smell of the ocean and the bright, long, sunny days. I miss the spirit of the place, the feeling that people were living for more than just their next pay cheque.

I get into bed as soon as we get home from visiting Millie and even though I'm exhausted, I can't fall asleep. I toss and turn, missing the rocking of the boat beneath me. Missing Hugh's gentle breathing from the bed below mine.

When Millie gets discharged the next afternoon, we bring her home together, all four of us loaded into the Highlander, Millie and I in the back seat. For the next few days, our family operates in orbit around Millie. We are at her beck and call, helping her get comfortable and ensuring she stays off her feet, welcoming in the home health nurse around the clock, and convincing Millie that her boss will be understanding when she calls her to ask for medical leave.

By the end of the week, Millie's request for full medical leave has been approved, and she won't be back at work for another month. She's heard from her co-workers, who inform her that before everyone left for the Christmas break, the lab was drowning without her. It got so bad, they said, that their boss wanted to hire an additional lab tech for benchwork.

Saturday is Christmas. We celebrate Millie's rebounding health. I donate to the turtle sanctuary on her behalf, and she loves it. Millie gets me a simple golden chain with a wave symbol engraved on the clasp. 'I don't want you to forget what you're capable of,' she writes in loopy script on a note she leaves in the box.

Somewhere in the middle of watching reruns of reality TV, I tell Millie I fell for somebody. I don't tell her it's Hugh yet. But I do tell her that he lives in Australia, that I miss him, and that I really screwed it up, and I don't know what to do.

'Ohmygod,' she starts talking so fast all her words run together. 'Who? Does he know you were me? I mean does he know you are you? Is he cute? Did you hook up? I knew it!' she cries, ending her barrage of questions on a triumphant note. 'I told you that,' she says, raising her eyebrows. 'Didn't I? I said you needed to get out of here. And now look – you met somebody!'

I roll my eyes at her. 'And I told you I wasn't ready. Now look . . . I met someone who lives literally as far away as possible.'

'You said you didn't want another Midwesterner,' Millie teases. 'Honestly,' she says, scratching Murphy behind his ears, 'I always thought you would end up with someone further from home anyways. I never thought you would be here forever.'

'You didn't?' I'm incredulous. My whole life has felt like a narrative of: *Of course, Andi will stay close to home*. Was I the only one thinking that?

'No,' she says simply, like it's the most obvious thing in the world.

'Now tell me everything,' she commands, but I'm saved by the bell because before I have to, our mom calls us down for dinner.

The antibiotics do the trick and Millie has no more hiccups on her road to recovery. We spend New Year's together, all of us relieved that we haven't had to go back to the hospital. I text Pippa, wishing her a happy holiday season, and she sends me back an adorable selfie of her and Andrew in what appears to be some kind of fake winter wonderland in the middle of London.

Before I know it, I've moved my life back to my apartment. My return to work approaches fast. I don't know how over a week has passed since I returned from Australia, which already feels like a lifetime ago. I don't know how I managed to survive each day, waiting for word from Hugh. With every hour that passes, my heart feels like it breaks a little more. I keep thinking the pain will lessen, but somehow my disappointment only deepens. I start to feel foolish. I don't know why I ever thought someone like him would be interested in someone like me.

I retreat further into myself. At first, everyone thinks that I have the post-trip blues. My parents suggest I plan another vacation, but Millie realises quickly that there's more to it.

'This is about the guy, isn't it?' she asks after coming to my apartment for the third day in a row to find me in the same pair of sweats. She's asked me about him over and over again, but even thinking about talking about him makes me want to cry, so I've shut her down each time.

All I can do is shake my head.

I think about Hugh constantly. Every time I drink coffee in the morning, I can hear his voice teasing, 'You're poisoning yourself with caffeine.' I find myself compulsively checking to see what time it is in Australia. I pull up the Boston conference schedule and check over and over again that he's still committed to present. I tell Murphy about him. I cry. I repeat the cycle.

Eventually, I'm ready to tell Millie. She comes over with takeout Chinese food and we sit on my couch,

Murphy between us. Millie listens, open-mouthed, the entire time. Only when I'm finished does she interject.

'Wow,' she says when I finish. 'Who would have thought . . .'

'Millie,' I feel a nervous heat rise in my cheeks, worried she'll criticise him. 'You don't know him.'

'I know he's my work enemy!' she cries playfully.

I relax. 'I know,' I groan.

'I can't believe this! Where's my loyalty?'

I hide behind a carton of fried rice.

'How serious is this? What if he's your lobster?' she teases, eyes wide.

'Do not *Friends* reference me right now,' I say. I feel my eyes start to fill with tears. 'Millie, I'm worried I'll never meet anyone like him.'

Millie softens. 'Oh, An, I mean, I don't agree with his research principles, but I do trust your judgement. So, however reluctantly, I will concede he may be better than I think. Why don't you mail him that letter you told me about? He deserves an explanation.' Millie's referring to a letter I had written to Hugh earlier that afternoon.

I waffle between wanting to send it immediately and wanting to give it to him in Boston. I'm holding out hope that if I can explain in person, Hugh will forgive me, which is more than worth the trip there. But I have a nagging feeling he'll cancel his trip, which is why I keep checking the conference schedule to see if his name is still listed.

'I know,' I whisper.

Millie smiles a wry smile. 'Can I tell you something?'

I nod.

'I always thought you were destined for big exotic adventures with a hunk like that,' she says, as she reaches across the couch to wrap me in a hug. 'Why do you think I sent you over there?'

Usually, a comment like that would make me panic. *But I'm boring*, I would think. I touch the necklace Millie gave me with my fingertips. If I'm exciting enough to pretend to be a marine biologist on the Great Barrier Reef, then I think Millie may be right. Maybe I'm destined for more than Columbus.

'Unfortunately for my wallet, I'm starting to agree with you,' I say, before taking a bite of sesame chicken.

Chapter 30

I go to my parents' house on my way home from my first day back at work.

'I've been thinking about something,' I say tentatively, easing myself down on the sofa next to Millie. Even though I'm feigning nonchalance, not a second passed in my grey cubicle where I wasn't thinking about how to present my idea to her.

'Mmm,' she says, still focused on the reality TV rerun.

'I actually want your opinion.' My heart flutters in my chest. My palms are damp. I'm nervous to ask this much of my sister, but I am determined to give it my best shot.

Millie turns towards me, resettling herself on the couch, giving me her full attention. 'What's up?'

I take a deep breath and spew the words out of my mouth as fast as I can. 'I want to apply to your lab. I know you said that they're overwhelmed, especially with you gone, and I've seen online that they're looking for a lab tech and—' I gulp down a breath of air, not wanting to stop talking until I get out everything I want to say, terrified that Millie will think this is a bad idea. 'And I think I meet the qualifications, I have the degree. And I know you're going to say it's a backwards step for me, but I've been thinking about it for a while, and I think it's just a lateral move. I can't work at Sunshine Foods forever.'

I don't know what reaction I was expecting, but it wasn't silence. Millie stares at me for a beat too long before she replies. 'You're sure this is what you want? It's a lot of grant applications. Sometimes you have to stay kind of late, and honestly, the pay stinks. And it's not like we're at a marine station . . .'

'Yeah, I'm sure. I can't quite explain it, it just feels right.' I pick at my cuticle. 'I know Columbus isn't the most glamorous place to do this . . . if you don't want me to apply, I won't.' I rush to say the words. 'I promise, I really don't want to get in the way and if you feel like it's your place, I understand.'

'Are you kidding?' Millie asks. I look up. She's beaming. 'I would love nothing more. I just wanted to make sure you've really thought it through. It *is* hard. Like sometimes it really sucks.'

I nod.

'But we can carpool!' Millie squeals. 'And I've been asking you to hang out with Bianca and me for ages and now you will finally have to!' she says. Bianca is Millie's best friend from work. Millie squeals again. 'Apply! Apply!' she chants.

So, I do.

The interview process is easy. Millie refers me and talks me through the phone screen. I get fast-tracked through to final stages, mostly because of a letter of recommendation from an old marine biology professor. When I'm offered the job, I cry with relief. I feel like even though everything with Hugh still feels terribly wrong, something in my life is starting to feel right.

On the day I put in my notice at work, I return to the letter I wrote to Hugh. I've only been back at work a couple of weeks after New Year, and when Matteo asks what I'm going to do, I tell him that I've accepted a position at a marine biology lab.

'You're moving to Australia?' he asks, so loudly that Becca's head pops up from her cubicle.

'I wish,' I joke. 'I'm starting at the lab here, where my sister works.'

Matteo nods, unaware of how much his comment pulled at my heartstrings. I wish I was moving to Australia. I would give anything to go back to the place that captured my heart, to hear the ocean again, to smell the salty air every day. The University of Sydney also has the best marine station in the world – every marine biologist dreams of working there. Even Millie respects it, despite the fact that Hugh works there.

'I always thought you were destined for something greater,' Matteo says cheerfully. He pulls me into a hug. He means it as a compliment, but it makes me want to roll my eyes.

For two weeks, my last two weeks of work, I revisit the letter to Hugh so frequently that it has torn edges and tear stains. On my last day, I decide to mail it, smudges and all. I send it to the address on his email signature. Vanessa had emailed all of us pictures of the formal dive logs, the air we consumed, the depth we dived to, the weather and the locations. Hugh had replied to the email thanking her, his Sydney address hovering surreptitiously at the end of his note.

I read back over the pages explaining why I lied to him and what he meant to me. I explain what I realised since coming home, that before we met, I thought that being in love meant that part of your identity became that person. I thought it was romantic, the idea that a 'couple' would lose part of their identities as they grew closer together. But then I met Hugh. And the more I fell for him, the more I felt like *me*.

The only change I make is adding a postscript. *I quit my job,* I write. *Thank you for seeing something bigger in me than a 9–5 cubicle. Love, Andi.*

Almost as soon as I start at the lab, the Boston conference comes up. Millie still can't travel, she's not supposed to go anywhere while they're monitoring her for risk of another infection, and she nominates me to go and present her research in her stead. Usually, the opportunity wouldn't go to the newest lab tech, but everyone else is either buried in work catching up after the holidays or doesn't want to prep a presentation. Now that I'm an employed marine biologist, Millie reminds me cheerfully, I can present research without feeling like a fraud.

I lean into preparation, trying to make the most of the opportunity. I'll be the only one from the team going, which makes me both more nervous (I would rather have someone to show me the ropes) and less nervous (I am glad none of my peers will be there to watch my lecture). I like having something to work on that I'm passionate about. I even use some of my old slide deck skills from Sunshine Foods to add a little creativity to what I'm presenting.

After I show my boss the first draft of my deck, she formally adds my name to the conference agenda. I start to check it habitually after that, wondering if Hugh will see, wondering if he will change his mind.

It takes five days. Exactly a month after I sent the letter, Hugh's name disappears from the schedule. I stare at my phone open-mouthed. My stomach drops. I try to use the breath exercises I've learned in yoga, now that I've finally started going to classes, but even they didn't calm the jack-hammering of my heart.

I know I'll have to accept that I need to let Hugh go, but it's easier said than done. When, a couple of days later, I hear someone with an Australian accent in the grocery store, it's all I can do not to burst into tears in the condiment aisle.

The next time Millie asks me about the conference, I almost tell her I can't go. I open my mouth to explain that some days I feel so sad I don't even want to take a shower, that going somewhere Hugh was supposed to be feels impossible, but my gaze catches on the new wrinkles that have formed across Millie's forehead and I hold my tongue. She teasingly pulls the 'I got a double mastectomy' card enough that I know that's what she'd do if I said I was having second thoughts.

'One day you'll have to stop using that,' I tell Millie after she guilts me into bringing her a latte on my way to work.

'You're the one who always falls for it,' she replies with a smile, happily sipping her steaming coffee.

The cold in Columbus is bitter for weeks in a row, but day by day I weather it for a little longer with Murphy. I stay quiet about not wanting to present, and instead try to focus on what good opportunity it is. I fall into a rhythm at the lab. I like my co-workers; most of the other lab techs are a little younger than me, but we go to the bar next to the office for trivia together every week and it's fun and lively and I feel like I'm finally getting back to having a life.

There's one co-worker in particular that I get along with really well. His name is Blake and he's twenty-four. I assumed I was too old for him to even think of me that way, but one day he asks me out. He does it so casually that I don't register it for a minute or two, and I leave him hanging a beat too long.

'I'm sorry,' I say finally. He has big brown eyes and long eyelashes. He's cute. Young, but cute.

'I'm kind of hung up on someone,' I explain. Ever since I found out Hugh cancelled his trip to Boston, the thought of him makes my heart feel like it's being squeezed by a giant fist. I'm not ready to be seeing anyone else. I'm in no place to date someone, especially not a co-worker.

But the hole Hugh left is slowly filled by my new job. Millie and I spend more time together now because we see each other at work, and the insecurity I used to feel in her presence, that I was constantly being compared and deemed the worse sister, has significantly dimmed.

It started lessening after the first week, when I told Millie I couldn't eat lunch with her and Bianca every day anymore. 'Can we do twice a week?' I offered instead.

'Why?' she had asked, clearly insulted.

'I think I need some separation,' I explained. 'It's not personal, it's just that when you're around I feel like I'm quieter . . .' I trailed off and tried again. 'You're just good at everything . . . sometimes it feels like there's no space for me.'

'But I love having you around,' Millie responded.

'Yeah, but . . .' I wriggled in my seat, uncomfortable.

'I get it,' Millie finally sighed, 'I'm sorry. I don't mean to take up all the space.'

'You don't need to apologise. It's not your fault,' I said, surprised to find that I meant it. 'I choose to act that way, and there's plenty of space for both of us.'

'I think so too, but still . . . I should have realised I was making you feel that way. I just love having you around, An. It's been so fun.'

'Yeah.' I shrugged. 'I'm having fun too . . . I just think . . .'

'I get it,' Millie said, laying a reassuring hand on my forearm. 'You're my biggest cheerleader. I thought I was yours too, but I think I put that on the back-burner when we're together, which isn't fair.'

'I'm an adult,' I remind her. 'That was my choice too.'

And now, maybe because I'm closer to Millie than ever, or I'm busy preparing for Boston, but whatever the reason, my loneliness is starting to subside. Millie figured out a way to livestream my presentation, which only made me work harder to make it perfect. I'm proud of how it's shaping up and excited to show my new team that I can do something apart from working heads-down in a research lab.

I run through my presentation with Millie for the final time. 'This isn't necessary,' I complain, reiterating *again* that our boss already OK'd the final draft. We're presenting on the regeneration of coral and implying that the butterfly wrasse is still alive, but without the dive log we can't say definitively that it is. Millie forced me to include some of the photos I took, even though none of them are clear proof. I look over the photos again. I find nothing.

'I want it to be perfect,' Millie says, clicking through slides. She settles on the one that has the least grainy photo of the reef. 'You're sure you don't have any better pictures?' she asks.

'Millie,' I say, rolling my eyes, 'yes, I'm sure. I've told you that a thousand times.'

'And no one else took pictures?'

I hesitate. 'I mean,' I say, 'Derek did.'

'You never told me that!' Millie says, leaping up from the couch. She's regained all of her vitality and previous mobility. She's even coming to terms with her new breasts, although she still refers to them as her 'chicken cutlets'.

'I didn't?' I ask. I can't believe I hadn't thought of Derek sooner.

I hastily search back into my email for the last one I received from the Coral Sea Dreaming tour company. In the string of CCs, it included Derek's email: dwilson@ texastech.

'Are you gonna ask him? The camera guy?'

'Yes! I'm going as fast as I can,' I say impatiently, taking the computer out of Millie's hands and plopping it into my lap.

I fire off a quick email, explaining why I need the pictures and asking if he minds just sending off whatever he took during the last day.

I am about to shut my computer, not expecting Derek to respond right away, when I hear the familiar ding of a message landing in my inbox.

'OMG,' Millie says, peering over my shoulder.

'We don't know if it's even him who's responding,' I remind her.

But it is. Derek has attached a zip file with over a hundred photos.

His message reads:

Hi Millie/Andi,

Nice to hear from you. I hope you're well. I attach a zip file of all the photos I took on the last day. If you're wondering how I could send them so fast (because yes, working in tech is quite time-consuming, I wasn't lying about that), it's because Hugh just asked for the same set of photos. If I'm honest, Natalie was worried she left a bad taste in your mouth after the trip. If you're reaching out to me for photos, I'm glad to assume that's not the case!

She was hoping to speak to you while we were on the boat, but she never got the chance to – she is spearheading a new campaign for a skincare line that includes sunscreen and she wants to pitch to her boss the idea of including a marine biologist as a user. Would the marine biologist in your family be interested? I'm going to pass along your email so she can send you more details.

Cheers!

Derek

Millie snorts with laughter when she reads the opening lines of the email.

'I told you,' I say, also laughing, 'he is *that* guy. You know how many times I heard about how much he works?'

'Skincare!' Millie squeals. 'Did she ask you to model?'

'*That's* why she kept talking to Hugh?' I shake my head in disbelief.

'You could have gotten free sunscreen?' Millie squints at me in disbelief. 'And you *didn't*?'

'I didn't know,' I say. 'God, I'm so dumb.'

'Is she the one you didn't like?'

'Yes. She gave me weird vibes and kept giving me weird looks.'

'All because she wanted to put you in a marketing campaign.' Millie starts to laugh. 'You can be so dense.'

I can't help but laugh too. But after a beat our laughter dies down again. 'But . . .' Millie says, trailing off.

We haven't addressed the elephant in the room.

'If Hugh was asking . . .' I say, but I trail off too. *Does that mean he's still thinking about me?* 'Do you think . . .' I say.

'Do I think he's going to Boston?' Millie supplies.

I gulp. 'Do you?' I squeak.

'There's only one way to find out,' she says.

Chapter 31

Four months post dive

I'm so jittery when I land in Boston that it takes me twenty minutes to find the spot where I'm supposed to meet my Uber. Boston is beautiful in April. The cherry blossoms are blooming and there are ducklings everywhere, but between worrying about my presentation and obsessing over Derek's email, I can't focus on enjoying the city.

I check into my hotel, drop my bags and head to a nearby yoga class I'd booked, hoping it will calm my nerves. Going to yoga has become such a regular occurrence for me now that sometimes I can't believe it was the result of a silly reminder I set in my phone, a promise I made to myself the first day on *Coral Sea Dreaming*.

The conference doesn't start until tomorrow morning, and tonight I will give my presentation one final run-through. Everything changed when I received Derek's pictures.

Millie and I had pored over them that night on the couch.

'How many does this guy take?' she complained after we scrolled through the first twenty.

'And this is just one dive,' I replied. We kept going. All we were scrolling for was a clearer photo of a school of fish on the reef, one that could accompany a slide on coral regeneration and emphasise the main point: a season of cooler water gave corals the chance to rebound and act once more as a refuge for the surrounding fish populations.

We both saw the butterfly wrasse at the same time. In the lower left of the photo, purple, yellow, the outline of a small fin barely visible on its underbelly. Millie screamed.

'Oh my God. Oh my God!' she yelled.

'No freaking way,' I whispered, still staring at the picture.

'All this time he just had this?' She zoomed in on the photo, beaming.

'All this time the dive log was useless?' I asked myself quietly, overcome with a combination of relief and heavy sadness. I tried to push it out of my mind – I knew Hugh's refusal to sign the dive log signified something deeper about our relationship. He refused to see beyond his black and white moral standard, and I would do anything to help my family, even something that was ethically questionable.

Millie and I had stayed up late that night, reworking the presentation around Derek's photo. Now that we had crystal-clear proof of the wrasse's existence, our presentation was shorter and more to the point – if corals have regenerated enough to sustain the regrowth of the butterfly wrasse population, then now is the time to focus on pollution from nearby banana farms. We still couldn't use the photo as stand-alone proof, but it made the presentation a lot stronger. Millie had even paid a satellite company to use their aerial photos of pollution leaching into the reef.

My presentation is scheduled for 10 a.m. – the earlier slots are given to less well-known presenters and usually less crowded, both of which are fine for me. Even though I could barely touch my breakfast, a dry hotel muffin, I still feel nauseated when I approach the podium. I'm early, and I introduce myself to the tech support guy, who lingers around long enough for me to do a quick dry run and familiarise myself with the slideshow technology, and then disappears off into the shadows, leaving me slightly sweaty, nervously pacing until it's time to start.

I peek around the side of the stage into the audience. My heart is hammering, and I know it's more than just nerves. I could never fully let go of the fact that Hugh could be here. That he could see me and recognise the girl that he fell for – now that I *am* a marine biologist. Now that I feel more like *me*.

But instead of seeing shaggy blond hair, I see the mousy brown hair of other marine biologists, trickling into the first of a series of lectures. None of them look at all excited about how their day is scheduled to go. Three minutes until my presentation begins. Millie is all set to watch it on a livestream, she's already texted me good luck. I check the audience again. The tech support guy is back and nudges me with his elbow, startling me to attention.

'Is something up?' he asks in a whisper. 'You're supposed to go on now.'

I walk to the podium, my heart hammering in my chest. This is my first chance to make my boss proud, to make a mark in my new field. The bright lights from the ceiling obstruct my view, so I can't see anything except the row in front of me. I smile and introduce myself. I start clicking through my slides.

I've practised so thoroughly that I've memorised the content that goes with each slide. I go on autopilot with my speech, blabbering on about the rate of regrowth and the different coral species present in the specific location where the butterfly wrasse were spotted.

I arrive at the slide with Derek's picture. Here is where I go off script, the only piece of my speech I hadn't prepared with Millie.

'Um,' I say, hesitating for the first time. I'm tempted to shield my eyes from the harsh lights, but I keep my hands at my sides, grasping the clicker a little tighter in my right hand.

I take a deep breath.

'I know it doesn't matter but I actually didn't take this photo,' I start out. Just like the rest of my speech, the audience doesn't react, so I forge ahead. 'I wasn't an employed marine biologist when I went on the trip where most of this research stems from, so my certification wasn't up to date. And the photographer was a hobbyist aquatic photographer. I went on the trip for my sister, the lead researcher on this presentation, to see if I could find the butterfly wrasse for her. I want to ensure I acknowledge the situation upfront so that in the future the integrity of this research will not be in question. While we are not explicitly certifying the existence of the butterfly wrasse, we are providing the photographic evidence for you all to come to your own conclusions.'

I know Millie is going to kill me for not getting her approval before I did this, but I felt like I had to make some things right. She never told her work explicitly who took the photo, nor was she passing it off as proof, so she can't really get in trouble, but the acknowledgement that the photo wasn't taken by a certified marine biologist definitely derails the presentation.

I take another deep breath. The audience fidgets in their seats, bored or unconcerned, I don't know which. It feels anticlimactic. I click the button and move to the next slide, ready to talk about banana farms.

Before I can start talking about pollution, I see a tentative hand in the audience. For a moment, I wonder if it's someone scratching the back of their head. I clear my throat. Then the hand shoots up more definitively. I process that it's a large hand. One that belongs to a tanned forearm. I can feel my heart rate quicken. *It can't be . . . can it?*

'Yes?' I call out to the dark crowd.

As soon as I hear the rumblings of his voice, a shiver runs down my spine. I would know that voice anywhere. It's him.

Chapter 32

'Ahem.' He clears his throat.

The lights are still blocking my field of vision. I take a step forward so that I can see. Hugh is standing up in the middle of the auditorium. I didn't know it was possible to forget how handsome someone is until I see him. I can tell he's unsure about what he's doing – he's not standing up as straight as usual, and his jaw is so pronounced it seems like he's clenching it.

The audience is looking to me expectantly. I open my mouth to speak but suddenly my throat is dry. I practically lunge for the water bottle on the table.

'I would like to clear something up,' Hugh says, turning to address the audience behind him. He has an easy way with crowds, I can tell already. 'I can second that the wrasse was spotted, and I've filed a petition for an exception so that my sighting and the photograph can count as proof of existence. I accompanied Andi on her dives and also saw the butterfly wrasse. Just wanted to make sure that was known.' With that, he sinks back into his seat.

I can barely finish the rest of the presentation, I'm so distracted. I fumble out the closing words and quickly click through the acknowledgement slides, desperate to get backstage, away from the lights, desperate to talk to Hugh.

Part of presenting at conferences involves being around afterwards for questions, so I force myself to exit stage right and linger to see if the participants have anything to discuss. My gaze is locked on a blond head about thirty feet away from me, a couple of rows up, when a young woman appears at my side. She introduces herself as someone working for a Boston institution and asks about a specific pollution statistic. I answer her briefly, giving her Millie's email in case she has any questions, and send her on her way. I look back up to see if I can spot the blond ahead again, but it's gone.

My phone vibrates in my pocket. A text from Millie:

No f*cking way. HE WAS THERE? HE INTERRUPTED MY (your) PRESENTATION? Are you so happy? TELL ME EVERYTHING. Are you guys talking? AHHHHH
   Told you that he can really steal a show. Now do you see why he's my nemesis?

I smile at my phone, glad she isn't mad. I type a message back:

Sorry I ad-libbed some of the talk track.

A hand taps me on the shoulder. 'Got a minute?'
Instinctively, I know it's Hugh. My insides melt as I turn around. 'Hi,' I breathe.
'Hey.'
We look at each other in awkward silence. I take in every part of Hugh's face. His eyelashes, his thick eyebrows, the curl of hair just above his right ear. I can

barely look him in the eyes, they're too strong and too magnetic. Already I feel like he's pulling me under. My knees start to wobble.

'So,' Hugh says, with the start of a smile playing at his lips. 'This is you now, huh?'

'I'm pretty sure *you've* always known me as this. But yes, this is me now.' I do a half curtsey and immediately feel mortified that I half-curtseyed. Thankfully, Hugh is smiling and doesn't seem to notice.

'Did you know I was here?' he asks when he looks up.

I shake my head.

'So, you were just gonna tell the whole room regardless?'

'It was the right thing to do.' I shrug.

Hugh laughs. I missed the sound of his laugh.

'I'm sorry about asking you to sign the dive log,' I say.

'I'm sorry I made you have to do *that*,' he says at the same time, gesturing at the stage.

'It's OK,' I reply.

'My personal feelings got in the way,' he adds, talking over me again.

We both start to laugh.

'Personal feelings, huh?'

'I wasn't planning to come,' he says. 'It's not like I had anything to present on anymore.' He chuckles awkwardly. 'And I didn't think you'd want to see me after how we said goodbye.'

'But I sent you a letter.'

'What letter?'

'The letter,' I repeat, feeling impossibly stupid and incredibly frustrated. 'It explained everything. Why I lied, what was happening with Millie . . . You never got my letter?'

Hugh shakes his head. 'No . . . but when my boss insisted I come with her to help with her presentation I figured it wouldn't be right to miss yours.'

I grin. 'I have to admit – I heard you emailed Derek, and I was hoping it had something to do with the conference.'

'Ah, yes, Derek.'

We both laugh.

'The truth is . . .' Hugh breaks off midsentence. He leans closer to me, his eyes lingering over my face, my lips. I feel like we are the only two people in the world. I grab his hand with mine, intertwining our fingers. For the first time in four months, it finally feels like I can breathe again.

'Yes?'

'Andi, I never stopped thinking about you. I missed you. I was hoping that I could find something of Derek's to help, to make up for how we said goodbye. That maybe I could reach out to you again . . .'

'Hugh,' I breathe. 'If anything, it's me that should be thanking you. After all, you did help me go from talking about cereal to *this*.' Although when I wave my hands around the cleared-out auditorium it doesn't feel much more impressive than my cubicle.

Hugh laughs. 'Hopefully, you're getting to do more than attend conferences. So what do we do now?'

'Well . . .' I pause, glancing at my schedule. The rest of my day is full of presentations that I wanted to attend but don't need to, and suddenly I'm not feeling inclined to stay inside.

'We can attend the talk on ITLOS regulations, or we can go grab food at a cute spot near the park?'

Hugh's eyes sparkle and I can tell he's trying not to laugh. 'ITLOS. Definitely.'

I swat at his arm.

'Food sounds perfect.'

'That was easy,' I say, picking up my bag and swinging it over my shoulder. 'Remind me why Millie says you're terrible to work with?' I'm whisper-laughing now. Hugh is drawing me closer, our torsos touching, his other hand wrapped around my low back.

'How is Millie?' he asks.

'She's good. She sends her regards.'

He laughs. 'I take it she saw my interruption.'

Our faces are drawing closer together. I feel like I can't breathe.

'She did.'

Hugh leans forward and touches his forehead gently to mine. 'When do you leave?' he breathes.

'Two days,' I say. I'm smiling so wide I feel like my face will split in half. Our noses brush.

'Then we better make the most of it.' He kisses me, first lightly, our lips barely grazing each other, then deeper, hungrily, so intensely I can feel it all the way into my toes.

'I really am sorry,' I say when we finally break for air. 'I'm sorry I wasn't honest and then I asked you to lie for me too. I'm sorry it took me so long to realise who I'm supposed to be.'

'Andi,' Hugh says, our foreheads meeting once again. 'You have been you the whole time I've known you, and I've loved every second.'

Chapter 33

One year post dive

I stare out the window of my studio apartment. If I squint, I can make out a sliver of the deep blue Pacific Ocean. I found a place right next to Bronte Beach, home to Hugh's favourite breakfast spot. I had to sell all my furniture at home (thankfully, most of it was from IKEA), but there's a used furniture store near my new place, and in no time, I've filled my flat with an old table and a soft armchair, a worn wooden bedframe, and mismatched nightstands. The only thing I bought new was a big plush bed for Murphy, as a treat for sticking with me as we moved across the world. Murphy and I walk on the beach path every day, and every time I smell the ocean air and watch the frothy white tide smash into the cliffs below me, I wonder how I got so lucky.

Sometimes I remind myself it wasn't all luck. It was constantly applying to vacancies at the University of Sydney until one stuck. It was spending days in Boston with Hugh laughing, remembering Derek's antics and Andrew's inability to control his own flotation. I finally got to tell Hugh how scared I was that Natalie would tell everyone I was Andi, which made him laugh so hard he had to wipe tears from his cheeks. '*That's* what you thought she was doing?' he asked. 'She was trying to convince me to try sunscreen made with *seaweed*.' He breathed out, before collapsing into laughter again.

When I whisper-called Millie from the bathroom the morning after our first night together, Hugh still sleeping under our mussed hotel duvet, she shouted, 'FOUR TIMES?' so loudly through the phone that I dropped it in the sink.

'You told me it was good but not that good!'

'Well, it's much better now that we're not in the sand!' I countered, laughing.

I told my family after I returned from Boston that I met a guy. That we were 'seeing where it goes, but he lives pretty far away'.

My mom wrinkled her nose at that. 'Does he live in Boston?' she asked, with as much disdain as a proud Midwesterner can muster when confronted with the Northeast.

'A little further than that,' I replied.

Millie snickered from her place next to me.

Eventually, I got an entry-level position, something I was technically overqualified for, but something that gave me an employment visa. I jumped at the chance.

And as much as I hate to admit when Hugh's right (which is all the time), he was right when he said I should move to Australia – it looks good on me. I feel stronger from my walks up and down the cliffs, I'm eating healthier food, and I have a sun-kissed glow, the freckles on my nose are out in full force. Plus, the coffee here is incredible.

The oven beeps, startling me from my thoughts. We're headed to Hugh's mom's house for dinner, like we do every other weekend. Hugh's mom, Gracie, lives in a little white clapboard house smack in the middle of the city. A jade tree sits on her front stoop, beautiful and gnarled. Gracie looks just like Hugh and always greets me the same way. 'Andi!' she says warmly, pulling me into a hug like I'm a long-lost friend.

Shaggy, Hugh's little brother, is already here and Hugh runs to greet him, picking up a rugby ball on his way and immediately initiating a game of toss. Hugh is in his element at home, his body relaxed, his limbs fluid, his eyes a bright, turquoise shade of blue.

I help Gracie set the table as stragglers arrive. Hugh's aunt and uncle usually come, as do the older couple that lives next door. Everyone assumes their positions – Hugh's uncle starts manning the grill, Heather, Hugh's aunt, starts refilling drinks. Shaggy darts in and out of the house, arranging bowls of coleslaw and salad on the table.

My phone buzzes in my pocket, which never happens at this hour considering most of my social circle is still in the US. It's Millie. I step out to answer it, panicked. My heart is racing. Millie gets scans every six months as a follow-up to her double mastectomy.

'Everything OK?' I say, as soon as the FaceTime connects.

'Andi!' Millie yelps as her face slowly comes into focus. 'I didn't know if you would answer but thank God you did – I have great news!'

'Millie, you scared me!' I tell her angrily, although I'm so relieved my anger is fleeting. 'It's so late for you,' I say, 'you never call me at this time.'

'I know but I just found out and I *had* to tell you.' She's practically jumping up and down.

'OK, what is it?' I'm sceptical. Millie's last great news was that she found her new favourite bagel place. Not that I don't support great bagels, but I didn't exactly think it met the bar for 'great news'.

'You really want to know?'

'Yes! Tell me. I'm at Hugh's mom's so I can't be on the phone for forever.'

Millie rolls her eyes, but she smiles. 'Cleveland's sending me to Australia for THREE MONTHS!' she shouts.

'You're kidding me,' I say, my face exploding into a grin.

'Nope!' She launches into an explanation.

'Ahhhhhh!' I scream as she talks. I'm so excited I can't contain it.

She tells me the cities she's visiting, the dives she's supposed to take for work, why she didn't tell me when she applied – it was a long shot, she wanted it to be a surprise . . . I zone out as she launches into her tourist visa application and how quickly she thinks it will process. Instead, I think about all the things we can do together, all the stuff I've been dying to show her.

Hugh heard my scream and has looked up from his rugby throwing, his eyebrows knitted together in confusion.

He must be able to hear snippets of the FaceTime because he mouths to me, 'Millie? Here?' He raises a single eyebrow – he still doesn't see eye to eye with Millie . . . at all. But they're learning to love each other, and that's nothing a little bonding time can't fix. Right?

He mouths at me again. 'She'll be staying with you, won't she?' He rolls his eyes, but I can tell from the crinkle in their corners that he's happy. He hasn't met Millie in person yet.

I roll my eyes back, nodding, but I can't keep the smile off my face.

'Is Hugh there?' Millie asks.

I nod. 'Yes.'

'Tell him the news!' she squeals. 'And that I read his latest article—' she blows a raspberry with her lips '— and I'm ready to prove him wrong.'

Hugh walks over to say hello.

While they talk, I think about what I want to do with Millie.

A weekend in Brisbane. Trips down the Gold Coast. Byron Bay. Even hitting a casino after we dive the Whitsundays.

I hope she's up for an adventure.

Author's Note

When I started writing this book, I was just coming off a vacation to the Great Barrier Reef. Throughout my trip I flip-flopped between joy and awe, but I couldn't help but feel an undercurrent of something deeper – worry, loss, despair and anxiety tinged my thoughts and my recollection of the trip. Our group shared many conversations about our worries for the health of the reef, for the state of the world, and for the future we were walking into.

But in every conversation we had with our boat captain, our first mate, our dive instructor, there was *hope*. There were stories of people doing great things, committing their lives to making the world better, healthier, and more sustainable.

I took liberties with this novel (the Butterfly Wrasse, for example, is not a real fish) but the problems our scientists and reefs are facing are real. There is evidence that coral reefs can regenerate, but often that requires our help. Humans can reseed and regrow corals to speed up the reef's natural recovery. Land-based runoff does affect marine life, and the Great Barrier Reef is facing pollution and water quality issues as a result. But we can change the policies that govern how we interact with and treat the land around us.

There is so much hope in this story, hope for love, for happier endings, and for health, but if you want to add a little more hope to the world, please visit citizensgbr.org, a non-profit focused on protecting the world's reefs. You have the option of donating time, expertise, or funds.

I will be donating a portion of the proceeds from every sale of this book, so rest assured that even just by reading it, you have done some good.

For cancer survivors and those affected by cancer — while the C-word appears in this story as a sidelined character, I know that is not the case in reality. I do not have the words to express the pain, the grief, the terror that it inflicts on so many. Please know that my heart is with you always.

Acknowledgements

When I'm reading, I often skip to the acknowledgements because they fill me with warmth and hope that there are so many people out there being thanked, and so many authors earnestly doing the thanking. I am so happy to express the gratitude that has been jumping around inside my heart.

To every single person who picked up this story – thank you. Reading is a balm to the soul and readers channel that transformative, healing, compassionate power into everyday life. I am indebted to each and every one of you.

Tanera, my absolute force of an agent – you have changed my life. Your belief in my ability as a writer has made me believe in myself. You are a dream come true for any author lucky enough to work with you. Laura, thank you for tirelessly reading every draft. The vision you and Tanera had for this book is the only reason it is what it is today. I am so proud to be a part of the Greenstone family.

And the rights teams who so passionately have advocated for this story – Mary Darby and Georgia Fuller – thank you so much for sharing Andi and Hugh with the world.

To all the folks at Bonnier who worked tirelessly to get this book into the hands of readers, thank you. Melissa, you are hilarious. I have never received an email from you that didn't make me laugh out loud. I will never tire of you leaving margin notes tying something I wrote to a Taylor Swift song.

To all the folks who had a hand in this journey — I have so much gratitude for you and if I were to name every single one of you the acknowledgements would be as long as the story itself. If you are reading this, know that I appreciate everything you have done for me. To Coral Sea Dreaming, a real life Liveaboard for the Great Barrier Reef, thank you for the trip of a lifetime. And no, this is not paid advertising, although I really wish it was.

To my Seattle family, thank you for listening to me prattle on about this endlessly and for always responding with the words of encouragement I needed to hear. Everyone deserves friends like you.

To my beta readers, my best friends, the people who infuse my existence on this earth with laughter, warmth, and exuberant, unbridled support and love, how will I ever thank you enough? You have read all my first drafts, you have picked me up after every rejection (there were five books ahead of this one), and you have jumped for joy with every celebration. This little paragraph doesn't come close to what you all deserve, so if I am so lucky, I promise to thank you again in another "Acknowledgements" section.

Dorka, thank you for telling me I couldn't do it. I'm so thrilled to get to tell you that I did! Cody, thank you for encouraging me even when I sent you sci-fi. Leah, thank you for your quiet and steady support, through everything. Kirk, if I write anything funny, ever, it will be because your friendship has given me more laughter than my own heart knows what to do with — thank you. Zoey, I don't know how your voice isn't hoarse from how hard you cheer me on, but boy am I glad you never tire of doing it. Grace, watching you believe in yourself made me believe in myself. There are no words to adequately express my gratitude for that. The world needs more women like you. Tams, you are my second set of eyes so often sometimes I wonder if you're just my first. Thank you for never leaving my side. I will never leave yours.

To my very large family, my cousins, my aunts and uncles, my in-laws and my bonus siblings and parent, every single one of you has made me who I am. To my grandparents, thank you for loving me so deeply with no reservations. Finishing a book takes a level of determination and persistence my grandmothers have in spades. They are the women who showed me how to keep going with deep compassion and soundness of spirit.

To my sisters, you are the best parts of every sibling dynamic I will ever write. You are my sounding boards, endless wells of laughter, the devil's advocates that I don't want but really need, and you have been supporting me since quite literally the day I was born. I am so grateful for that. Dad, knowing a parent is proud of you is the *best* feeling a child could have. Thank you for giving that to me in spades, regardless of whether or not this book sells a single copy. Mom, thank you for making us bring books in the Honda Odessey instead of watching movies. You are the beginning of my love of the library, of reading, of the written word, of holding a book in my hand and thinking *finally*, I get to sit down and read. I love you all endlessly.

CLAIRE KERSHAW

Whit — when people ask me how I knew I wanted to be a writer, my answer is always that I didn't know until after I had fallen in love with you. Until we met, all I dreamed about was finding someone to share life with. You are miles better than anything I ever dreamed up, and when loving you became my reality it made room for my other dreams, like this one. Thank you for sticking by my side through it all. You make my life feel like the best, most swoon-worthy romcom. I love you.

Get ready for

APPLE OF MY EYE
by Claire Kershaw

Coming August 2025